Quaker
Testimony

❀

Evelyn Rodewald

*With thanks for your
support!*
Irene Allen

Also by the Author

Quaker Silence (Random House)
Quaker Witness (Random House)
No Stone Unturned: Reasoning about Rocks and Fossils
(W. H. Freeman and Co.)

Quaker Testimony

Irene Allen

St. Martin's Press
New York

Design: Nancy Resnick

Library of Congress Cataloging-in-Publication Data

Allen, Irene.
    Quaker testimony : an Elizabeth Elliot mystery / by Irene Allen.
        p.   cm.
    ISBN 0-312-14709-0
    1. Women detectives—Massachusetts—Cambridge—Fiction. 2. Quakers—Massachusetts—Cambridge—Fiction. 3. Cambridge (Mass.)—Fiction.   I. Title.
PS3551.L3935Q32   1996
813'.54—dc20   96-19599
                                                          CIP

First Edition: September 1996

10   9   8   7   6   5   4   3   2   1

This book is dedicated to

James Stewart Thayer, whose early generosity to the author
was crucial to the development of this series

and

E. Anne Robinson, who has helped guide Elizabeth Elliot
through each of her adventures.

Acknowledgments
✣

It is a pleasure to acknowledge the inspiration of the many war-tax resisters in New England, Quakers and non-Quakers alike. I only wish this story could do justice to the faithful lives I have seen in Massachusetts.

My parents have been exceedingly patient and generous to me as I labored on this story; my debt to them is incalculable. Clifford Harrison has been, as always, a rock in a weary land.

My Harvard roommate, Sarah S. Ruden, edited the manuscript and provided the poem about Saint Augustine, originally published in *The Lyric* (Fall 1991) and reprinted here with the permission of the editor. My friends Anne Robinson, Sharon Rogers, Elizabeth Zbinden, and Muriel Dresser have been helpful to the growth of this story. Jim Thayer, Lincoln Hollister, and Karl Schurr provided excellent technical advice about guns and gunpowder, subjects to which I am deeply resistant. I appreciate the kindness infused within their timely replies to my questions. Clyde Taylor encouraged me to address some of the shortcomings in the story's penultimate draft; his comments were crucial to the rewriting process.

My brothers and sisters outside the Religious Society of Friends have been most helpful, and it is a deep pleasure to acknowledge their generous ecumenism. An Episcopal rector taught me the outlines of just-war theory and introduced me to the writings of Daniel J. Boorstin. Mennonite authors sharpened my thinking about the dilemmas of taxation in modern society and pointed me toward the possibility of courageous faithfulness. A Catholic Sister explained the mechanisms of conversion to Catholicism and helped me to understand several important points of vocabulary. A Catholic Father gave me copies of the Pope's statements about the Gulf War.

All factual errors and doctrinal lapses remaining in this book are strictly my own.

Quaker
Testimony

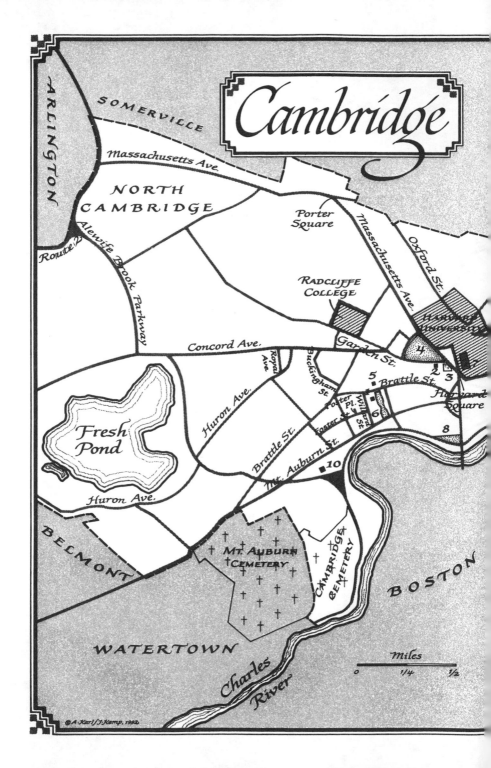

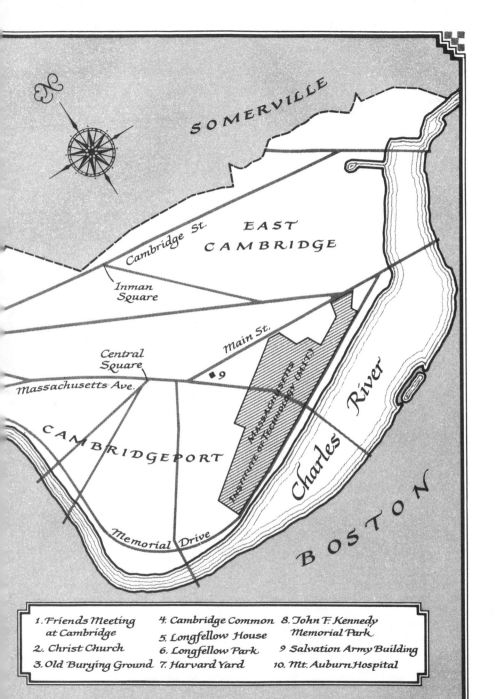

1. Friends Meeting at Cambridge
2. Christ Church
3. Old Burying Ground
4. Cambridge Common
5. Longfellow House
6. Longfellow Park
7. Harvard Yard
8. John F. Kennedy Memorial Park
9. Salvation Army Building
10. Mt. Auburn Hospital

1

%

We utterly deny all outward wars and strife and fightings for any end or under any pretence whatsoever. And this is our testimony to the whole world. We do certainly know, and so testify to the world, that the spirit of Christ, which leads us into all Truth, will never move us to fight any war against any man, neither for the kingdom of Christ, nor for the kingdoms of this world.

George Fox, a founder of the Religious Society of Friends, in a Statement of Quaker Pacifism to the English Government, 1661

Almost from the beginning the Quakers realized that their [pacifism] would put difficulties in the way of their running a government . . . Men who set too much store by their dogmas and who will not allow themselves to be guided by the give and take between ideas and experience are likely to suffer defeat.

Daniel J. Boorstin, historian unsympathetic to Quakerism, writing on the early history of Pennsylvania

Elizabeth Elliot turned over in bed when the formidable clock radio next to her head began to play somber classical music. It was an expensive radio, more elaborate and with higher fidelity than anything she would have purchased, given to her the previous Christmas by her two grown sons. She glanced at the instrument's dials to confirm that it was half past six. She lingered in bed a moment, but there was no escape from the day that she knew might bring deep sorrow to two Quakers she greatly respected.

The thick heat of August had not yet descended on Cambridge, and Elizabeth felt good herself as she stretched her sixty-seven-year-old bones. She threw back the clean but old sheet, yellowed from hundreds of launderings, and walked over the aging gray carpet past the curtains stirring in the early morning breeze. She glanced out the open window and saw that the day was fair.

Because she might be representing Friends Meeting at Cambridge to government agents this morning, she dressed carefully in a crisply pressed, short-sleeved white blouse and a navy cotton skirt. Hose and navy shoes completed her outfit. Elizabeth believed that navy complemented her thick thatch of gray hair and her increasingly colorless face. Looking in the bathroom mirror, she was satisfied.

She went downstairs, had a quick breakfast with a strong cup of tea, then filled Sparkle's bowl with dry food. The diffident cat, not in evidence at the moment, was presumably curled up somewhere in the safety of the basement. Sparkle had been a stray kitten, adopted by Elizabeth's late husband, a man only slightly less tenderhearted than his wife. Sparkle had never fully acclimated to domestic life. She still spent much of her time out of the sight of humans. Elizabeth was fond of the cat as a remembrance of Michael and lavished gentle attention on her whenever she appeared.

As a morning devotion, Elizabeth read several pages of a history of the Quaker colony in Pennsylvania. Usually she read something more spiritual, but she had recently found the book among her late husband's things, and it was proving both interesting and relevant. The high ideals of Quakerism had made Penn's colony difficult to govern, particularly because Quakers had welcomed Scots, Irish, and Germans into their community, promising religious freedom for all. Some of those settlers had repeatedly asked of the Pennsylvanian government things which were contrary to pacifism. The clash in colonial times between the need for compromise in a complex world and the demands of the Gospel was important to Elizabeth because modern Quakers were still struggling with similar issues.

When she had read as much as she could in one sitting, she set aside the book and began to rise to leave the house. Her eye caught the flash of a cardinal in the backyard that had come to look for the steady supply of sunflower seeds Elizabeth provided. Sparkle lived her life inside, so her mistress was free to feed the birds without worrying for their safety. The cardinal, one of the regular visitors, took what it wanted and departed.

As she stood up, Elizabeth's eye fell on a large Christmas cactus hanging in the kitchen window. Looking at the clock to make sure she had time, she went to the back hall to get the watering bottle. Her cacti had led troubled lives. Some years they had bloomed wonderfully in the winter, a most welcome sight in the darkness of a Massachusetts December. But this past year they had wilted pathetically and had not bloomed at all. Elizabeth had considered throwing out the sickly plants, but she was unable to condemn anything she had cared for to an early death. During the spring, the cacti had improved, but today they definitely looked yellow and limp. Elizabeth put her right hand into the box of dry fertilizer, bringing out a handful. With her left she put a little back into the box and, satisfied with this attempt at measurement, dropped the remainder into her water bottle and dusted off her hands against each other. She filled the bottle at the kitchen sink and walked quickly through the house, dividing the water among the cacti and several African violets in the living room.

Locking the front door of her house and deliberately not looking at its peeling paint, the Clerk of New England's largest Quaker Meeting turned and stepped onto the uneven, redbrick city sidewalk. She walked down Concord Avenue in the direction of Cambridge Common. It was easy to enjoy the cool morning temperatures, enhanced as they were by unusually low humidity. The air felt light. The day would, with luck, not be a scorcher.

Cutting through the grounds of the Episcopal Divinity School, she came out on Brattle Street at Longfellow Park and looked across the street at the Meetinghouse, bathed in the morning sun. Religion had always been important to both Elizabeth Elliot and her late husband. Since the Elliot children had grown up and her husband had died, Meeting work had become even more central to Elizabeth's life. She put almost all of her time and energy into service for the Religious Society of Friends. It had not been a surprise when, two years previously, Cambridge Quakers had asked her to be Clerk, or head, of the Meeting. The job carried no pay but guaranteed lots of work and serious soul-searching as Elizabeth tried to live up to her ideal of what a Quaker should be.

There was no need to stop at the Meetinghouse before eight o'clock on a Monday morning. No mail would have come, and even Harriet, the Meeting's secretary, would not arrive until nine. Elizabeth continued on Brattle, walking along Cambridge's famous Tory Row, past grand old houses which had stood since before the British redcoats had marched through Cambridge on their way to Concord and Lexington in 1775. She walked to the corner of Brattle and the simpler, but equally old, Willard Street.

Enjoying the gentle light and the slight morning breeze, Elizabeth wondered what she might expect from a certain widower in Meeting. Neil Stevenson and she had been keeping company since the previous winter, and she knew they were reaching the point where their relationship must either become deeper or wither. But she was genuinely unsure what was in Neil's mind. Like most men she had known, Neil avoided talking about emotions, preferring subjects which seemed to Elizabeth impersonal. He talked avidly about intellectual questions, politics and Quaker history, but never in a way that illuminated his own interior life.

The pair had never discussed their future. This was, perhaps, as Neil wanted it, but Elizabeth felt uneasy about their mutual silence. Unlike Elizabeth, Neil was well-to-do, and she often felt that his money came between them. His wealth conflicted with her notion of Quaker simplicity. Especially since she had become Clerk, her conscience about such matters had been heightened, and she believed, like early Quakers, that owning more than one needed was destructive to Christian life. She had noticed with sorrow the increasing tendency of wealthy Quakers to ignore tithing and more generous gifts. The Meeting's budget made it clear that almost no Friends parted with ten percent of their income, most especially those Quakers who were well off.

Elizabeth knew that having and holding money was somehow important to Neil, important in a way she did not understand. To complicate things, both Neil and she had grown children with their own needs and expectations. Elizabeth knew that marrying a wealthy man might lead to resentment from his offspring, afraid for their inheritance. Besides, she was not sure she wanted to remarry. She remembered her long marriage with Michael fondly and still felt grief over his death, but being a widow had its advantages. She was, for the first time in her life, free to order her daily life, her activities, and her modest financial arrangements without consulting anyone else. It was an unexpected luxury for a woman of Elizabeth's generation and one she enjoyed greatly. She sighed as she walked, wondering how she and Neil would arrange matters between them.

She turned southwest off Willard onto Foster Street, just as a loud boom reverberated through the quiet neighborhood. Elizabeth looked up, searching for a plane in the sky. Sonic booms were uncommon in Cambridge in recent years, and Elizabeth could not see a plane. Her back was now to the Meetinghouse, which she could have seen if she had turned around. Foster Place, the Clerk's destination, was a tiny dead-end lane perpendicular to Foster Street. It was the home of two Meeting members, Sheldon and Hope Laughton. Most of one side of Foster Place was occupied by the stately, three-story Laughton house and the large yard that surrounded it. The house, of white clapboard, dated back to the Civil War. Sheldon and Hope, both handy and energetic people, had done much work to restore their home and refinish the original oak of the interior. This morning Elizabeth was going to spend time with Hope, one Friend with another, giving her emotional support as the Laughtons waited for the possible seizure of their beautiful and historic house by federal agents.

As she walked up Foster Place, Elizabeth cluck-clucked at several cigarette butts on the ground beside a telephone pole. The older she became, the more careless she thought Cantabrigians were with their trash. As she walked gingerly across some gravel spilling onto the brick sidewalk from an unpaved driveway, she thought about the Laughtons. She expected that, by this time in the morning, Sheldon would have taken little Catherine to day care. During the summer, his work as a landscaper and gardener began early in the morning. Before Catherine was born, Sheldon had worked as a geologist. He had often flown to the wilderness of Alaska and other western places, and like other practicing geologists had been out in the field at first light. Early hours still came easily to him. It was therefore no surprise to Elizabeth that the driveway at the Quakers' house was empty. She knew that the Laughtons' old station wagon was their only car, and that it was also Sheldon's work vehicle.

A mourning dove cooed calmly as Elizabeth walked up to the front door. The world here on Foster Place seemed dignified, still, and peaceful. She rang the doorbell. There was no answer, and after a moment she rang again. She made a fist with her left hand, the one less affected by arthritis, and rapped on the door. There was no answering sound from within.

Elizabeth knew that Hope would not have left the house on this, of all days. She stepped back from the door and walked around the house to her right, her vague apprehension prohibiting her from stopping to admire the large rosebushes. She walked carefully in her dress shoes through Sheldon's well-tended grass to the backyard. At one of the kitchen windows she peered in, expecting to see Hope at her breakfast, perhaps unable, in the large house, to hear the Clerk's modest attacks on the front door. But all she could see was the glare of the sun in the east window and the shadowy outline of cabinets against the far wall. Retreating from the window, she stepped over to the back door and knocked loudly. She waited and knocked again, wondering if the government might have evicted the Laughtons from their house during the night. But if that were the case, Elizabeth reasoned, Hope or Sheldon would have called her this morning, as Clerk of Meeting, to inform her of their homelessness. Besides, if there had been a middle-of-the-night eviction, the Laughtons' furniture would be standing on the street. In other cases Elizabeth had seen, that had been the final result of this kind of witness.

Puzzled, Elizabeth frowned and tried the kitchen door. It was locked. She realized she had not tried the handle on the front door. She continued her circle tour of the property to check on anything she might see or hear. But all was quiet on the north side of the house, just as elsewhere, and she returned to the front yard without understanding the situation any better.

The oak and leaded-glass front door, surprisingly, was unlocked. Elizabeth opened it slowly and entered, calling out, "Hope? Are you here, Hope?" Her voice seemed small in the large foyer. She closed the massive door and called out again. She caught a faint but familiar odor, which registered deep in her mind as foreign to the house. Puzzled, she breathed deeply but could smell nothing more. Again she called to Hope, but silence was the only reply. Her voice had disappeared up a big oaken stairway and been lost somewhere on the second floor. If Hope were here but on the third floor, might she have missed the doorbell and Elizabeth's calls? The Clerk felt a mixture of annoyance and apprehension as she walked up the staircase and said once again, "Are you here, Hope?"

She found the smaller staircase to the third floor at the back of the house, a more humble set of stairs appropriate for the servants of the last century. She called upwards in a loud, almost stern voice. Not even a cat appeared. Elizabeth returned to the first floor and, looking around carefully, walked toward the back of the house. She paused by a beautiful antique piece of furniture in the center hall. It was a Shaker-style cabinet, and on top of it lay a book. She idly looked at the title and saw it was *The Confessions of Saint Augustine*. Surprised that the dark volume had nothing to do with Quakerism, she picked it up.

The inside front cover indicated the book had been purchased from one of the secondhand bookstores in Harvard Square. Sheldon had inscribed his name in it. As Elizabeth opened the volume to the title page, a piece of paper fluttered to the floor. She leaned over to pick it up and could not help but read the verse which had been written in pencil on it:

The Conversion of Saint Augustine

What in particular he read
was not the miracle. Instead,
The child's voice chanting on next door,
The sun's voice on the garden floor

Rang like a fever in his head.
("Pick it up, read it," the child said.);
He swore, he turned around to look
For some distraction, and a book

Lay open on a bench below;
He read, "Take thy companion go—"
But no, exactly what he read
Was not the miracle. Instead

It was the page, his eyes, the light:
God gives the power to read and write,
He knew and knew until he died
("Pick it up, read it," the child cried).

She looked carefully at the paper. The poem was not attributed to anyone, but Elizabeth assumed Sheldon was the author, for he often wrote poetry. She thought it odd for a lifelong Quaker to be writing about a man she could only think of as a Catholic. Still, she admired the verse. She put the poem back in the book and turned from the Shaker cabinet toward the kitchen.

Standing at the door of the kitchen, Elizabeth thought for an instant that she was going mad. She next considered the possibility she was hallucinating. Gripping the wide doorframe for support, she closed her eyes. She asked God's help, and slowly her mind began to function more smoothly. Tentatively, she concluded that what was before her was real. Gingerly opening her eyes and pushing her glasses up her nose, she forced herself to look and to see.

Hope Laughton lay on her back in the center of the kitchen floor, a large, moist red hole in her blouse. Her mouth was open. Blood was seeping slowly onto the yellow kitchen tiles beneath her.

Holding as tightly to the doorframe as her arthritic hands would allow, Elizabeth took a deep, steady breath and decided that the first thing she must do was determine if Hope was alive. She stepped across the tiles and knelt down beside the younger Quaker. The pointed toe of Elizabeth's right shoe was moistened with blood as she looked at her fellow Friend's face.

Hope was not breathing. Elizabeth picked up her nearer hand, which lay on her chest not far from the wound, and felt for a pulse. There was none. Not a spasm, not a stir of life remained in the body. Still holding Hope's hand, Elizabeth instinctively and wordlessly prayed. Then she called herself back to the practical. As she gently put the hand back where it had lain she saw that her own hand was bloodied. Horror and unreality again gripped her as she stood up, thoughtlessly wiping her hand on her skirt like a little girl. Just as mechanically, she looked around the kitchen for an explanation. She guessed that Hope's injury was a gunshot wound, but there was no sign of struggle and no gun.

Dazed, the Clerk stepped slowly across the kitchen and picked up the telephone to dial 911. Her foot overturned a small paper sack on the floor below the telephone. It tipped over, spilling scores of small, cellophane-wrapped objects. Bright and varied colors tumbled out onto the floor. At first, Elizabeth did not recognize the objects, although she knew she had seen them before. In an instant, she remembered a young woman on a subway platform handing out such packets to passersby. From the woman's cheerful but vulgar patter as she gave away her wares, Elizabeth had gathered they were condoms. And here were the same individually wrapped objects, incongruously spread across the kitchen tiles.

Elizabeth did not pause to put them in their bag but reached again for the telephone. Just as she raised the receiver, the doorbell rang. She hesitated, then hung up the telephone and took one step toward the front hallway. As she did so she heard footsteps in the large foyer and a man's voice calling out, "Government agents! We're here under the authority of the Internal Revenue Service. We have a warrant for eviction!"

Elizabeth froze in place on the yellow tiles. She made an inarticulate murmur in reply, realizing as she did so that she could not be heard. Still, she was paralyzed. With deep and searing panic she realized that she was not even able to pray. Time all but stopped flowing. Several men's voices mingled in the front of the house, and then a tall man in a suit appeared at the kitchen door.

"Mrs. Laughton, I presume?"

She mutely shook her head. The man's face turned a chalky color when he caught sight of Hope's bloody body.

"Jesus Christ!" he said without reverence. Then, quickly, he drew in a breath and yelled, "Guys! Back here!"

No fewer than four men instantly appeared behind him. Darkness began to wash over Elizabeth. She felt nausea and what she thought was the final night envelop her. Her last memory before she fainted was of the faces of the men crowded in the doorway, each painted with shock at the crimson scene they saw beyond her.

2

Friends are urged to support those who witness to their governments and take personal risks in the cause of peace, who choose not to participate in war as soldiers nor to contribute to its preparation with their taxes.

Advices on Peace and Reconciliation
from New England Yearly Meeting's *Faith and Practice*, 1986

(One) fatal flaw to the influence of Quakers on American culture was . . . a preoccupation with the purity of their own souls and a rigidity in all their beliefs. This hardened them against the ordinary accommodations of this world.

Daniel J. Boorstin

Elizabeth regained consciousness painfully and by degrees. She did not hurry the process. She knew that she was lying on the Laughtons' kitchen floor and that there were several men she did not know standing around her. She did not move or even open her eyes, but tried to remember what had led to this. Two days previously, on Saturday morning, she had gone to the Meeting-house to gather with interested Friends and see what could be done to help the Laughtons. The couple maintained one of the most courageous Quaker witnesses the Clerk had seen. As she lay still and quiet on the hard tiles, Elizabeth's mind found its footing, and she rapidly remembered all that had happened at that meeting.

It had been hot and densely humid. Elizabeth was the first to arrive at the Meetinghouse. She had unlocked its doors, both front and side, and propped them open to catch any breeze the Lord might send. Against her better judgment, she had struggled with two of the old, stiff windows of the building and opened them as well. Her back ached dully from that task.

Sheldon and Hope Laughton and their close friend Otto Zimmer came to the Meetinghouse together. Sheldon was a sober and fearless Quaker, about fifty years old, who had been a part of Cambridge Meeting since childhood. He was a big man, looming over lesser Friends in several ways. Elizabeth had known him for decades. They were not close, but they had worked together on Meeting projects many times over the years. Sheldon was a serious man. He wrote poetry and had, at times, an eye for the world both more critical and artistic than that of many Friends. Some of his poetry had been published in Quaker journals, but lately, Elizabeth had been told, he was not submitting any.

Hope Laughton, Sheldon's small and wiry wife, was some ten years younger than he. Her diminutive frame did not dominate a room as her husband's did, but her fierce sense of integrity had helped move the Meeting toward some of its more difficult decisions. Hope was an ecumenical spirit, working for the multifaith soup kitchen at Christ Church in Harvard Square. But she was as committed a Quaker and a pacifist as anyone in Meeting, and Elizabeth both liked and respected her. Hope had her preschooler, Catherine, clinging to her right hand when she came into the large worship room that comprised the structurally simple Meetinghouse.

Otto Zimmer was a dark-haired and bearded man in his thirties, with a short temper and an urge to preach. Elizabeth did not know him as well, but she was aware he was serious and tenacious about all matters connected with taxes and the military. He was a "convinced" Friend, meaning he was a convert to Quakerism from another denomination. No one was a prouder Friend than he, a pattern familiar in many branches of Christendom where those who convert take up their cross in a most uncompromising way. Otto was both bright and educated, but Elizabeth thought he had not yet found ways to use his talents. He worked at simple jobs, presently as a hospital orderly, but he had the self-assertion more commonly found in men holding powerful positions. In spite of his habit of underachieving, Otto had a big ego. He might, in time, become an important Friend if he could learn to listen to others and if he matured into self-acceptance. Elizabeth did not, however, always have high hopes for Otto's future.

All three of the Friends who stepped from the bright heat of the outdoors into the stagnant heat of the building were war-tax resisters, belonging to that small minority of Quakers who felt called by the Spirit to obstruct the federal government's collection of taxes that paid for the military. Quakers had, from their earliest days in seventeenth-century England, refused to participate in war. The strength of the Quaker view of pacifism had helped the Society of Friends weather the storms of early persecution and the droughts of later assimilation.

In recent times, a commitment to the Quaker peace testimony had led some Friends to withhold a large part of their taxes from the IRS rather than be a part of the government's preparations for war. Because Sheldon was self-employed as a landscape gardener and Hope worked intermittently during the school year for Quaker organizations that did not cooperate with withholding, they were able to keep most of what they owed in federal income tax in their own possession. In April of each year, with the prayerful support of part—but by no means all—of the Meeting community, the Laughtons sent the money they chose not to pay in taxes to peace groups and relief agencies rather than to the IRS. Some Cambridge Friends, particularly many of the wealthier and older members, disapproved of the Laughtons' criminal behavior. Others applauded their integrity and courage.

The government, of course, did not accept the Laughtons' act of conscience. Over the years, the IRS had taken money from the Laughtons' checking account and seized and sold a Toyota the pair had been given by Hope's parents shortly after their child was born. These measures, however, were not the end of the matter, because the sum of back taxes, interest, and substantial penalties grew rapidly. For their part, the Laughtons did not buy a new car, but simply borrowed a battered station wagon from an old Friend who retained ownership of the vehicle, thus making it impossible for the IRS to seize. Hope closed the pair's checking account, and the Laughtons, at considerable inconvenience to themselves and the world, lived on a cash-only basis. They paid their bills in person and cashed their paychecks at Quaker-owned businesses. Thus the government was frustrated in its attempts to seize property from the Laughtons, and on more than one occasion the pair was threatened with criminal prosecution. The threats were delivered by mail and on the telephone by the unfortunate IRS agent in charge of the case. Mercifully, nothing like criminal charges had materialized.

At the Meetinghouse on Saturday, Otto had been the first to speak. "Sheldon and Hope have heard again from the IRS. They're going to be forcibly evicted from their home next week."

"I'm so sorry," said the Clerk simply, nodding first to Hope and then to her husband. The government's action was one she had long anticipated, but her heart contracted in sorrow nevertheless.

"It's a difficult time," said Hope softly. Little Catherine had let go of her mother's hand and wandered over to the sunlight of a western window of the Meetinghouse. A moment passed before Hope continued. "Last spring when the IRS auctioned our house, everything still seemed distant and unreal to me. But I heard yesterday afternoon from an IRS agent. They'll come on Monday to throw us and our stuff out, if necessary. The man who called is one of the nicer guys we deal with, Evan Beringar. I think he was trying to give us warning so we could be emotionally ready. And so we could prepare Cathy for what's going to happen. But even knowing in advance, it'll be hard."

"Not that you can trust anything the IRS guys say!" Otto interjected. "And you can't be sure of their motives. Before the auction they spent a lot of time trying to scare you, remember."

"Yes, they did. Or perhaps they would say they were trying to warn us how serious this all was. Tax collectors aren't our enemies, you know," said Hope.

"Jesus was fond of one of them," mused Sheldon to no one in particular.

"But last spring was a difficult time," Hope concluded, "and some of the IRS men were most unpleasant."

The previous spring had brought on a crisis between the Laughtons and the government that had been almost enough to make Elizabeth regret that she had agreed to be Clerk of Meeting. The IRS, over several years' time and with plenty of warning to the Laughtons, had taken the necessary legal steps to claim their house in lieu of payment of their back taxes. The house had belonged to Sheldon's parents. Elizabeth was sure that it was important to the Laughtons' plans for the future, especially for their old age. They were not wealthy people. Because Sheldon was self-employed and Hope worked only intermittently, they were not covered by a pension plan. The house was their only asset.

Like all real estate in the better parts of Cambridge, the Laughtons' house had appreciated in the 1960s, doubled in value in the 1970s, and tripled in the next decade. Although the recession at the end of the Reagan years had hit New England harder than other parts of the country, a house like Sheldon and Hope's did not drop in value; it simply appreciated more slowly for a time. It was so close to Harvard Square that many yuppies would have bought it at any price and numerous real estate dealers would have purchased it with an eye to carving it into condominium units. Despite the recession, when the IRS laid claim to the Laughtons' house, it might have expected to get eight hundred thousand dollars or more for it.

The government's auction of the property led to a lot of work for Elizabeth. She had written to Meetings throughout New England and told them of the upcoming auction, asking that the Laughtons be kept in the prayers of all Friends. No doubt many Friends did pray, and, in addition to that, more than two hundred had come to the auction, arriving many hours before the proceedings were to begin. The Quakers who felt most uncomfortable with war-tax resistance stayed away; those who had come were supportive of the Laughtons even if they disagreed with the couple's specific choices or lacked the courage to follow the same calling.

The presence of many Friends radically changed the commercial atmosphere of the event. Quakers spoke to potential bidders as they arrived and explained the reasons for the forced sale of the Laughtons' home. Sheldon and Hope were introduced to anyone willing to meet them. People listened to their quiet explanations of what had led them to this sad situation.

Clearly, many Friends argued, if our government killed only one person per decade, Quakers might not feel called to withhold their taxes. But if the government had a policy of systematic butchery, all Christians might reasonably resist it in every way possible, including refusing to contribute to the tax system supporting the government's actions. Did the government's invasion of Panama and Grenada, the war in Vietnam, and the extensive bombing of Baghdad constitute systematic evil of the sort that must always be resisted? Even if the government's actions in its foreign policy were truly immoral, was it permissible to withhold part of annual taxes in light of all the good the government did for society? To put it another way, how would Quakers have felt if Catholic Americans had withheld part of their taxes during the period the government paid for abortions for the poor? Should Friends have done that? These and other multifaceted questions were discussed by Quakers and non-Quakers alike as they milled through and around the Laughtons' home.

Although most of the potential bidders had a difficult time grasping the religious commitment of the Laughtons, they could see the matter was not a simple business transaction. It was clear that, to hundreds of sober and thoughtful Quakers, the cause was an act of faith. Would-be bidders drifted away, unwilling to confront Quakers, even gentle and respectful ones, in such large numbers.

In truth, as Elizabeth knew, what had brought out the horde of Quakers was only partially a respect for the Laughtons' witness. Many Friends, especially those from families which had been Quaker for generations, came to the auction out of loyalty to the Society of Friends and to defend, in a gentle sense, two of its members against outsiders. Elizabeth knew that the throng of Quakers present that day could not have reached agreement about whether the Laughtons' actions reflected God's will. But they could agree that the Laughtons were Quakers and that Quakers had a long tradition of conflict with the government. When threatened by the authorities, Friends had an understandable inclination to put aside disagreement, at least for a day, and present a united front to the crassly secular world around them.

Someone had alerted the news media about the forced auction, and Boston's TV and newspaper reporters were on hand by the time the event was to begin. Despite media presence, the Quakers maintained a dignified air. Crowding was so great that the bidding was postponed three hours in the hope that some of the Quakers might depart as the day wore on. As a matter of fact, no Friends left, but a number of potential buyers did.

During that three-hour period, Elizabeth, as Clerk of Cambridge Meeting, had been interviewed by numerous reporters. She had tried, over and over, to explain the Quaker peace testimony in terms intelligible to the format of news reporting. She felt frustrated by the reporters' desire for short quotations, but she answered their questions about the Quaker view of nonviolence and the possibilities of living within the spirit of the most radical parts of the Gospels. She was not sure she had communicated all that was in her heart, but she had tried.

For her own part, Elizabeth had always paid her federal taxes in full. Unlike the Laughtons, she did not feel clearly called by

God to criminal action. But she felt more than a little discomfort in explaining the Laughtons' actions to the press because she sometimes feared she was a hypocrite, giving lip service to Quaker pacifism while failing to live up to its implications. She also felt a quiet pride in her community, a serious and thoughtful congregation which had produced a couple of deep integrity.

When the auction finally took place, only one person participated. A Boston lawyer bid a hundred thousand dollars, the minimum that the IRS required, and was awarded legal ownership of the large and gracious house. Some Friends, especially younger ones, had wept openly at the result. Elizabeth had foreseen something of the sort and was not as disappointed. Persons outside the Quaker community, after all, were often unprepared to respond to Friends' concerns, especially when a great deal of money could be made. The lawyer, Elizabeth thought, was likely acting on someone else's behalf, someone who did not share the Friends' vision of simple sufficiency.

Sheldon and Hope had a total tax liability two times a hundred thousand dollars because of the penalties, fines, and interest that had accrued over the years. Elizabeth knew that the amount bid for the house, even if paid on the spot, would not end their legal troubles.

Additionally, Sheldon and Hope had always made it clear to the IRS that they would not simply vacate their home. They intended to use passive resistance against the government as long as they were alive, whatever the result of court rulings and auctions. So forcible eviction was inevitable, and, from what Hope said in the Meetinghouse, it was now imminent.

"The IRS may not come on Monday," said Otto. "They often bluff and make you worry for nothing. But they'll come soon." He went on excitedly, "And that won't be the end of it! We got a lot of attention for our position last spring. The auction was free publicity for war-tax resisters all over New England. All Quakers will probably be audited next year! Despite the fact that all the Meeting did was pray and talk to the press, not exactly activities the Constitution prohibits."

Elizabeth frowned. She knew that her own taxpaying habits might be the product of her fear of poverty and prison. But she also thought it both good and right to be in compliance with the law whenever possible. All Quakers could agree that it was important to cooperate with the government unless explicitly led by the Spirit in other directions.

"I'm sure the authorities care less about our thoughts and prayers," she said, "than they do about law enforcement. Governments, good ones at least, value the rule of law." Elizabeth had never liked Otto, and for a moment she was afraid her dislike might be evident in her tone.

"Are you defending the system that gave us nuclear bombs and the Cold War? Military spending is what the government does with more than half of our tax dollars!" Otto leaned toward her as he spoke.

Elizabeth Elliot knew the categories of the federal budget as well as Otto did. She gathered herself together to respond to his bullying and said, without annoyance, "Our leaders are elected by the people. Are you setting yourself up to judge everyone? All your fellow citizens? Some of them are quite serious Christians, remember."

Otto only shook his head, leaned back, and would not condescend to answer. There was hope, thought Elizabeth, that he might mature, but at present he was one of the more belligerent pacifists she knew.

The Clerk turned toward Sheldon. "I truly am sorry," she said. "As you know, I've always felt clear about paying my taxes, but I deeply respect your actions. And I admire your courage. What can the Meeting do to be helpful?"

"Hope and I have discussed that," replied Sheldon evenly, unperturbed by the tension between the Clerk and Otto. "We'd like a few Friends to be at our house each day until the seizure. We can't be sure when it will come—that's one of the hard things about dealing with the IRS—but probably it's very soon."

"We won't physically resist in any way, of course," said Hope, "but when the federal agents come we'd like not to feel alone in this."

Elizabeth murmured a phrase of understanding.

"We should have sit-ins every day!" said Otto sharply. "Make the *Boston Globe* cover them! Think of all you two have accomplished. Since you've done this much, why not continue?"

"We've done all we're called to do," said Hope, as quietly and peacefully as her husband. "They can take our house. I don't feel clear about having anyone arrested. And I don't want drama, just some moral support." She held out her arms to Catherine, who toddled into them.

"I'm sure Friends will respect your wishes," said Elizabeth, praying briefly that Otto would do so.

Ruth Markham entered the Meetinghouse and joined the group. She was a Friend who worked at Harvard University as a secretary and taught in the First Day School, the Quaker equivalent of Sunday school. Catherine ran up to her and cheerily said hello. Several more Quakers soon came, and the Laughtons' situation was discussed at length with each new arrival. Eventually pen and paper appeared from a Friend's purse, and Otto began to make a list of who could be at the Laughtons' house at what time. It was agreed that there would be no resisting the federal agents nor courting arrest. With that understanding, Elizabeth had every wish to cooperate as Clerk.

"When can you come?" said Otto pointedly to Elizabeth.

"Whenever Friends wish. I'm retired, and my time is free," answered Elizabeth steadily.

"Come on Monday morning," said Hope. "That's the earliest

the IRS might arrive, and it will be a hard time for me. Sheldon has to go to work, you see, to finish a big job he has in Lexington."

"I'll be there," Elizabeth answered soberly.

Hope smiled.

"I'll leave just before seven and take Catherine to day care," said Sheldon. "It opens at seven. We don't want her on hand to see our belongings moved out onto the street." He added to Hope, "I'm sure some of my Pax Christi friends would come, too, if you'd like."

Elizabeth did not understand and looked at Hope for clarification.

"No," said Hope dismissively, "this is for me. You won't be there, after all, and I'd appreciate Quaker rather than Catholic company." Her husband nodded.

Otto had continued around the group, getting one or two persons to agree to stay with Hope each morning and afternoon for all the days of the upcoming week. There had been many hugs and a few tears. Little Catherine had begun to cry, perhaps because of the stagnant heat of the Meetinghouse or perhaps from the obvious emotions of the adults. Her squalls had encouraged the gathering to break up.

Elizabeth's memory of what had brought her to the Laughtons' house was now clear. She was alert but perfectly still as she lay on the kitchen floor and listened to the government's men around her discussing what they should do. They had expected to evict people, not find a scene of violent death, and their confusion was evident.

3

The problems posed by taxes collected for military expenditures have long troubled Quakers and other Christians. The U.S. federal government currently spends about sixty percent of its budget on war preparedness; this spending has established an enormous industrial and scientific complex directed toward highly lethal violence. Voluntarily contributing tax dollars to the federal Treasury has proved impossible for some Friends.

Leaflet on War Taxes
Friends Meeting at Cambridge, 1989

Elizabeth had fully regained consciousness and decided to act. She stirred and opened her eyes.

"She's with us again." Someone squatted down beside her saying, "Lady, can you sit up?"

Elizabeth struggled to a sitting position on the floor. Unlike when she had awakened in bed this morning, her joints were stiff and painful. The cool, hard kitchen tiles had not done her good. She felt her back creaking as she moved, and she did not want to stand immediately.

"We've called the police," said the tall man in the suit who had mistaken her for Hope. "They'll be here in a minute. I don't know what the hell is going on, but you'd better get your wits together before they arrive."

Elizabeth rubbed her temples. Slowly, she began to remember the details of what she had discovered in the house. She shuddered despite her stiffness.

"Why don't you get up and come into the other room," said a kinder voice. A weathered face appeared before her and smiled tentatively.

Elizabeth slowly stood, her age evident in her every motion. She was careful not to look behind her, but followed the gentler IRS agent into the living room.

"You stay with her, Evan!"

"Don't worry," he replied and motioned Elizabeth to sit down on the sofa in the large living room in the northwest part of the house.

Elizabeth looked around mechanically, her glance passing over the Peruvian weavings that decorated the wall. Hope, before she became a wife and mother, had worked in Peru for the American Friends Service Committee. A framed pen-and-ink drawing of a llama hung over the mantel. Elizabeth's eye stopped on it for a moment. Both she and her informal guard heard sirens entering the neighborhood.

Elizabeth asked, "You're here to evict the Laughtons?"

"Yup, that was the plan. We've got the authorization. We expected there might be a crowd of people here to protest it. But all we found was you and Mrs. Laughton in the kitchen."

"I don't know what's happened here. I was going to wait with Hope, to keep her company this morning, in case you gentlemen came." Elizabeth shook her head at the apparent absurdity of the plans which had been laid on Saturday.

Two large uniformed officers of the Cambridge Police Department surged noisily through the front door, followed closely but more calmly by Detective Stewart Burnham of the Homicide Department. The man in charge of the IRS squad, standing in the foyer, gave a rapid explanation to the three newcomers. He motioned to Elizabeth and toward the back of the house. Detective Burnham stepped over to the Quaker with a puzzled expression on his face.

"In these circumstances, I can't say it's good to see you again, Mrs. Elliot. What's happened here?" His gray suit was open, and his tie partially loosened in honor of August warmth and humidity. Elizabeth, who had known Burnham from a previous occasion when another Quaker had died mysteriously, had never seen the detective looking so casual.

"The couple who lives here expected to be evicted by the IRS sometime this week," she said, looking directly at the detective and speaking quietly. "They are Friends, Detective, and the Meeting has tried to support their witness. We each signed up to be here for half a day to help Hope Laughton wait. Sheldon is at work, you see, but Hope really only works during the school year." She stopped, afraid she was beginning to ramble. Again, she rubbed her temples, trying to clear her head.

After another conference with the government agents, Burnham disappeared into the kitchen. He gave several orders to the uniformed policemen, then returned to the living room and again turned his attention to the Quaker.

"I'm told Sheldon and Hope Laughton live here but have forfeited this house to pay back taxes," said the detective. It was a declarative sentence, but there was a note of question in his voice.

"That's right. They're war-tax resisters," answered Elizabeth quietly.

"Come again, Mrs. Elliot? I don't follow the jargon you people use."

Elizabeth apologized and briefly explained. She related the story of the auction of the house the previous spring and the Laughtons' desire to force the government to evict them. "It's part of a general response called passive resistance," ended the Quaker. "Some Friends are sure that it's the Gospel."

"I'm acquainted with the people who owned this house," Evan offered, "because we've had a lot of dealing with them the past few years. Although I don't agree with their actions, they're decent and generous people. It's clearly a religious question for them."

Points of theology did not interest Stewart Burnham. "When did you arrive here, Mrs. Elliot?" he asked briskly.

"About eight o'clock."

"Do you know the time more exactly?"

"No, not to the minute. Everything was quiet. The car was gone from the driveway. The station wagon the Laughtons use, I mean. Sheldon goes to work early, and it was agreed he would take little Catherine to day care this week so she wouldn't see the government men. These scenes are difficult, and it's not something for children."

"That's right," said Evan quickly.

The detective nodded. "That part at least I can understand. But how did you get in here?"

"The front door was unlocked. I knocked and rang but there was no response, so I came in to see if Hope was here. I looked upstairs. Then I found her in the kitchen." Elizabeth felt a spasm of nausea.

"Why didn't you call the police?"

Elizabeth explained that she had tried, but that the IRS men had interrupted her.

The detective sighed and shifted his weight onto his heels. "We'll take you downtown for a full statement. I'm not charging you with anything. Of course, you have a right to a lawyer. You can get one to come to the station and have him with you when you give your statement. You'll have to have someone bring you a different set of clothes. I can see the blood on your skirt and on that shoe. We'll have to test the bloodstains and test your hands for traces of powder. So call one of your friends and get them to bring you something else to wear. You'll be detained until you give a statement, let us examine your hands, and surrender your clothes. By the way, do you know who is responsible for the big bag of condoms on the floor?"

"No, I don't know anything about them. I tipped over the bag by accident."

"Does birth control tie in with Quaker teachings? It's not forbidden, I take it." There was a hint of derision in the detective's voice.

"It's not forbidden. But killing someone most certainly is."

Burnham turned from Elizabeth. Evan Beringar helped her to her feet and ushered her to the door.

At the Cambridge police station in Central Square, Elizabeth's hands were coated with a thin layer of wax. The procedure was an intensely degrading one. She felt at the mercy of the police and their technical people, unsure what was being done to her. She stammered out a question about the wax, and the man who was manipulating her hands explained that it would remove any gunpowder traces from her hands. The coating was peeled off, and then her fingers were inked and her fingerprints taken. She looked at her hands, smeared with purple ink, with dismay. She was allowed to wash, and she did so carefully and thoroughly, vigorously scrubbing each finger.

She was given a chance to use the telephone in a tiny, bare office. Without hesitation or reflection she called William Hoffman, a lifelong Friend who was a member of the bar and now sat as a judge for the Commonwealth of Massachusetts. Luckily, he was in his office and not in court. She explained in a few clumsy words the tragedy at the Laughtons' house and her own predicament.

"How can I get a lawyer?" Elizabeth concluded, bewildered that she, of all people, was asking such a question.

"I'll call my old law firm, and they'll send someone down. With luck, it will be Doug Gibson. He's good. Don't answer any questions at all until a lawyer shows up. None whatsoever. That's important, Elizabeth! This is not a question of Quaker honesty. It's a legal matter. Will you promise me you won't speak to anyone until a lawyer is with you?"

Elizabeth promised. Then with hesitation, she mentioned that she needed a different set of clothes and a pair of shoes so that the police could retain what she was wearing. She recommended he call Ruth Markham, who would be at work at Harvard, and ask her to walk over to Elizabeth's house and fetch a new set of things.

"How can she get into your house?" asked the judge.

"Tell her there is a key taped under the mailbox."

Despite the situation, Bill laughed at the Clerk's idea of security. He promised to reach Ruth and said good-bye.

Doug Gibson, whom Elizabeth had met once before through the good offices of Judge Hoffman, arrived at the police station at ten o'clock. He was dressed in business clothes but managed to give them a casual air. His unruly hair and small potbelly made him look more human than many lawyers. He and Elizabeth were allowed to speak to each other privately in the small interrogation room. Mr. Gibson listened to the Quaker's explanation of the morning's events in thoughtful silence.

"It's most unfortunate, of course, that the IRS men arrived before you called the police," he said when Elizabeth had concluded her narrative. "But being found with a murder victim isn't proof of anything. The whereabouts of the murder weapon will be important, but only time will resolve that. I must ask, Mrs. Elliot, did you have any reason to want Hope Laughton dead?"

"Don't even think such a thing!"

The lawyer smiled and ran a hand quickly through his unkempt hair. "OK, let me ask the question another way. Would you gain anything, no matter how trivial, from her death?"

Elizabeth paused, then said slowly and deliberately, "Even if I hadn't found Hope's body, this death would be nothing but grief for me. It will be distressing to the Meeting, particularly if any Friends are suspected of being involved. As Clerk, I have more headaches than you can imagine from much lesser problems. I

don't see how even the police could think that I might gain anything."

"Are you a particular friend of Sheldon's?"

Elizabeth shook her head and explained that although she had
known Sheldon since he was a boy, it was not a close friendship,
just the acquaintance of one Friend with another at Meeting.

"Did Hope know anything about your life you would prefer not
to be made public?"

This time the Quaker fathomed, in a dim way, the point of the
question. She only shook her gray head in wonder at the lawyer's
idea.

"Did you owe Hope money, by any chance?"

"No," answered Elizabeth. "In fact, when the Laughtons were
evicted, Friends would have given them money to help tide them
over. They have nothing. I'm sure they haven't been in a position to lend anything to anyone."

"Good. Let's talk to Burnham and get this cleared up. Tell the
whole truth. If there are any questions I don't like, I'll stop you,
but if I'm silent you go ahead and answer."

Stewart Burnham joined them. He had dozens and dozens of
questions for Elizabeth. He covered her job at Friends Meeting,
her relationship to the Laughtons, and her ambivalence about
war-tax resistance. Most importantly, he wanted an almost
minute-by-minute account of her movements that morning from
dawn until the IRS men arrived at Foster Place. Doug Gibson,
feeding several pieces of chewing gum into his mouth, made no
objection, and Elizabeth was glad to answer everything. She explained her breakfast and reading at the kitchen table, mentioning the importance of the history book to her as a counterpoint
to the Laughtons' current witness to pacifism. She said that she
had stopped to water her plants, according to her Monday habit,
before she left the house and walked to Foster Place. She repeated
several times that she had knocked and rung at the Laughtons'

front door but, receiving no answer, had let herself in. Calling and walking upstairs had led to nothing, and when she walked toward the rear of the house she had found Hope's body in the kitchen.

At the end of an hour the questioning was over. Within a few minutes, a secretary produced a typed statement of Elizabeth's account. Elizabeth Elliot, for the first time in her sixty-seven years, signed her name to a police document. As she was signing, a man came into the interrogation room and handed the detective a piece of paper.

The detective was clearly startled at what he read. He looked at Elizabeth and said that there had been abundant quantities of gunpowder on both her hands.

"How do you explain this?" asked Burnham sharply.

Doug Gibson leaned forward and stopped chewing his gum, but he did not restrain his client from answering.

"It makes no sense," said Elizabeth. "I have never picked up a gun in my life, much less fired one."

"There was more powder on your hands than I'd expect if you'd been at a firing range all morning."

Elizabeth, with the certainty given to those telling the truth, calmly replied, "I've never held a gun in my hands in my life. Never. It's not something a Quaker would forget, Mr. Burnham."

"May I ask something?" said Doug Gibson.

Burnham eyed him narrowly, but nodded.

"Did you wash anything with ammonia this morning? Do any cleaning, I mean in your home? Or touch any fertilizer?"

The detective looked at Elizabeth closely. She thought for a moment and then remembered her dull-looking Christmas cacti. She explained how she had watered her plants, first adding dry fertilizer to her watering can.

"That makes sense," said Burnham slowly. "There's too much nitrogen on your hands for a single gunshot. The test is for nitrogen, actually, not for gunpowder itself. There's nitrogen in the powder, you see."

"And in other things, too," Doug Gibson interjected.

"Indeed," said the detective dryly. "Still, Mrs. Elliot, it's a good thing I know you. Circumstantial evidence is against you."

"My client was found with the murder victim, it's true," mused Gibson aloud, "but no weapon was found with her. And she had no motive for harming Hope Laughton. Quite the contrary."

Burnham smiled in detached amusement. He asked Elizabeth to write an addition to her statement detailing her handling of fertilizer. Then he said she was free to go once she had surrendered her clothes. But he cautioned her not to leave Cambridge. Doug Gibson, looking at his watch, gave Elizabeth his card and excused himself, inviting her to call him the next day or at any time if the police contacted her again.

Ruth Markham had arrived during the questioning and stood waiting in the hall outside Burnham's office. She had brought a grocery bag with a change of clothes for her friend. She was allowed to hand the bag to Elizabeth as a police matron took the Clerk to a room where she could undress.

"I'll wait for you!" Ruth called out. In her distress at seeing her friend in police custody, she looked fiercely at Burnham and snapped, "Harassing an old woman for a change of pace, eh?"

Burnham was too wise to respond. He said instead, in carefully civil tones, that Ruth could wait in the lounge at the end of the hall.

4

Friends set definite limitations to the authority of their rulers. If occasion arises when it is necessary to refuse obedience to unjust laws, such conscientious objection should not be entered into lightly or hastily, and should be made with love and forbearance toward those who disagree.

New England Yearly Meeting, 1950

Elizabeth was sagging with fatigue when she appeared at the door of the tiny lounge at the end of the hall. She was dressed in the clothes Ruth had brought. The outfit was a navy blue print blouse and a pair of royal blue cotton slacks that Elizabeth would never have worn together but which, at present, filled the need. Fortunately, Ruth had brought a pair of sandals. Elizabeth had been required to surrender even her hose to the police matron, and she was glad not to have to wear closed-in shoes without stockings of some kind.

She was now free to depart and said so to Ruth, who sat waiting for her, fidgeting with impatience.

"Thank you for bringing me these things," said Elizabeth as the two women walked down the wide marble stairs of the old building to the first floor.

"I hope my choice was OK. I just took what looked practical. Here's your house key. You shouldn't keep it under the mailbox, you know. It's the first place a thief would look." Then in a sharper tone Ruth asked, "But what on earth has happened?"

Elizabeth explained as briefly as possible. Ruth adjusted quickly to the news of Hope's death. She was not hardhearted, Elizabeth knew, but she always maintained a tough exterior.

"Did Bill get you a decent lawyer?" asked Ruth abruptly, after

Elizabeth had explained her discovery of the corpse.

Elizabeth assured her that he had.

"How can you know? He may be an old wreck in need of business. These lawyers are a pack." Seeing the distress on Elizabeth's
face she said briskly, "But what's done is done." More gently she
continued, "You look worn out, Friend. Too bad the Meeting for
Healing isn't until Saturday." Elizabeth was unsure whether Ruth
was speaking facetiously. The Meeting she had mentioned was a
grave matter to the Clerk, since it was one at which the needs of
the membership could be publicly brought before God. But some
Friends thought petition and intercession to be the lowest forms
of prayer and looked askance at Meetings for Healing.

Before Elizabeth could think how to respond, Ruth asked in a
matter-of-fact tone, "Have you had lunch?" The two women had
emerged from the front door of the police building. It was not a
torrid day, but the morning's cool temperatures were a thing of
the past. The concrete around them reflected the sun and made
Elizabeth feel more poorly.

"No, I've had nothing since breakfast," she answered, "and
that seems like an eternity ago. Let's go someplace air-
conditioned." It was an extravagance by Elizabeth's simple standards, but the day seemed to call for extremes. She added, "Some
lunch might help me."

"Of course it will!" said Ruth. "Come across the street to the
cab stand. We'll take a taxi to Harvard Square."

Elizabeth allowed herself to be put in a taxicab, transported to
the well-chilled Green House Café in Harvard Square, and established there at a corner table. Ruth suggested what she might
order and hurried the waitress. Elizabeth was glad to relax momentarily in the face of Ruth's gift at taking charge. But then she
began to feel distracted. "We must tell Sheldon what's happened,"
she said, "but I don't know how to get in touch with him." She
was near tears. "He needs to know."

"Elizabeth," said Ruth sharply, "he needs to be told. But the police will do that as soon as they can. When he copes with the news, he'll find a way of telling Cathy. None of that is your responsibility, Friend! You look bad enough right now without more worry. So give yourself a break, at least until you've eaten."

Elizabeth took a steady, deep breath and put her hands briefly to her face as if in prayer.

Once food was in front of her, she became sharply hungry. Color returned to her face as she ate a large bowl of soup and half a sandwich and drank a glass of apple juice. As Ruth demolished a dieter's special plate of cottage cheese and fruit, Elizabeth felt the transforming power of food hitting her bloodstream. Within a minute she was both much calmer and felt a wave of deeper, more certain energy.

Ruth stopped chewing long enough to muse aloud. "The question is, if the killing was done by someone in our community, who would have a motive?"

"No matter who did this terrible thing, it's difficult to imagine a motive for murder," replied Elizabeth firmly.

"Yes, especially difficult for someone like you. But I can imagine killing someone. If I were angry enough, or afraid for my life. All of a sudden, I mean. But it's tough to see how a woman as gentle as Hope could have put someone into a blind rage. And how could she have made anybody so afraid they would kill her?"

"Perhaps she surprised a burglar. Someone hanging around the house who saw Sheldon and Cathy leave and figured the house was empty."

"Yes. If the gun can be traced, that will clear it up, but I don't suppose that burglars register their guns."

"No," responded Elizabeth, "and anyway, I think a pure and simple burglar wouldn't carry a gun. But a man who wanted to kill would do so, of course. This could be some lunatic, don't you think? A passing stranger, coming in off the street to fill some perverse need, like you see in the papers."

"Actually," said Ruth, "what you see in the papers is almost never random violence. People who kill almost always know the victim, usually intimately."

"I confess, I skip those things in the *Globe*," said Elizabeth quietly.

"Not me! I read 'em all!" declared Ruth. "Which brings us to Hope's husband and, I suppose, our Meeting. That's going to be the suspect pool for the police, you can bet on it. And the first question will be whether there was a lot of premeditation involved or if the killer only decided on things this morning."

Ruth paused to sip her coffee, giving Elizabeth time to think.

"Very little premeditation, I would guess," said the Clerk at last. "If the killer is a Quaker, I think he came to the end of some road this morning, and could see no way to go forward but to commit murder. The decision may have swept over him quickly. A bit like depression. When someone is really deeply depressed, the only option they can see is suicide. From the outside, you and I know there are other choices, but they don't. But what was it about Hope that gave someone no alternative but murder?"

Ruth put down her cup. "That's a good point about tunnel vision. But if you're right, and it was a desperate decision to kill, I think it will be harder for us to understand. You're a good student of human nature, Elizabeth, but a passion of the moment will be tough even for you to deduce. At least if the killer can remain calm."

"If it was a decision made in a hurry, the killer made one or more mistakes. Stupid things that will weigh on him."

"Or her," said Ruth.

"Yes, yes," replied Elizabeth distractedly. "We may see the mistakes or find the killer trying to correct his errors."

"One of the neighbors may have seen someone come to the house," mused Ruth.

"Yes. That would be most helpful, of course. But it was truly quiet when I walked down Foster Place this morning. No people moving around, no cars even. Residents of that neighborhood are the kind who have places on the Cape or the Vineyard."

"True," said Ruth. "They aren't here at this time of year, enjoying the heat in Cambridge with us plebeians."

Neil Stevenson, Elizabeth's gentleman friend, had a summer house on Martha's Vineyard. He had wanted Elizabeth to spend August with him there, but she had declined, not wishing to have any appearance of evil between them. Neil therefore stayed in town, the better to spend time with her, and Elizabeth was strongly conscious of his sacrifice. She had never known someone with a house on the sea to voluntarily spend the last soggy part of the summer in Cambridge.

"The police will check with any neighbors who are here," said Elizabeth. "That's the kind of thing they're good at." Her tone changed sharply as she added, "I wonder if little Cathy could be in any sort of danger."

"There's no way of knowing at this point. How will the police find Sheldon if they don't know where he's working today?" Ruth said, picking up her coffee again.

"I don't know. They asked where he took the child, but I couldn't tell them that either," replied the older woman, gently shaking her head.

"Ha!" cried Ruth, setting down her tepid coffee with a clatter. "I can! I've been doing nursery duty for First Day School this year, and I know Cathy Laughton. Hope came by to pick her up a few Sundays ago, and I asked her where Cathy had learned to write the alphabet. All the kids learn the letters from *Sesame Street*, but Cathy writes all twenty-six letters—in correct order, mind you— anytime she's near a crayon. Hope says she learned it all at Inman Day Care. The program wins awards because they blend Montessori lessons with a twelve-hour day care schedule. Every day. That's where Sheldon took her this morning, I'm sure."

"If they're open at this time of year . . ." Elizabeth mused.

"Friend," said Ruth with exaggerated seriousness, "day care is a fifty-two-week-a-year business. We're not living in 1961 anymore."

Elizabeth ignored Ruth's tone, accustomed as she was to her friend's un-Quakerly manner of speech. "Let's walk to my house," she said, comfortable about thinking aloud with a Friend, "and get my car. You're right, of course, about violence being frequently quite domestic. The police will think of that, too, and they'll ask what Sheldon has to say for himself. I hope he'll be able to prove where he was this morning. But it's hard to see how he can demonstrate what went on inside the house early in the morning, unless Cathy knows and can tell us. Let's see if we can find the child at the day care. If she can report how her mother was just before her father and she left, we may be able to clear Sheldon of suspicion." She continued with more certainty. "At least clear him in the Meeting's mind, if not in Detective Burnham's. And Sheldon's standing in Meeting should be protected, if possible, both for his and for Cathy's sake." She looked up at Ruth. "Or do you need to get back to Harvard? Forgive me for forgetting this is a workday for you."

"Harvard can limp through one day without me. When Bill Hoffman called this morning, I put a 'Back in an Hour' sign on my typewriter. But I didn't say which hour. Let's go. I doubt that the police will listen to the evidence of a three-year-old, but if we handle this right, she may be able to tell us the truth. That's what the Meeting will need."

The pair left Harvard Square and walked up Concord Avenue. The short trip was a warm one, but now that she had something definite to do, she felt much better. She and Ruth got in her '77 Chevrolet, wincing at the heat inside. With the windows wide open, Ruth directed Elizabeth to the day-care center near Inman Square, just outside Cambridge in Somerville. They arrived at a large modern building and were fortunate enough to find a place on the street to park in the shade.

"God smiles on you," said Ruth as Elizabeth parallel-parked. The Clerk decided not to invest any of her limited energy in eldering her friend about her flippancy.

While Elizabeth was struggling to lock the car, Ruth got out and walked up the steps and through the double front doors. Elizabeth caught up to her as Ruth poked her head into a room just off the main hallway that had the word OFFICE on its door. Elizabeth was content to stand in the hallway, surprised at the size of a modern day-care facility. Her elementary school had been smaller and, she thought, considerably better looking, perhaps because it had been designed by practical people unconcerned with architectural statements.

Ruth stepped back from the office door and motioned the elder Quaker to follow down the hallway. At a door marked ROOM 4, she knocked and went in. Elizabeth followed close behind. Two slender women, casually dressed and quite relaxed, were seated at the front of the room, chatting in near whispers while about twenty small bodies lay spread around the floor on mats. The Quaker visitors had come at nap time.

"May I help you?" asked the closer of the two women as a few small children raised their heads to look at the newcomers.

"I'm Catherine Laughton's Sunday school teacher and a friend of her parents," said Ruth softly before Elizabeth could speak. "We'd like to speak to Cathy. There's been a tragedy at her house this morning."

The younger woman's brow furrowed. "Let me see if she is awake. Please wait in the hall, and I'll bring her out."

Minutes later, little Cathy, her teacher in tow, emerged from the room.

"Hi, Luth!" said the child, pulling absently at the elastic in the waistband of her bright red shorts. Her printed top had dark food stains spread evenly across her gently rounded stomach.

"Hello, Cathy!" said Ruth. She looked up at Cathy's youthful teacher and said in her most commanding tone, "Please listen carefully and remember everything that's said." As she turned her attention again to Cathy, her sharp-edged personality miraculously softened. She knelt down to the child's height and said warmly, "I'm sorry if we got you up from your nap."

"I don't like nap," said Catherine Laughton seriously.

Ruth smiled. "Neither did my boy when he was your age. Can you tell me about this morning at home? Your daddy brought you here today, didn't he?"

Cathy put a stubby finger in her mouth and nodded.

"When you and your daddy left the house, what was your mother doing?"

The child removed her finger and said, "Mama was eating blekfast."

"Where did you say good-bye to your mama?"

"In the car. Mama put me in the car seat."

"Where was your daddy when Mama put you in the car seat?"

"In his seat."

"In the car?"

The little girl nodded, looked at Elizabeth critically, and returned her attention to the more familiar Ruth.

"What happened next?"

"We came here."

Ruth glanced up at the teacher as if to emphasize what the child was saying and returned her attention to Catherine. "Did you see your mama go into the house?"

Catherine nodded and said, "She wabed at us from the window."

Ruth quickly hugged Catherine, and Elizabeth saw tears in the secretary's normally hard eyes. Ruth stood up and, taking the child by the hand, moved a few feet down the hall. Elizabeth, who felt relief for Sheldon and deep compassion for his motherless child, brushed back tears and said to Cathy's teacher, "I'm Elizabeth Elliot, head of the Quaker Meeting that Catherine's parents belong to. May I ask your name?"

"Denise Johnson. What's all this about?" asked the young woman, belatedly beginning to display some distrust about the proceedings.

"It's police business, I'm afraid," said Elizabeth quietly, grateful to Ruth for moving the child down the hall. "A man from Cambridge's Homicide Department, a Detective Burnham, will call you in the next day or two and ask you about this. It's a matter of clearing Catherine's father of suspicion of a horrible crime. If you can, please write down everything you heard here while it's still fresh in your mind."

The young woman nodded her ponytailed head. She seemed to accept Elizabeth's words as they were intended. Elizabeth motioned for Ruth, who returned with the three-year-old. Denise and Cathy went back into Room 4, Cathy turning to wave goodbye to Ruth.

Ruth regained her adult manner in an instant. "Whatever the cops may think, we know Sheldon didn't harm Hope Laughton. And you didn't either."

"We can thank God that Sheldon seems above suspicion," Elizabeth replied reverently. But then she added, "The terrible thing is, someone is the murderer. May we have the strength to face what that may mean."

Elizabeth gave Ruth a ride to the north part of Harvard's campus on Oxford Street, where, with a grunt, the secretary extricated herself from the sagging vinyl-covered seats of the old Chevrolet. From the curb she leaned into the open window of the car and brusquely informed Elizabeth that if little Catherine needed somewhere to stay, she would be welcome with her.

"I could take her to Inman Square during the day when I have to be here at work. She's used to that day care, and since she knows me, my house might not be a bad place for her. Until things sort themselves out for Sheldon."

Elizabeth thanked Ruth for the thought. "By the way," she asked, "do you know what Pax Christi is?"

"It means the peace of Christ, doesn't it?"

"I guess so. But I think it's an organization."

"No, I can't help you. It's not Quaker, that's for sure. Since when do Friends know Latin?" She laughed derisively. "But now back to the grind," she said, turning away and trudging up the sidewalk to Harvard's paleontology building.

After dropping off Ruth Markham, Elizabeth drove home and parked her car. The motor of the old Chevy ran on for several seconds after it was switched off, but she was too absorbed to notice.

The sun was still high in the sky. Elizabeth's relief at Cathy's report gave her new strength to face inconveniences like the August heat. She collected a large stack of Monday mail from her box and went into the house, wondering if she should put her spare house key back in its usual place or find another spot for it. She decided on the same place and found some new tape. Long ago she had unconsciously chosen to ignore the ever-rising street crime in Cambridge, and luck or divine intervention had protected her house from burglary and her person from robbery. She had confidence nothing would change.

In her living room she automatically glanced at the mail. To her surprise there was a thick envelope from Rebecca Nichols, her roommate in college. Rebecca had been a shy Baptist girl when she arrived at Wellesley from rural Washington State. Elizabeth's quiet Quaker ways had soon put her roommate at ease, and they had become fast friends. They roomed together for four years, sharing every confidence. Elizabeth had married Michael, a good Quaker man, while Rebecca had returned to the Northwest and gone to work in a bank. Her abilities had carried her upwards, despite the perceptions so many held of her sex in those days. Seattle's postwar economy expanded with each decade as trade with Asia blossomed, and Rebecca flourished along with her bank. She was a senior vice president by the time she was fifty— and that in an era when women bankers were as rare as Quakers in the Marines.

In the first several decades of their acquaintance, Rebecca had not been as serious as Elizabeth about religious life, claiming that since she had been born again, like any good Baptist, somewhere in the passage through adolescence, nothing more could be demanded of her. But after arriving at the top of the business world she had written to her old roommate that she was once again attending church on Sundays. Although there were few high-ranking businesspeople in the Baptist tradition, Rebecca was well used to being unusual, and she joined a large, progressive Baptist church in her downtown neighborhood. Elizabeth could not help being delighted for these changes in her friend's life.

The Quaker knew from the heft of the missive that something serious was on Rebecca's mind. She sat down and opened the envelope. The letter was handwritten, unusual for Rebecca, and it ran:

> Dearest Elizabeth,
> I'd like to speak to you, but it's too late in the evening to call. It's always late in the East by the time I get home from the bank, and even tonight, upset though I am, I don't want to risk disturbing your rest—so I'll write down my troubles.
> Everything at church is terrible, just terrible. I can hardly bring myself to think about it. You remember, don't you, that five years ago I was on the pulpit committee? We needed a new pastor, and four other members and I did a nationwide search for one, the normal thing for us Baptists. The process of finding a preacher

is a bit like falling in love: you need someone who fits with the congregation and can be a father figure for it even while he guides the church through whatever rough spots it encounters.

We were very pleased to eventually find a man who seemed just right in every way. He was a pastor in his forties with a pleasant wife and two school-aged children. He was originally from the Midwest, although the church he came from was in California. He could preach well, but he wasn't in any danger of succumbing to fundamentalism, the disease that's infected so many Baptist churches. He was a very able man: he was a licensed psychologist as well as a clergyman, and he set up a practice here in our church with the blessing of the congregation. He saw clients who otherwise might not have been able to afford that sort of help— Baptists, of course, but also a variety of church people referred to him by clergymen from other congregations in the area. He still preached on Sundays and did so very well. In short, we thought he was doing more than most pastors do to earn their bread, and even if we didn't understand exactly what he was doing during the week we assumed it was all for the best.

And maybe part of his weekday work was worthwhile, who knows? I still can't believe he's a thoroughly evil man!

But nothing less than evil has been happening in his ministry, I'm afraid. It's wrenching to admit it, but at least several of the younger women and teenage girls who came for psychological help to our church office ended up in sexual relationships with the pastor.

From what I know of doctors and patients, things

can get intense on both sides, but it's the responsibility of the professional not to lose control. Indeed, don't psychiatrists get kicked out of the AMA for this sort of thing? I think having sex with patients is recognized as the worst thing a therapist can do. It's the professional aspect of the wrongdoing that really gets to me. Where can women go if not to a doctor or a pastor for help? They had every reason to trust this man, and their trust was cruelly misused.

Naturally there are other elements to the situation. The man is an ordained Baptist minister and, of course, is married. Really, it's all too distressing. He'll lose his job with us on Sunday; the deacons have called a congregational meeting in order to fire him. The regional association of Baptist churches, when it gets its act together, will refuse to recognize his ordination anymore. And I assume his license to practice psychology is in jeopardy. Heaven only knows what his wife will do.

I still think he was partly a good man. He cared about the ministry and about the congregation. That was genuine, Elizabeth! But we all of us are bent, and people do have deep talents for rationalization. He's harmed everyone he's cared about now, and probably destroyed himself. I really wonder if he'll live through this.

It's not an unusual tragedy, I know. You can see that by just glancing at the papers. But it's devastating when it envelops your own church. It will be especially hard for the children. The well-behaved ones, at least, look up to him, and he's been the Sunday school teacher for the high school group for the past several years.

Damn it! That makes me wonder! If he harmed any
of our own high school girls I'll kill the swine! I'm
sorry, Elizabeth, but I'm terribly angry. Our trust has
been betrayed, and I was one of the people who recommended hiring him in the first place, you see.

Perhaps Friends are wise not to have clergy. You do
avoid some problems. But surely even Quakers can't
always avoid sexual misconduct. Don't tell me there's
no sin in Meeting life!

It's very late now and my head is splitting so I'll stop
here without inquiring politely how you and your children are. Hope to speak to you soon.

Love,
Rebecca

Elizabeth set the letter down slowly. She was distressed for her
friend, but in light of the current problems in Meeting she knew
she could not give her whole attention to Rebecca's pain. It was
a terrible thing, surely, for a trusted man to behave in such a way.
There was nothing but danger, as far as Elizabeth could see, in
ordaining people. After being told they spoke for God, and did
so in a way no one else in their congregation could, was it any
wonder so many clergymen succumbed to the worst part of their
own egos? And doctors of all sorts ran the risk of playing God with
their patients rather than respecting the individual's right to self-
direction. Combining a doctor's power with a pastor's authority
could certainly lend itself to gross abuse. Quakers, perhaps,
avoided some of what Rebecca called "misconduct" by refusing
to locate significant power in any individual. A Quaker Clerk was
little more than chair of the Business Meetings, and a person was
Clerk for only a few years. But that was not to say, of course, that
Quakers were less prone to the sins of personal life than church
people. They simply could do less harm to their brothers and sis-

ters in Christ since no Friend had authority over any other.

Elizabeth set aside the letter, making a mental note to return to it when her own life was in better order. The rest of the mail consisted of catalogs and bills. Putting the whole stack on her desk, she went upstairs and changed into anklets and walking shoes which she could lace up firmly. She decided not to take the time to change her slightly mismatched clothes, reasoning that the people she would encounter on her proposed errands would not expect the best her closet could produce. She went downstairs, locked the front door, and walked down Concord Avenue toward the Common. She made use of Episcopal property, as was her habit, to take a short cut to Brattle Street and Longfellow Park. The Meetinghouse looked the same as ever, unaffected by the events of the morning. Its solid bricks were stolidly reassuring.

5

We state again our opposition to all forms of violence and oppression. We call on our government to avoid the support and the appearance of support of oppressive governments abroad and oppressive measures at home. Some of our members seek to call attention to the involvement of our government in institutionalized violence by refusing to pay all or a portion or their [federal] taxes. While we do not now feel that all members are called to take this action, such a witness may represent a true leading for an individual. In cases in which the Yearly Meeting has tested the leading of an employee to make such a witness, it shall place all or a portion of the taxes withheld from the employee in the New England Yearly Meeting Peace Tax Fund or some other appropriate fund, rather than voluntarily turning over such funds to the government. The Yearly Meeting takes this action in order to assist in calling attention to the involvement of the government in violence and in support of individual calling, and not from any desire to frustrate civil authority.

Document from Business Meeting,
Friends Meeting at Cambridge, 1993

Elizabeth crossed the driveway to the colonial-style brick house next door, which was owned by the Meeting. The Meetinghouse itself was one large room, useful for allowing two or even three hundred Quakers to worship together but less useful for smaller gatherings. The house next to the Meetinghouse was used as an office and for classes of the First Day School. It also had a kitchen, two small parlors, and bathrooms. The Clerk entered and said hello to Harriet Parker, the Meeting secretary. Harriet was on the telephone, which was a relief to Elizabeth, who did not want to get into a conversation. She quickly checked the Clerk's mailbox and found it jammed. A number of letters were awaiting her attention. She leafed through the stack of envelopes, discarding junk mail but opening the other items. There was a call for more Quakers to do prison visitation, and a request that Friends hold a vigil on Boston Common in opposition to the death penalty. An ecumenical rape crisis center in Cambridge was asking the Meeting for financial assistance, and there was a handwritten letter from an eighteen-year-old asking for advice about resisting draft registration. The draft had ended long ago, but under the Reagan administration a law had been passed requiring eighteen-year-old males to register in case the government decided to call them up for military service. This posed questions of conscience for people hardly more than children. Each letter would need thoughtful attention, and Elizabeth felt momentarily overwhelmed by the burdens of the Quaker testimony to nonviolence. Pacifism had never been an easy witness, of course, but the complexities of the modern, interdependent world seemed to multiply a Quaker's responsibilities without multiplying the time and energy needed to respond to God's will.

During the buildup of tensions occasioned by the Laughtons' tax resistance, the Clerk had feared that she and the Meeting were not up to the demands of the Quaker tradition. Pausing with the mail in her hands, she reflected that a good Friend had now been killed, just as her witness to the IRS was being put to a severe test. Both events were unusual, and although there was no logical connection between the two evident at the moment, Elizabeth was sure that the timing of the murder and the confiscation of the Laughton property were not the result of chance. She could have been wrong, but in her long experience, extreme and unusual events were often interconnected, although not necessarily in a simple way.

It was tragic, if she were correct, that Friends' attempts to live within the peace testimony of the Gospels could be connected to such violent evil. Elizabeth softly quoted an old hymn her mother used to sing around the house, murmuring, "What needless pain we bear." Throughout her life, she had, at times, been sure she did not have the strength required to be a Quaker, and the demands on her today reminded her of her constant failure to be a true light in a dark and complex world. But after a moment's paralysis, habit and discipline, if not faith, regained control of her mind. She put the envelopes into her purse, waved good-bye to Harriet, still on the telephone, and went back outside. Her head was heavy as she left Longfellow Park and walked up Mt. Auburn Street to the hospital.

The walk seemed much longer than it had seven years earlier, when Michael Elliot was spending his final days at the hospital. At that time, Elizabeth had made the trip twice each day. She did not remember the walk as so taxing. Of course, she had been younger then, and the air pollution in Cambridge was not quite so bad.

When Elizabeth reached the hospital she sat in the air-conditioned lobby for a few minutes and had a soft drink from a machine. She arose with more energy. Walking to the end of the hall, she asked a woman behind a counter labeled PATIENT IN-FORMATION, "In which room may I find Miss Silverstone? She's been here several days."

Consulting a computer screen and without looking up, the young woman answered, "In room four-oh-two. Up the elevator, down the hall, on the left."

Elizabeth took the elevator and walked slowly down the brightly lit hallway of the fourth floor. She was passed by two nurses busily talking to each other and paying no attention to the quiet visitor. She reached room 402. Knocking brought no response, but knowing her eighty-six-year-old friend's increasing difficulty with hearing, Elizabeth opened the door and looked inside. There were two beds in the room, the first smoothly made up and empty. Patience Silverstone was in the second, next to the large windows at the end of the room. She caught sight of her friend and motioned through the bars of her bed for Elizabeth to enter. The younger Quaker walked quickly in, concern evident on her face.

"It's wonderful to see thee," said the older woman, her eyes smiling.

"I heard you had fallen," Elizabeth replied as she looked around at the clean but plain room. Its beige walls and obligatory framed print of a nature scene reinforced the idea that Mt. Auburn Hospital was a bureaucratic institution, first and foremost, and only secondarily a place for healing. "I didn't see you at Meeting yesterday, and in the evening Jane Thompson called and told me what had happened. Why didn't you telephone me?" asked Elizabeth, with chagrin.

"I know how busy a Clerk is, and I was sure the news would reach all Friends soon enough," said Patience calmly. "But it's good to see thee now," she added with warmth.

"What happened?"

"Don't be angry with me! On Saturday morning, I stood on a chair to reach my big roasting pan, and I fell." She tapped the cast on her leg. "My hip is intact, God be thanked, but my leg is broken, and I'm bruised from head to toe. The doctor says he can't put one of those metal pins in my leg. The break is wrong for it. So the cast will have to stay on for a while."

Knowing how difficult it was for bones to heal in the elderly, Elizabeth shook her head sadly. "I'm sorry, Friend."

"My thanks," said Patience. "Young people do keep their balance better."

"Indeed. Which is, of course, a reason for reconsidering one's habit of climbing on chairs." She smiled. "But I can't criticize. I know I do things around the house that frighten my sons." Her gentle eyes searched the patient's face. "Are the nurses here treating you well?"

"Oh, yes. The staff is kind. The boys in the ambulance and the emergency room people were gentle. My doctor came right away to see me."

"Are you in pain?"

"Not much more than usual, actually," said Patience with a small laugh. "They've given me some sort of anti-inflamatory drug for my leg. I'm not sure it does the break much good, but it really helps my arthritis." She held up her hands and wiggled her fingers. "I may have more freedom of movement than thee."

"In your hands, perhaps," Elizabeth answered with a smile. She nervously touched her own hands together. They still reminded her unpleasantly of the police tests. "But I assume you won't be leaving this bed soon," she said as she pulled her mind back to her friend.

"No," said Patience equitably. "But I think I look better than thee at the moment. Is something wrong?"

Elizabeth nodded and sat down beside the bed. "I can scarcely tell you this, the news is so difficult. And here you are injured and in pain. But still, it's important Meeting news, and I know you would want me to tell you." With tears in her eyes, Elizabeth haltingly relayed the news about Hope's death and her own discovery of the corpse.

Patience was shocked and grieved. "Oh," she said with a sob, "to think of how many Friends thee and I have seen come to the end of life. But a death such as this one!"

"Yes, this end is a tragedy. And for more than one person."

"Indeed. I know we should believe that all things work for the best, but sometimes it just doesn't seem that way in this world. She was just a child herself!" said the Meeting's oldest member, her voice cracked with emotion. "Such a waste of a good Quaker." But Patience had lived too long to be permanently disconcerted by death, however unexpected and tragic. "It's a terrible thing," she said more firmly. "And most terrible, of course, for Hope's little girl."

Elizabeth sighed her agreement. She explained that Ruth and she had spoken to Cathy at her day-care center. Elizabeth relayed the girl's exact words.

"That may not count as real evidence to the police, but it should clear Sheldon of suspicion in Friends' minds," said Patience. "Not that one could suspect him! But still, I'm glad he drove away when Hope was alive and well."

Elizabeth concurred.

"Who will raise the little girl?"

Elizabeth smiled at her friend's assumption that a father could not rear a child. "I assume Sheldon will raise her, Friend. Men do such things these days. But perhaps at the moment Hope's sister will take her. I know Hope and she have been close, and she would be family. I hope something like that will work out because, between the homicide department and the IRS, Sheldon's life over the next several days will be complete chaos."

"Should I know Hope's sister?"

"Yes, she's Constance Baker of our Meeting. Her husband is Titus Baker, the man who used to work in D.C. for the Friends Committee on National Legislation. The Bakers don't attend regularly. In the last several years, Titus has often been in Central America with the Friends Service Committee, and Constance doesn't come to Meeting without him. But they're members of our Meeting."

Patience nodded her head. "I know who they are. If Constance doesn't have too many children of her own, perhaps she can help Sheldon for the present."

"She has no kids, I'm sure of that." It had once occurred to Elizabeth, chatting with the Bakers after a Meeting some years ago, that Constance was quite lonely. Titus's frequent absences, the Clerk had thought, left his wife alone most of the year. Children would have made the situation different, but not all women were blessed with them as Elizabeth had been. "But if she doesn't feel up to it," she continued, "Ruth Markham just volunteered to take Catherine while Sheldon organizes a new life."

Patience considered. "I have never appreciated Ruth as a Friend. She is too short-tempered and sharp-tongued for my liking. But she does do a lot for our community, I must admit."

"Indeed. And our Meeting will need lots of help in the coming days. Sheldon or I will be the police's prime suspect, I'm sure. I was found with the body, and it clearly was a recent death. Hope was still as warm as you and I are now. I touched her to check for a pulse, you see. The police will use their methods to fix the time of death, but it was only shortly before I arrived, I'm sure. And as for Sheldon, unless it's perfectly clear where he went after he dropped Catherine off at the day care, I'm afraid the police will suspect that he came back home and shot his wife. Husbands killing wives will hardly be a new idea to the police."

"But Sheldon and thee had no motive!" Patience objected.

"Hope's death will not benefit me in any way. But Sheldon may benefit, through life insurance policies, for example. Although the Laughtons were not the sort to be heavily insured, living as they did, dependent on the Spirit. But still, there may be some financial motive the police will turn up." Elizabeth looked out the window and continued in a lower tone. "What worries me is that the murder may be bound up with the Laughtons' tax resistance. The timing of Hope's death and the crisis with the IRS is probably not just chance."

"It could be," said Patience slowly, also looking out the window at the distant seagulls circling over the Charles River. "But I admit both events are so unusual, it's tempting to try to explain them together." She looked back at the younger Quaker. "And tax resistance does get Friends into intense situations."

The Clerk sighed. "I sometimes wonder if we taxpaying Friends have really examined our conscience. Maybe we just don't have the courage to ask the Spirit for guidance."

"Perhaps," said Patience slowly. "But everything about breaking the law is complex."

"I admire the Laughtons. The tax system is more difficult to face than the draft, really. Taxes come up each year, over and over again, whereas young men facing the draft can choose conscientious objector work or go to prison and be done with it."

"Yes," replied Patience. "There's no relief from the tax dilemma, except destitution or death. And the pressure from maintaining that kind of witness is intense. Hope and Sheldon are true Quakers, but think of what they had to endure at the time of the auction last spring!"

"But can God call them to do more than they can manage?"

asked Elizabeth rhetorically. "Surely not. If this tax resistance is truly of the Spirit, then they will be sustained. That must be our faith."

"Such faith is touching," said the elder Quaker with a smile. "But I've seen just how human Friends are. Could it be surprising if one of the Laughtons broke down? Do you think, for example, that Hope could have killed herself?"

"No. I've thought of that, but there would have been a gun beside the body if it were suicide. Unless someone took it away, I suppose." Elizabeth rubbed her eyes and longed for a strong cup of tea. "It looks like murder, not suicide, and in that quiet neighborhood I doubt that a thug would come in off the street to shoot Hope."

"Sheldon owns a gun," said Patience quietly.

Elizabeth started. "Sheldon Laughton?"

The bedridden patient nodded as much as her stack of pillows allowed. "I learned of it some years ago, when he was spending his summers working as a geologist in Alaska. I eldered him about it, asking what sort of witness it made, a Quaker carrying around a gun! But he said he needed it for bears in the North and for rattlesnakes, I think it was, when he did a job in Nevada. It still seemed wrong to me, but that may be easier to say in Cambridge than out West."

"What kind of gun was it?"

"I've no idea."

"The police will learn of it. It's probably in the house somewhere. Unless we're fortunate and Sheldon got rid of it when Cathy got big enough to get into things. He might have done that, for safety's sake."

There was a pause in the two women's conversation. The elder Quaker coughed deeply. A bell rang down the hall and then subsided. Elizabeth saw that her friend's eyelids were drooping. She sat silently for a moment, dropped briefly into prayer, and then concluded that the visit had reached its end. She stood up and promised to return soon.

"It's always good to see thee," said Patience, "but I know how busy a Clerk is. Come when there's time."

"I'll be back in the middle of the week," said Elizabeth. "Until then you'll be in my prayers. On Saturday, you know, we have a Meeting for Healing. I'll bring your situation to it, of course. But by then I hope your pain will have lessened."

"God be with thee," responded the elder Quaker and smiled.

6

The politics of eternity works not by might but by spirit; a Spirit whose redemptive power is released among men through suffering endured on behalf of the evil-doer and in obedience to the divine command to love . . . such love suffers long, is always kind, never fails.

American Friends Service Committee, 1955

It was late afternoon when Elizabeth walked up Concord Avenue after her visit with Patience. The heat had abated a little, and the sun was lower in the sky. Still, she was hot when she reached her house, and her blouse was more than damp. She poured a large glass of ice tea from a jug in the refrigerator. She disliked coffee and drank soda pop only under duress, but tea, both hot and cold, was as refreshing and renewing to her as the sight of the Meetinghouse on Sunday morning. Encouraged by her first sip of the icy brew and by the agreeable prospect of a whole pitcher beyond her glass, she sat down by the telephone and opened her battered xeroxed copy of the directory of Friends in the Boston area. Otto Zimmer answered on the first ring. Elizabeth identified herself and said she had tragic news to tell him.

"I know already," replied Otto grimly. "I had signed up to come stay with Hope this afternoon, remember? When I got there, at twelve, the police were all over the place. They wouldn't let me in the house. They'd been searching the yard before I arrived, I think, and they'd just found a gun in the bushes. The rosebushes, at the front of the house. I got a glimpse of it, a big revolver. Then a man named Burnham told me Hope was dead and asked me lots of questions about where Sheldon could be found." Otto coughed or choked back tears. "I don't know where Sheldon is working at the moment, but I know he'll pick up Cathy at her day care when he's done. I gave them that address. Then I got worried, thinking that Cathy would be taken away to some foster home if they arrested Sheldon when he showed up for her. So I called Constance Baker, Hope's sister, and told her what had happened. She volunteered to wait at the Inman Day Care until Sheldon comes. She's Cathy's aunt, so I expect the police will allow her to take the child home for the present."

"Good," murmured Elizabeth. "But why do you think the police will arrest Sheldon?"

There was silence on the telephone line. Elizabeth shifted her sweaty grip on the receiver.

"I suppose I thought he was the obvious suspect," said Otto, strain evident in his voice. "Most murders are done by immediate relatives, aren't they? And I'm afraid he owned a revolver, left over from his days as a field geologist. I can't imagine that Sheldon is guilty, but the police may suspect him. They'll need to question him, at least."

"Oh, yes," agreed Elizabeth, "they'll question him in minute detail. I'm glad Catherine is taken care of for the present. She'll have a lot to adjust to now, poor thing, with her mother gone."

A clear sob escaped from Otto as he said, "She was a good woman. A real Friend. I can't imagine why she was killed! Do you think the man that bid on the house could have wanted the Laughtons out badly enough to harm her?"

"No," said Elizabeth quickly and firmly, impressed by the suspects Otto could so rapidly create. "The IRS was going to evict them this morning. The man could have taken possession of the house tomorrow if he had wanted."

"Who could have harmed her, some lunatic who got into the house?" asked Otto. "I don't see how anyone could have done such a thing. She was the best person I knew. Caring and gentle. And terrifically courageous. She was special, a very special woman." His voice trailed off into sobs.

Elizabeth wondered, for an instant, exactly how special Hope had been to him. Out of respect for the Friend's obvious grief she decided not to push him further on that subject, and she asked quickly, "Otto, what is the 'Pax Christi' that Sheldon referred to on Saturday?"

"It's a Catholic peace group," sputtered Otto, regaining composure as he added, "Pretty big, really. I don't know anything more except that Sheldon thinks highly of it."

"Has he worked for them?"

"No, I don't think so. It's very Catholic, not ecumenical. I assume a Quaker would not be welcome."

"Perhaps he knows some of the members, that's all. It's not connected with the Catholic Worker organization, is it?"

"No. The Catholic Worker people are radicals. Good pacifists, but living in poverty and working in soup kitchens. Pax Christi is a pretty mainline group. I think it's got serious peace concerns, but it's not strictly pacifist. And it's not radical in any way, at least not by our standards. It's got bishops on its board of directors, I remember Sheldon telling me."

"What will become of Catherine now, do you think?" asked Elizabeth abruptly, interested in seeing if Otto's distress would return with the change of subject.

She took another swallow of icy tea as Otto answered steadily, "Sheldon will raise her, I'm sure. What else? God comfort her now!" He sobbed, but quickly recovered and closed the conversation, asking Elizabeth to call him if she learned anything definite from the police. She let him go.

After hanging up, she finished her tea while musing thoughtfully. Then she called Neil Stevenson. She had no need to refer to the Friends' telephone directory this time, since she knew Neil's number by heart. He had been to her house for Sunday dinner only yesterday, but it seemed an age since she had heard his low, quiet voice. She told him the sad news about Hope Laughton. Neil listened carefully and offered to come over to

Concord Avenue if Elizabeth was feeling shaken. She declined his offer, although she appreciated it, saying truthfully that she was feeling much better now.

"Sheldon did a lot of work in my yard last spring," said Neil, trying in his own way to adjust to the tragedy by speaking of something certain and unemotional. "I was very pleased with the job he did. I have no idea, though, where he might be working in Lexington, and I don't think the police will be able to find him today. He almost always works for private individuals, you see, so he could be anywhere out there."

Elizabeth explained that Sheldon would be detained by the authorities when he went to the Inman Day Care to pick up Cathy.

"I know that when my wife died I wouldn't have wanted to speak to the police for any reason. But maybe his little daughter will give him a reason to hold on."

Elizabeth thought that likely and said so. The couple hung up, promising to get together the next day for lunch in Harvard Square, as was their increasingly frequent custom.

Elizabeth listened to an interview program on National Public Radio and warmed up a portion of Sunday's casserole. Sparkle appeared and curled up in a vacant chair as Elizabeth considered the day's events. The Quaker explained to the cat what little Catherine had said, and how glad she was that Sheldon appeared to be in the clear. Sparkle, used to Elizabeth's quiet monologues, began to purr. Elizabeth fell silent and stared out the window into the backyard, mechanically noting a goldfinch at the bird feeder. Minutes passed before she came out of her reverie and had her simple meal. As she was finishing washing the dishes, the doorbell rang, and, wiping her hands quickly on a tea towel, she went to answer it.

Detective Stewart Burnham stood on her front step in the glow of the setting sun. Out of a lifelong habit of hospitality Elizabeth began to smile, but she stopped when she saw the detective's stern face, set in rigid planes and angles.

"Do come in," she said simply, opening the aluminum screen door, which flashed dully in the sunlight as it swung open.

Detective Burnham stepped into the dark front hall, taking a paper from his suit pocket.

"I have a warrant for your arrest, Mrs. Elliot, for first-degree murder. You have the right to remain silent, and anything you say can and will be used against you in a court of law. You have the right to have your attorney present during questioning. If you so desire and cannot afford one, a lawyer will be appointed to represent you. Do you understand these rights as I have explained them to you?"

For Elizabeth, the day had begun at the Laughtons' house with concern that she had taken leave of her senses, and the idea of madness now returned with full force. She backed haltingly away from the detective and sat down on the stairs to the second floor. Putting her hands over her face, she tried to breathe deeply.

"Do you understand your rights?"

Elizabeth said nothing.

"You have to answer! Do you understand your rights as I have explained them to you?"

Elizabeth Elliot nodded slowly, her head still in her hands.

"How dare you talk to the Laughtons' little girl like that!" His voice was intense and angry. "What she says to me from now on is meaningless. For all I know, she'll only repeat what you put into her head!"

Mechanically Elizabeth looked up and focused on the open door in front of her. She shook her head. "Her teacher heard everything that was said on both sides. It's obvious, Mr. Burnham, that when Cathy left her home this morning with her father, Hope was alive and well."

"Nothing is obvious now! I can't take the word of some young day-care worker, considering the subtleties of what you may have done. You've been helpful to my office in the past, Mrs. Elliot, I admit that. But now you've gone much too far. My first thought was that this killing was done on the spur of the moment by an intruder. But you've given me good reason to think otherwise. And whether I like it or not, you're my best suspect for the murder. You may have dusted your hands with fertilizer to hide the trace amounts of nitrogen from firing one shot. Anyway, I know you're hiding something!" Burnham's voice rose another notch in pitch and intensity. "Why on earth did you lie in your statement this morning?"

"Lie?" said the bewildered Quaker softly, focusing her vision on her accuser but with no understanding of his question.

"Your statement is false. I don't know what you had to do with the events at that house, or who you are trying to protect. But I'll find out. A neighbor to the Laughtons saw you in their backyard before the IRS men arrived. You were looking into the kitchen window. There's no point in denying it; we found the imprint of your left shoe in the dirt under the window. There's dirt of the same color on the shoe we have at the station." He added pitilessly, "It was the other shoe that was bloody, so perhaps you didn't notice the mud when you surrendered your clothes."

"I did look into the kitchen window," said Elizabeth slowly, comprehending part of what was at issue.

"Why didn't you admit that in your statement?" asked Burnham quickly, his anger in no way diminished. "You said you went to the front door, received no answer, and went inside."

"And that was right!" said Elizabeth with the self-confidence born of speaking the truth. "I simply didn't think to tell you that I'd walked around the house to check if anybody was in the backyard or if I could raise an answer at the back door. I knew someone must be home! The IRS was expected, you see, and the Laughtons are not people to run away."

"Why lie?" said Burnham angrily. "What did you see through the window?"

Elizabeth looked directly at the detective and calmly replied,

"When I answered your questions in Central Square this morning I simply didn't think of everything. Please remember, I had had a terrible shock and fainted. Yes, I walked around the back of the house and looked in the kitchen window. I could see nothing. I knocked at the back door, but there was no answer. I tried it, but it was locked. Then I remembered that I hadn't tried to open the front door, so I went around to do that."

"I can't believe you, Mrs. Elliot, given how much your story has changed. You must come with me."

"May I get my purse? It has some of my blood pressure medicine in it, and I'll need it if you're going to keep me any length of time."

"I'm keeping you until you tell me the truth! Get your purse, by all means."

The detective's car, a dark Crown Victoria, was parked directly in front of the Elliot house, contrary to Cambridge traffic laws, which allowed no parking on that side of Concord Avenue. Traffic—and traffic regulations—so dominated the lives of Cantabrigians that the sight of the car on the wrong side of the street was almost as disorienting to Elizabeth as the idea that she was under arrest. The strangeness of the day continued to mount in her mind as the detective put her into the back seat of the car and closed the door that, Elizabeth mechanically noted, had no inside handle. For the first time in the old Quaker's life, she was truly at the mercy of the authorities.

At the police station Detective Burnham reached Doug Gibson on the telephone and told him to come immediately to Central Square. The detective then took Elizabeth to the same small, windowless interrogation room, where she waited alone until her lawyer appeared.

"What's happened?" asked Mr. Gibson. He listened intently to the Quaker's explanation, then blew out his breath thoughtfully and said, "The neighbor's evidence is important, I'm afraid. I sure wish more neighbors had been around, and looking out their windows, so someone else would have been seen near the house, too. Well, answer Burnham's questions when I let you, but if I tell you to be silent, don't say a word."

"I have nothing to hide," Elizabeth said with a hint of exasperation and more than a hint of fatigue.

"It's not a question of hiding anything. It's a matter of your rights, guaranteed by law."

Elizabeth began to say that mankind's law was of little importance to her, but she stopped herself and sat silently. Burnham came into the small room and sat down across from Elizabeth and her lawyer. He went over her statement line by line, asking at the end if she cared to amend it. She nodded and added to the statement, carefully writing out a description of her brief trip to the Laughtons' backyard. Doug Gibson read it, nodded, and handed it to the detective. Burnham questioned her again and again about the events of the morning. Elizabeth's fatigue deepened, but she answered as best she could. She stated every detail she could remember, with no objections from her lawyer. The third time through the story, she even remembered the sonic boom that had startled her when she was turning off Willard Street. She mentioned that she could not see the airplane that would have accounted for it, but Detective Burnham was not interested.

Just when Elizabeth thought the questioning was over, Burnham barked at her, "Who did you see through the kitchen window? It was someone from your Meeting, wasn't it?"

Before Gibson could respond, his client said, "I didn't see anyone! I suppose Hope was there, on the floor, but the sun was on the windows, and I don't think I could see the floor anyway."

Gibson relaxed.

"Who did you see in the backyard?" the detective queried.

"No one," said the Quaker deliberately, and added, "Did the neighbor who saw me see anyone else?"

Burnham looked at her narrowly.

"Do you have any other statements from neighbors?" asked Gibson.

"Everyone else in the neighborhood is away on vacation," said Burnham, shaking his head. "Which is why I have to value every bit of evidence I have. And the neighbor who saw your client is a good witness." Abruptly, he turned toward Elizabeth and asked, "Why did you want Hope Laughton dead?"

"I didn't! That's preposterous!" said Elizabeth, failing to hide her indignation. Gibson smiled and let her continue. "I was going to Foster Place this morning to support Hope Laughton in her tax witness." She felt something akin to anger, a most uncomfortable emotion for her. "Why would I want to kill a Quaker, a good mother, a Friend so serious about her testimony that she was an inspiration to the whole Meeting?"

"I don't know, but I'll check for every conceivable motive," responded Burnham with sincere exasperation. "False statements, nitrogen on your hands, and tampering with the evidence of a three-year-old witness! Damn it, Mrs. Elliot, you're going to regret this! I'll get to the truth!"

"God willing," said Elizabeth seriously, "the truth will become clear. Then you'll see that I'm telling you everything just as I remember it. Little Cathy and I are not liars, Detective."

Burnham stood up. "You'll be taken to a cell here for the night. There's no way to get bail determined this late in the evening."

"That's not acceptable!" said Gibson sharply. "My client should be released on her own recognizance."

Burnham stopped. "As you know, I don't have the authority to decide that. Bail, or waiving it, will be decided tomorrow. In fact, I can promise the preliminary hearing will be tomorrow, too. That's the best I can do."

"Detaining someone like Mrs. Elliot overnight in your cells is shocking!" said Gibson, rising from his chair.

"She'll be in with the women, remember. It's not a bad floor. And I'll get her an empty cell if there's one left." He turned abruptly, looking away from Elizabeth, and strode out of the tiny room.

"I'm sorry," said the lawyer with uncharacteristic feeling. "I'll see you at the preliminary hearing tomorrow. We may be able to get the charge dropped completely. About half of all criminal cases in this state don't go on beyond the preliminary hearing because the cops don't have solid evidence. They don't have a good case against you, and that's what I'll argue. But even if we lose and the charge stands, we'll get bail named. Can you post bail? It may be substantial."

Elizabeth thought of her carefully balanced checking account and shook her head. "I live on Social Security, in the house my husband and I had together. That's all I have." She realized with a start that her resources, at least potentially, had recently increased. "But I do have a friend from Meeting, a wealthy Quaker, who would put up bail for me, I'm sure."

"Even a large sum?"

"Yes," said Elizabeth simply. "Anything a judge could name, I think. Would you call him and tell him what's happened?"

"Of course."

Elizabeth dictated Neil's phone number from memory. A matron entered just then, so she didn't have time to consider if she should try to add a personal message to her friend.

Elizabeth was led up to the floor above the detective's office. There was air-conditioning in the lower parts of the building, but here on the cell floor the warm and increasingly humid air was dense. Her clothes and purse were taken from her, but she was allowed to keep two doses of her prescription medicine. The rest was confiscated, Elizabeth could only assume, to prevent any suicide attempt. A police matron gave her a loose-fitting nightdress and a jumpsuit, both bright orange. She was put in an empty cell next to two young women.

"You'll get your own clothes back in the morning for your hearing. Lights out in ten minutes!" said the matron as she walked away. Elizabeth was left to wish that she had had on better clothes when Detective Burnham had come to her house. She would now have to appear before a judge in the mismatched blouse and slacks Ruth had picked out.

It was stuffy but not terribly hot. The two women next to Elizabeth were loud and talkative, and the Quaker could not help hearing what they said. Each sentence was laced with profanity, and she cringed as she straightened the sheet and blanket on her bunk and lay down for the night. The younger women, she thought, were not completely sober. Because so many horrifying things had happened in one day, Elizabeth was not as shocked by their language as she otherwise would have been.

After the main lights were turned off, leaving a small bulb in the hall still burning, and the women next door grew quiet, Elizabeth calmed her mind by reciting Psalm 100. "Know that the Lord is God; it is he that made us and we are his," murmured Elizabeth. "We are his people, and the sheep of his pasture." Then she prayed for Hope, in Quaker fashion silently holding the dead woman in the Light for several minutes. Next she prayed for Sheldon and little Cathy. Gathering herself together, she prayed for the murderer, whoever he might be. Finally, Elizabeth prayed for herself. Her need was great, and she poured it out to the semi-darkness around her. She asked for guidance, for the comfort of God's presence, and simply for the strength to endure whatever the next day might bring. By the time the Quaker had finished her prayers, the women in the next cell were silent. Elizabeth closed her eyes and was soon blessed with a deep sleep.

In the small hours of the morning she was awakened by her neighbors, who were angrily shouting at each other. "You goddamn bitch!" one yelled. The other woman screamed in pain.

Elizabeth sat up and felt her powerlessness. Her sheet was damp from sweat; the air in the cell was stagnant and thick. The main lights came on, but the din did not diminish. A police matron ran down the corridor toward them.

"Knock it off!" she bellowed in a voice Elizabeth thought would have done justice to a heavyweight champion. "Both of you, shut up! You, come out of there!"

"She's a pervert," said one of the women. "I wanna move."

"Goddamn bitch!"

"Shut up, I said!" barked the guard, who by this time had opened the cell and had one prisoner in the corridor. She locked the cell again and strode down to unlock the door that protected Cambridge from Elizabeth Elliot. She pushed a disheveled young woman in, saying, "Now look, if there's any more trouble I'll know why, 'cuz this old lady doesn't make a peep. There better not be any more noise!"

"God help us all," murmured Elizabeth as the guard departed. The young woman climbed into the unoccupied bunk as the main lights went out again.

"Jesus. Maybe I can get some sleep now."

Since the young woman was speaking to herself, Elizabeth did not reply. She heard her cell mate stretch out on the bunk. Within a few minutes, her regular breathing announced she had found the sleep she sought. Elizabeth, however, had never felt more awake.

I don't think I'm afraid so much as confused, she thought. *Whatever those two women did to get themselves arrested, can this sort of system help them?* She turned on her side and felt the misery of her situation rolling over her. *When I was in prison, you visited me,* she recalled from the Gospels. Now she had a new perspective on the passage. *This place is degrading, a real assault on anyone's self-respect. If even I feel it, think of how it must affect the younger people!* She rolled onto her back and looked around the dimly lit cell. *Of course, there may have been better reason for arresting these two than there was for arresting me. Who knows what they may have done. But whatever it was, this kind of experience can't promote the good in anyone.*

In early American history, as Elizabeth was acutely aware, it was Quakers who had urged society to build penitentiaries where wrongdoers could be isolated in a quiet atmosphere, there to consider their misdeeds and do penance for them. This was, Friends thought, a more useful response to criminals than the floggings, beatings, and stocks of old England. And, contrary to anyone's expectations, the whole American penal system had been structured according to ideas original to the Quakers. Alas, the experiment had long ago proven a complete failure. Prisoners seemed to be increasingly isolated from goodness the longer they remained in the system designed for their penance and salvation. Elizabeth knew that in recent decades Quakers had urged new and fundamental changes in the prisons of the United States. But she wondered, now that she was under lock and key, if the Religious Society of Friends had as much knowledge of incarceration as it should to make truly useful recommendations. Really, she must take up some of these thoughts with the Meeting's Committee on Peace and Social Concerns.

Elizabeth pursued her thinking further. It seemed clear to her, and not for the first time in her life, that all police work was based on violence. Few prisoners would cooperate with the police were it not for the implied threat of billy clubs and guns. Elizabeth was not an anarchist, and she believed that some sort of policing was necessary. But she liked to think of such issues in terms of family discipline, the way a mother would envision them, rather than accept officers patrolling the streets and arresting people with the threat of violence. But she knew she had few answers to the many problems which Cambridge, a complex and densely populated city, experienced. Still, she felt sure that the present system did more harm than good.

Elizabeth emerged from her thoughts on this subject as her cell mate began to snore softly. "God help us all," she repeated and soon dozed off in the muggy semidarkness.

7

In modern times some Friends have refused to pay at least that proportion of federal income tax which corresponds to the proportion of the national budget spent on military matters. That the government has ways of collecting these amounts without consent has doubtless discouraged some other Friends from attempting refusal.

Henry Cadbury, author and member,
Friends Meeting at Cambridge, 1953

Elizabeth awoke abruptly in the morning to the sound of a harsh clanging down the hall. Within an instant, the previous night's depression returned. She sat up on her bunk, put on her glasses, and saw that her cell mate was already up.

"Got a cigarette?"

"I'm sorry," said Elizabeth, "I don't smoke." After a pause she added, "May I introduce myself? My name is Elizabeth Elliot."

"Hi ya, Liz. I'm Kelly. What's a lady like you doing here?"

"I've been arrested on a murder charge," said Elizabeth as she slowly swung her legs over the edge of the bunk. She winced, more at her arthritis pain than because of her admission.

"Christ!" said Kelly with obvious pleasure. "Did you blast your old man?"

Elizabeth shook her head. "Nothing like that. I didn't do anything, actually, except discover the body of a woman who had been killed. Before I could report it, some men came and found me. The woman was a member of my church."

"You're probably not shitting me," said Kelly, disappointment evident in her voice. "You seem too simple for this place. Some of us belong here, but they bring in the wrong sort of people every once in a while. I hope it gets cleared up, Liz."

"Thank you. I have faith that it will."

"I don't know about faith! Not with these guys!" Kelly's mood changed as she added matter-of-factly, "But I'll get out today for sure. They got me for holding some pot for a friend. They were looking for crack—my old man sells it—but they couldn't find any. I was the only one home so they took me in for the grass. It was only a couple joints, see, so I'll be out as soon as I get a hearing."

The appearance of a policewoman in the hallway saved the Quaker from having to respond. Elizabeth and Kelly were allowed to walk down to the end of the hall and shower, then returned to their cell, where a cold breakfast and their own clothes awaited them. They dressed quietly, and Elizabeth saw that creases now covered both her blouse and her slacks. She smoothed her clothes with her hands as best she could, fiercely regretting that they were not fresh and sorry again about Ruth's choice.

Kelly lay down on her bunk, ignoring the food, but Elizabeth inspected breakfast. The coffee was tepid, and clearly there was no hope of tea. To her surprise, she found she was close to tears. But she ate, and Kelly was soon called out of the cell.

She departed with a jaunty wave and a "Good luck, Liz!"

Alone in the cell, Elizabeth let herself cry. She had a good and thorough bawl. When the sobbing was over, she was calm. Soon she, too, was called out of the muggy cell, the police matron explaining that her lawyer had arrived. She was led to a small, bare room on the same floor. Doug Gibson was there, chewing gum. The preliminary hearing was set for two o'clock that afternoon, he explained, and he said he would meet her in the courtroom. He said that he had reached Neil the previous evening and he had promised to have any funds needed ready for their use by the end of the business day. Elizabeth reminded herself not to forget Neil's generosity. His wealth clearly had some good uses, although she still saw several points of conflict between money and spiritual life. Her lawyer, however, did not allow her to ruminate on these problems.

"About half the people brought to a preliminary hearing are released and the charges dropped," Gibson said. "So keep your spirits up. Your hands had far too much nitrogen on them, and you lack motive. Those things should be noticeable even to the dim-witted judge we've drawn. The police, by the way, have found what's probably the murder weapon, in the roses outside the house. It's good you weren't near those bushes when the IRS men arrived. Keep your chin up, Mrs. Elliot, and I'll see you at the courthouse."

Elizabeth thanked her attorney and was ushered back to her cell. It grew warmer. She thought about the man so willing to raise her bail. She could see him, in her mind's eye, at his bank, liquidating investments.

Half an hour later, the matron again took Elizabeth to the spartan visitor's room. The Quaker, hopeful that Neil's transactions had been quick, thought that it must be he who had come to see her. She was led to a different visitors' room, where Sheldon Laughton, not Neil, was seated behind a grill waiting for her.

The big man was disheveled and distressed. His words poured out. "I spent the night here myself," he began. "The police met me at Cathy's day care yesterday afternoon. They told me what had happened at our house. I was overwhelmed. Cathy went with Constance, who was waiting for me, too. I don't understand what happened. Was Hope alive when you got to our house yesterday?"

Elizabeth explained, as gently as she could, what she had found at Foster Place.

"Who would want to kill her?" asked Sheldon in obvious disbelief. "Everyone loved her. It's just not real to me." He paused and ran a hand through his hair as if to clear his head. "This Burnham man, why doesn't he think of obvious things like a burglar? Why on earth does he suspect you?"

Elizabeth related her unfortunate misstatement about going directly in the front door of Sheldon's house. "I doubt he really believes I'm the murderer. But he thinks I lied, that I saw a person inside, through the kitchen window. He thought he had no choice but to charge me and bring me here. I answered all his questions. I saw no one through that window, Sheldon. I wish I had! Can you believe what I've told you?"

"Absolutely," Sheldon replied instantly.

The Clerk smiled faintly, encouraged by a Friend's obvious and simple faith in her. "I am terribly sorry about your loss. I'd like to give you my condolences. I don't understand what happened yesterday, but I do know our community was terribly injured. You, however, have lost more than the rest of us."

"Thanks," Sheldon choked out. "She was a part of me. I don't really grasp that she's gone. But someone did this thing, and I hope he can be brought to justice."

"Indeed. And that will happen, Sheldon, someday or another. We must have faith on that point. God does not abandon the innocent when they are so cruelly wronged." She paused and looked at the big man. "May I ask you about a couple of things?"

"Of course."

"I understand you had a gun when you worked in the West. Did you get rid of that when you took up landscaping?"

"No. I always hoped to return to geology. When Cathy got older, you see, and I could be away for longer stretches of time, I thought I'd go back. I do consulting by myself as an independent geologist. In the Arctic, there's a bear problem, so I kept my gun. It's a big revolver, forty-five caliber. A rifle would be better for bears, but that's harder to carry in the field. When you have to pack rock samples out of some place in the back-of-beyond, you want something you can put in a holster, not tie to your pack where you can't get to it quickly. I keep the revolver upstairs in the closet where I've got my other geological equipment. It's unloaded and on a high shelf where Cathy can't get to it."

"Is there ammunition with it?"

"Yes, a box of cartridges."

Elizabeth changed the subject. "You said that you also spent the night here. On what charge?"

"Burnham brought me here for questioning, straight from Cathy's day care. He had a warrant to search the car, and when he did, he found about a hundred needles in the glove compartment. I volunteer on Saturday mornings in Boston with an AIDS program. We pass out condoms and clean needles in Roxbury."

Elizabeth did not know Sheldon was involved in that kind of work, but given the sensitivity to social questions he and Hope had always shown, it did not surprise her. She knew, from reading the paper, that possession of needles without a prescription was against the law. It was rare, however, in these AIDS-plagued days, that the law was enforced against those who distributed clean needles.

"The Meeting doesn't know about my volunteer work," continued Sheldon. "Hope and I discussed it and decided not to mention it to anyone. You know how some Friends feel about promiscuity. And needle programs can be criticized for promoting drug use. I got into this last summer, when my old college roomie, who lives in California now, wrote and told me he was HIV positive. He didn't say how he might have contracted it, and when I finished his letter I realized I didn't care. Handing out information isn't enough, Friend, not for young people especially. Many people are going to do what they are going to do, about sex and about hard drugs. But we can make a difference as to the consequences.

"But I regret being silent about it now. It will get around Meeting that I've been charged with needle possession. I don't know what some Friends will make of that."

"Yes," said Elizabeth, understanding now the presence of hundreds of condoms in a bag in Sheldon's kitchen. "You and I both may have quite a bit of trouble with the Meeting. But in the end, Friends know one another for what they are. Detective Burnham will be another source of trouble, since he won't rest, I'm sure, until someone is convicted of Hope's murder. I'm glad, to tell you the truth, that his attention is focused on me for the moment, because it gives you a little time. But he'll check your story out, down to the last detail."

Sheldon looked away. It seemed he had aged a decade since Saturday's meeting.

"What's happening now?" asked Elizabeth. "Are you free to go?"

"Yes. Burnham charged me under a drug paraphernalia law, and I've just come back from my preliminary hearing. I'm released on my own recognizance."

"Good," said Elizabeth with even more warmth than was present in the sweltering room.

"I saw your name on the list at the courthouse. You're up for two o'clock. So I came back here and asked to see you."

"I'm glad you did. Things don't look too good for either of us, but we have to go forward in faith." The Clerk explained that Otto Zimmer had seen a gun taken from the rosebushes at the Laughton home. "It may be yours, Sheldon. Otto said it was a big revolver. Other than you and Hope, who knew that you had a gun?"

"Lots of Meeting people knew of it, and most of them felt free to elder me about it at one time or another. I've been lectured a lot about the incoherence of a Quaker owning a gun. That's a Sierra Club attitude, Elizabeth, nothing to do with the peace testimony. And the Sierra Club is about as elitist and anti-Quaker an organization as you can get. In the wilderness, especially in the North, a geologist needs something to protect himself against grizzlies. There's nothing George Fox would say to criticize that!"

"Who would know where you kept the gun?" asked the Clerk.

"Well, lots of Friends have been in and out of our house. At the time of the auction, for instance. And this summer we've had lots of meetings with war-tax resisters from all over New England. Quakers and other denominations, too. We've been blessed with lots of support, especially in the pacifist community outside the Society of Friends. As you know, a lot of Cambridge Quakers think we should obey the law. They've criticized our witness, speaking to both Hope and me on many occasions. And sometimes not speaking to us—we've both felt snubbed in a number of situations." He paused, visibly upset. "But other people have been supportive of our stand, even if they don't fully agree with our actions." Sheldon brushed back a bead of sweat that threatened to trickle into an eye and straightened his big frame. "But anyone who came to the house and looked for the gun would have found it quickly enough."

"What's Pax Christi?"

Sheldon looked startled. "The largest Catholic peace organization in the country. Didn't you meet my friend who works for it? At the auction of our house last spring?"

"I'm afraid I met too many people that day to keep them all straight. Far too many reporters."

"This guy you'll remember: Jose Condoro. He's about six foot three, has a light Puerto Rican accent. And he's black."

There were painfully few blacks in the world encompassed by New England Quakerism, and the neighborhood around Harvard University where Elizabeth had always lived was almost entirely white. Elizabeth seldom had occasion even to say hello to someone of another race and did, therefore, remember a man such as Sheldon described. She nodded.

"He's been an excellent friend to me this past year as the IRS crisis built up. I don't know what I'd have done without him. He's faithful. That's the only word for it. Maybe because of where he's from and all he's been through, he understands the Gospel in a way no Quaker I know seems to."

Elizabeth was silent, unsure how to respond. She knew he was speaking the truth as he saw it, not trying to provoke her as Clerk.

Sheldon looked away as he concluded, "Sorry if I get carried away. It's just that I really respect the Pax Christi people. And they've done a lot for me."

"I can see that," said Elizabeth uneasily. "I'm sorry if you find Catholics have been more helpful to you than Friends. I didn't realize there were Catholic pacifists."

"There are," said Sheldon eagerly, "and many more who might not be pacifists but are opposed to the wars our government gets into. Don't you remember what the pope said during the Gulf War?"

Elizabeth admitted that she did not.

"He was against the buildup of men and materials over there, and he opposed the war after the bombing started. After Bush announced his attack, the pope said that Western leaders should 'immediately abandon this war unworthy of humanity.' Sometimes Quakers talk like they invented the peace testimony, but even a conservative pope showed us what the traditional Church can do."

Elizabeth, who often lived within the sectarian notion that preaching peace was an almost exclusively Quaker occupation, made some mental adjustments. "I'm interested in that," she said slowly. "I admit, I don't recall the pope speaking on the Gulf War at all."

"He spoke against it in the strongest terms, again and again. He doesn't get covered much when he speaks against our government's foreign policy. The news played him up a lot when he visited Poland and said Mass for all the Solidarity people before the Eastern bloc fell apart. Then he looked like a good, anti-

Soviet pope. But when he speaks for peace in a way our government doesn't like, the newspeople just don't cover it."

Elizabeth was aware of the passion with which Sheldon was speaking. She also was aware that a lot of time had passed in the muggy interview room. Afraid that their time might be running out, she abruptly changed the subject. "Is Hope's sister taking care of Cathy?"

Sheldon changed topics easily. "Yes. Constance was very close to Hope. She and her husband have been unable to have children, so she's devoted to Cathy. Titus has been out of the country a lot, for the Friends Service Committee. He's in San Salvador right now, I think. Anyway, Constance doesn't work, so she's had a lot of time for Cathy. She's been a second mother since the child was born."

"I see. One last thing: Did Mr. Burnham ask you where you went after you dropped off your daughter at Inman Square?"

Sheldon blinked. "I drove straight from the day care to my job in Lexington. I've been working at the house of Charles Whiting, a Harvard professor, just retired, who wants his whole yard relandscaped. But no one there can vouch for me until about ten A.M., when the professor came out to speak to me. It's a big yard on a steep slope, and you can't even see a lot of my work from the house."

The police matron reappeared at Elizabeth's elbow and announced that the visit was over. The Clerk was led back to her close but lonely cell.

As good as his promise, Doug Gibson was at the front door of the courtroom when Elizabeth was escorted in for her preliminary hearing. He said some encouraging words which the Quaker didn't fully hear, absorbed as she was in scanning the room for Neil. She saw him, seated next to a window, and felt better even before he waved at her.

After a wait of a few minutes, the charges against Elizabeth Rebecca Elliot were read aloud by the court clerk. The prosecutor explained the circumstances of the murder, insofar as they were known. Doug Gibson argued that the evidence of Elizabeth's connection to Hope's death was wholly circumstantial; that she had gone to the house by arrangement with the deceased, an arrangement known to many people in advance; that his client was in the act of telephoning the police, as her fingerprints on the instrument showed, when government agents had interrupted her. He also said that she was a woman of blameless character, a lifelong resident of Cambridge who was respected by everyone who knew her. Finally, he pointed out that his client had more nitrogen on her hands than any suspect he had ever known, too much to be suspicious. Most importantly, he said, she had no possible motive for killing Hope Laughton.

The judge seemed to be daydreaming during the lawyer's speech. When Gibson sat down, he asked the prosecutor several questions about the gun. He was told it was a .45-caliber revolver, found in the rosebushes at the front of the house, and licensed to the deceased woman's husband. Ballistic tests were under way to see if it was the murder weapon. Mr. Gibson rose and pointed out that Elizabeth, if she were the murderer, would not have been likely to emerge from the house, discard the gun, and then return to the body and await discovery with the corpse.

The judge looked down at his papers and said, without animation, "Lack of motive seems significant here. And the tests on the gun are not yet complete. The murder charge against Elizabeth Elliot seems premature to the court and is hereby dismissed. Next case!"

Elizabeth thanked her lawyer and then was glad to relax into Neil's arms in the hallway outside the courtroom. The familiar smell of his aftershave and the feel of the starch in his shirt against her face were welcome. The nightmarish depression of incarceration dropped quickly away. Her smile was broad and most genuine as she put her arm around his waist and walked with him out the front door of the courthouse into the midafternoon heat.

"Your lawyer called last night," said Neil. "Don't worry about his bill, by the way. I've arranged that he'll send it to me. I've been running around today getting cash together for bail. That's the only reason I didn't come to see you this morning. What's happened?"

Elizabeth related all the events between their telephone conversation the previous afternoon and her appearance in court. Neil, clearly shaken, drew her across the street to his car.

"Let's take you home," he said as he held the passenger door of his Buick open for her, "and keep you away from witnesses and away from Foster Place! I don't want Burnham to have any excuse to do anything more. You'll have to promise me to stay away from trouble from now on."

Elizabeth let him close the door and enter the car from the driver's side before she answered. "I know you only want the best for me, Neil, and I'm grateful for your concern. I'll have to consider what you said about Mr. Gibson's bill; you two can't just arrange that between yourselves. But you are the only person who could and would raise my bail, I know. Thank the Lord that wasn't needed, but still, I won't forget what you were prepared to do. But, Neil, my life must be my own. I'm the person responsible for my decisions. And I'm Clerk, and I'll do what I think is best for the Meeting."

Neil looked stung. But he was a sufficiently seasoned Friend to be silent. He drove Elizabeth to Concord Avenue. As they approached her house, Elizabeth smiled at her quiet driver and invited him to pull up behind her car in the driveway and come inside for something cold to drink.

In the familiar kitchen, the tension between the two friends eased. Fixing two glasses of ice tea and adding a generous portion of sugar to Neil's, as he liked, Elizabeth spoke reassuringly to Sparkle. The cat had spent the night alone and emerged from the basement as soon as she heard her mistress. She rubbed against the Clerk's ankles and, in a wholly uncharacteristic moment of exuberance, even gave Neil some feline affection.

Elizabeth sat with Neil on the living room sofa. "I'd appreciate your thoughts about this mess. It seems to me there are two issues. I want the Meeting to know what has happened and to be assured that there is no evidence either Sheldon or I have done anything wrong. Secondly, there's the problem of trying to help the police not make too many more mistakes."

"There's a third issue, too, and that's your own safety," said Neil. "And your situation with respect to the law."

"I have no intention of spending any more nights in jail, I assure you."

Neil realized he must be content, at least for the moment, with that. "As for the Meeting," he mused, "some of the stuffier members are going to disapprove, in the strongest terms, of several things. The wealthier, law-abiding part of Meeting was never behind the Laughton's witness. I think that's inevitable. The comparison between the Laughtons and us more normal folk is invidious enough that some Friends look for reasons to back away from their brothers-in-Christ. Most of us feel guilt about cooperating with the IRS, but we'd rather feel guilty now and then than live as the Laughtons were doing."

"Exactly."

"But now we find Sheldon has been distributing both condoms and needles around town, and carefully hiding that from Friends. It won't increase his popularity with the part of Meeting that distrusts him to begin with. It will be very convenient to suspect him of his wife's death. It was his gun, wasn't it? The fact that he owned a gun is enough for some Quakers to suspect him of anything! And you, Elizabeth, will be in a tough spot, too. You've been charged with murder. Imagine how that will sound at Business Meeting tonight!"

"Business Meeting! I'd forgotten this was Tuesday!" She was distressed.

"It's unfortunate timing. You'd best let me go home now and call a few weighty Friends. I'll explain the situation. They'll respond better if all this isn't presented to them out of the blue tonight. But I'm still not sure how you and Sheldon are going to preserve your good names."

"Do make some calls. And thank you. Do you have the courage to call Hugo Coleman?" asked Elizabeth, naming one of the Friends with whom she was almost always at odds.

"For you, dear, I will call even Hugo. Thanks for the tea. I'll see you at the Meetinghouse at seven."

Elizabeth rose and kissed him, then saw him out the door. She waited until the blue Buick was no longer in sight before she retreated back into the relative cool of the house. Sparkle was nowhere to be seen as the Clerk refilled her tea glass. She went upstairs, took a quick shower, and changed into a brown linen skirt, a white blouse, and hose. She felt much more human. She made sure all the windows on the second floor were open. After tonight's Meeting, she hoped, the air would be cooler. She turned on a fan in her bedroom window.

With a glance at the clock, Elizabeth made a quick decision. She hurried downstairs once more, sliced some cheese, and made a sandwich. This she gulped down. She found a name and address in the telephone book, locked the front door, and departed in her car for Lexington.

The house of Professor Charles Whiting was on a south-sloping hill near Lexington Center. She saw the house number on a mailbox by the curb. Elizabeth parked her car. There were no other cars on the street; in suburban Lexington, parking was not the problem it was in Cambridge. Much of the front yard of the Whiting home was not visible from the house because of the change in slope of the hill on which the house sat. Lots of land-scaping work was under way near the sidewalk. A large expanse of fresh earth ran up to the break in the slope. Sapling sugar maples had recently been put in near the curb, with wires running away from each to the ground. Bushes were planted on the house side of the sidewalk. The owners, perhaps, were not content with visual privacy and wanted to keep people off their property altogether.

Elizabeth walked slowly up to the house. As she neared it, she could see signs of more landscaping work along the west side. She approached the front door. There was no answer to the doorbell or to her knocking.

Elizabeth wiped her forehead with her hand and sighed. She had made the hot trip for nothing.

As she stood on the front steps she looked down toward the street. She could not see the fresh earth near the street and could barely see her car. Across the street she saw a woman seated on the porch of a small house, apparently looking at her.

"I have nothing to lose," thought the Quaker and raised her hand in a tentative wave.

After a moment, the woman across the street waved back. Elizabeth walked quickly down the hill and crossed the street.

"Hello," she said as she came up to the porch. "My name is Elizabeth Elliot. I was just driving by, you see, and I knocked at the house up there, wondering if they could give me the name of who-ever has been doing landscaping for them." Elizabeth rationalized her lie by telling herself that the deceit did no harm to the woman and was a much simpler and more plausible explanation than the truth.

"The Whitings are probably out on the town. They eat out al-most every night."

Elizabeth nodded. "You wouldn't happen to know who they hired?"

"I do. I know everything about this neighborhood. Lived here all my life." She eyed Elizabeth. "Are you a local?"

"Yes," said the Quaker. "I live in Cambridge. I was born there and raised my family near Harvard Square."

The woman went on in a more confidential tone. "I don't recommend that workman. He won't speak to me. Not a friendly soul at all. Thinks I'm a busybody. I tell you, none of them work like they did in my day. Take that guy. Sometimes he comes just after seven A.M.. Makes sense, you know, to beat the heat. But half the time, he doesn't show up till nine or ten. I asked him, 'You got another job you're doing?' but he won't answer. I think he's being paid by the hour. The Whitings are dumb enough to do that. Harvard people. So he charges 'em from seven onwards, but half the time he sleeps late. Probably a drunk."

"Yesterday morning . . ." Elizabeth began slowly, unsure how to direct this loquacious woman.

"My point exactly!" she cried. "He didn't come till well after nine. It was maybe a quarter to ten when I heard that old station wagon. Just a few minutes after it pulled up at the curb, old man Whiting came down and spoke to him. I'll bet the guy pretended he'd been there since seven."

"Thanks for your help."

"He's not the type you want to hire, I tell you." The woman smiled as if in triumph.

Elizabeth returned to her car. The traffic into Cambridge, against the rush-hour tide, was not heavy, and she pulled into Longfellow Park at ten minutes before seven o'clock. It seemed as warm as it had been at three, but the Clerk was too deeply troubled about Sheldon to notice the heat. She still had hopes he was not a killer, but for one reason or another he had lied to the police, and, worse still, he was lying to his Quaker friends.

"Maybe my faith in him is misplaced," she said aloud as she parked.

8

We feel bound explicitly to avow our unshaken persuasion that all war is utterly incompatible with the plain precept of our divine Lord and the whole spirit of His Gospel, and that no plea of necessity or policy can avail to release individuals or nations from the paramount allegiance which they owe to Him who hath said, "Love your enemies."

Richmond Declaration of Faith, 1887

Just before Business Meeting was scheduled to begin, Elizabeth went to the office in the house next to the worship building and, letting herself in with her Clerk's key, hunted for the Meeting's directory of members. She looked up Sheldon and Hope's phone number and dialed it. As the telephone rang, she rubbed her free hand against the one holding the receiver. She still had unpleasant memories of the police testing her hands.

Sheldon answered the phone, and after exchanging pleasantries, Elizabeth began by saying, "I wondered if the police would have let you back into your house by now."

"Yes, they've done their work here. But Cathy and I won't be staying. It's difficult for me, being here, knowing what happened to Hope. Constance has invited us to stay at her house. I'm just packing up some things, no more than one station wagon full, and then I'll leave. Constance is really very kind. She's taking care of Cathy at her home right now so I can work here more efficiently."

Elizabeth said she was glad. "I'd like to stop by and talk to you tomorrow, Sheldon. When could I find you at the Bakers'?"

Sheldon said that he would be there all afternoon and that she could stop by anytime. Elizabeth wished him well with moving and hung up.

Before she left the office, she borrowed pencil, paper, and a copy of the book regulating Quaker life in New England called *Faith and Practice*. Then she walked across the drive to the Meetinghouse through the warm evening air. She entered the simple building and took her place at the front of the worship room. It was the spot from which the Clerk traditionally presided over Business Meetings. Sitting at the head of the room was both a burden and a privilege. Despite the hardships the Clerkship brought her, however, Elizabeth could not fully suppress her pride in having a post given to her by the people she valued most. Such pride, she knew, could border on the sinful, and she tried to set it aside whenever she recognized it.

She looked around the worship room and saw Neil, seated on a bench with Hugo Coleman. She smiled at her friend's good intentions. Bill Hoffman was sitting alone on a bench by the side door, as always. Jane Thompson, who lived between Elizabeth's house and Fresh Pond Reservoir, was present, as was Harriet Parker, the Meeting's secretary. Otto Zimmer, quite ashen, was seated in a corner. Elizabeth felt an impulse of compassion toward the man, despite his distasteful characteristics. He looked terrible, sitting on the bench with his eyes closed, his pasty face creased with tension. She walked over to him in the silent room and held out her hand, touching him lightly on the shoulder. Otto's eyes snapped open and he jumped, halfway rising to his feet. Elizabeth had never seen such strain in a Quaker at worship.

"I'm sorry," she said, her voice barely above a whisper. "I only meant to greet you."

Otto relaxed slightly and nodded. Elizabeth smiled and turned away, regretting the disturbance she had caused but wondering about Otto's state. As she walked over to her seat, she saw that many other Friends were now scattered around the worship room. It was time to begin.

The Clerk opened the Business Meeting by reading from New

England Yearly Meeting's Queries on social responsibility.

" 'Do you respect the worth of every human being as a child of God?' " she read in a firm voice. She glanced up and saw Ruth Markham entering the Meetinghouse. " 'Do you uphold the right of all persons to justice and human dignity? Do you endeavor to create political, social, and economic institutions which will sustain and enrich the life of all?' " Again she looked up and saw that Wally Orvick, Hugo Coleman's shadow and echo, had entered. In a strong and clear voice she continued, " 'Do you fulfill all civic obligations which are not contrary to divine leadings? Do you give spiritual and material support to those who suffer for conscience's sake?' "

As Clerk, Elizabeth had the authority to be quiet after the readings as long as she liked. Tonight she prolonged the worshipful silence for as long as she dared. At last she said, "Friends, we meet in Business format tonight to finalize changes in our First Day School program. But before we begin that task, the Meeting needs to be informed of recent and tragic events in our community.

"As some of you know, Patience Silverstone, our oldest member, fell in her home late last week and broke her leg. She is at Mt. Auburn Hospital and, I'm pleased to say, is in good spirits. But our prayers are needed.

"Yesterday, a more unusual tragedy visited us. Hope Laughton was killed in her home on Foster Place." There was a collective intake of breath in the Meetinghouse from all the Friends whom Neil had not warned via telephone. "She died shortly before the IRS arrived to evict the Laughtons for tax delinquency. It would be appropriate for the Oversight Committee to contact Sheldon about a Memorial Meeting. In light of the unusual circumstances of the death, I think we should be careful to give ourselves, as a Meeting, plenty of time to absorb this tragic news before we choose a date for the memorial.

"I'm sorry to say, it's natural for the police to initially suspect the people closest to a murder victim of involvement with the death. I'm afraid that Sheldon owned a handgun, for use against animals when he worked as a geologist out West. Some Friends knew about the gun, and it may be that it was used in the killing. Tests are being done on it. But I want to say that Ruth Markham and I spoke to little Cathy Laughton a few hours after Hope's death. Cathy is only a preschooler, but she was clear about two things. Her father and she left home together, as they always did when Sheldon takes her to day care. And when they left, Hope was alive and well. Cathy saw her wave good-bye from the window as her father and she drove away. That much is absolutely clear.

"There is more I must say about Hope's death: I discovered the body and was found with it by IRS agents before I had a chance to call the police. Last night, I was charged with murder."

The silence in the Meetinghouse was thunderous.

"I was held overnight in police custody," continued the Clerk. "Today those charges were dropped. At present, I think that both Sheldon and I are obvious suspects for murder in the mind of the police detective in charge of the case, Mr. Stewart Burnham. Until and unless the case is solved, we will not be free from suspicion. Sheldon has also been charged under a drug paraphernalia law because, when his station wagon was searched, the police found he had numerous needles in his possession. He tells me he has been working in Boston in an AIDS prevention project, distributing both needles and condoms on the street." She looked around the room, making eye contact with each Friend who would look at her before she concluded, "The prayers and support of all members are needed in this matter for everyone connected to the tragedy."

Wally Orvick rose to his feet to be recognized. "Question, Clerk," he said.

Elizabeth nodded to him.

"This is all news to me. I don't know how to respond. The Laughtons' house is not two blocks from here, isn't it? And this neighborhood is hardly the type crippled by random violence. Can that be changing? Is cocaine or something being sold around here?"

" 'Nothing is new under the sun,' " quoted Ruth from her seat. She stood up, saying, "It's easy to wish that violence is random or done by other people. Friends always want to think that way, as if we could never be a part of something evil. No one knows what happened at that house, but we have to face the possibility that the killing says something about us, about our community, in one way or another. To automatically assume otherwise is the worst kind of sectarianism." She looked quickly around the worship room. "But I don't mean to say I have any worries about Elizabeth. She was simply in the wrong place at the wrong time."

"Friends are glad you're not being held by the police," said Wally in Elizabeth's direction. "But may we ask why the charges were dropped?"

"There was insufficient evidence against me in the mind of the judge," answered Elizabeth calmly.

Wally was still on his feet. "But there had been enough evidence to arrest you?"

"That was the judgment of the detective in charge of the case. His views are reviewed in a preliminary hearing, by a judge."

"Not Bill Hoffman?" someone in a back bench asked.

Elizabeth smiled. "No. Another judge."

Hoffman rose to his feet, looked at Wally, and said, "It's not unusual for charges to be brought and then dropped. If a charge is dropped, it's dropped. Legally, our Clerk has not been charged."

"Except . . ." said Wally.

Ruth Markham rose and said, with barely concealed fire, "Elizabeth does what she feels led to, and does so with more courage and dignity than most of us. Friends might be mindful of that!"

Hugo Coleman was on his feet before Ruth finished speaking. The Clerk sighed her recognition of him.

"We all are concerned for the Laughton family. Their loss weighs on our hearts. But as a Meeting, we must consider what kind of public witness we make, not only by our actions but by how those actions look to our neighbors. The Apostle Paul warns us to avoid the appearance of evil, not just evil itself."

Elizabeth had to concur with that idea, since it was the verse she had had in mind when she declined to spend August in Neil's summer house. She dropped her gaze to her hands.

Hugo looked sternly around the worship room, his air of authority crackling in the humid atmosphere. "I feel clear in asking our Clerk to step aside for the present. She need not resign, but we should appoint an acting Clerk until this matter is cleared up. For the head of a pacifist organization, we need someone who is not accused of violence. It is with no disrespect for Elizabeth that I ask we have a new Clerk."

There was a deep silence as Elizabeth's heart contracted in pain.

Jane Thompson, still seated, said, "I have confidence in Elizabeth. Whatever the police may think, she is Clerk because we felt called by the Spirit to name her as our Clerk. Nothing has changed, in my opinion, about that calling."

"Exactly," Ruth said hotly from her seat.

"Friends!" said Elizabeth. "No one will speak who hasn't been recognized."

Bill Hoffman stood up. The Clerk nodded at him.

"These are still very early days in the investigation of Hope's death. It's stressful for everyone involved, including the police. The murder charge was dropped because it wasn't well considered. Such things happen. No charges are made at present against our Clerk, and we have no reason to assume that they will be. I feel clear that Elizabeth Elliot continue in the office to which the Spirit led us to appoint her."

Wally rose and was recognized. "I don't see how we can discuss this with Elizabeth presiding over Business Meeting. Clearly we need an acting Clerk for tonight!"

Neil Stevenson stood. Because he so rarely spoke in Meeting, the Clerk felt obliged to recognize him, although she also felt awkward in doing so, and might have preferred he be silent.

Her friend looked around the room and said, in a soft but clear voice, "We've been presented with a situation we're not prepared for. Friends' method of decision-making requires patience and listening. Nothing that is happening here is in that spirit, and therefore it isn't of the Spirit. Our Ministry and Counsel Committee is scheduled to meet Thursday evening, is it not? Perhaps it could begin the consideration of all the issues surrounding Hope Laughton's death. It's a complex situation and one Friends need to consider thoughtfully, not angrily. If Ministry and Counsel finds a sense of how we might proceed, it could report to our next Business Meeting."

Neil had made a recommendation in keeping with long-standing Quaker tradition, and he sat down in respectful silence. Divisive discussion was usually addressed in a committee before being brought to Business Meeting. Since both Wally Orvick and Hugo Coleman were on Ministry and Counsel, the Meeting's most important committee, it seemed unlikely they would object to the suggestion. As Clerk, Elizabeth was also on that committee, and she began inwardly to squirm as she thought of being in a small room with Hugo and Wally, charged with discussing the effects of her Clerkship.

Bill Hoffman stood again. "Because of my profession, and all that it takes from my life, I've resisted being put on committees, as the Nominating Committee of this Meeting is fully aware. But I would like to volunteer to meet with Ministry and Counsel this

Thursday. There are often misunderstandings about the law and the actions the police take, and I think I could be useful in explaining any questions that come up."

Friends nodded all around the room. A sense of unity, the normal goal of Quaker Business Meetings, was developing. Elizabeth relaxed slightly as she considered the help the judge's presence could be.

Bill was still on his feet. "If the Clerk desires, she need not come to Thursday's committee meeting. Clearly all this must be painful for her. But this Friend hopes she will be present. And this Friend still feels absolutely clear that she be welcome to continue as Clerk."

"That Friend speaks my mind," said Ruth Markham quickly.

"And mine," said Harriet Parker, quietly but firmly.

Wally Orvick stood and was recognized. "I hope the Clerk, as a member of Ministry and Counsel, comes to all the meetings of the committee. Neil speaks my mind when he says that we have been suddenly presented with something we're not used to dealing with. Taking some time to consider this situation seems right to me. And I would welcome Bill Hoffman's help with any legal questions that might come up."

Elizabeth looked around the room while inwardly sighing. No one seemed to have anything further to say.

"Let it be recorded that . . ." She paused, trying to think of words to describe the situation.

". . . that all questions related to Hope Laughton's death," said Hugo Coleman, pleased with his generosity to the Clerk.

". . . that all questions related to Hope Laughton's death," said Elizabeth quietly, "be referred for the present to Ministry and Counsel, with the hope that the committee will consider the situation and, with the help of William Hoffman, will advise Business Meeting of its thoughts when next we meet, two weeks from today."

After a moment Wally rose to his feet. "The other thing for us to think about is the charge against Sheldon Laughton. That charge was not dismissed, is that correct?"

"That's right."

"Perhaps the Membership Committee would want to consider Sheldon's status in our Meeting."

There was a low moan from around the room, and all Friends present, including Hugo Coleman, shook their heads.

Ruth growled from her seat, "Those remarks are not well considered."

Impressed by the negative response he had engendered, Wally quickly said, "Perhaps the idea is not useful. But we do need to consider, in one way or another, the reputation of our members. Especially where things like criminality and drug use are concerned."

"Yes," said the Clerk slowly, "we do need to consider the issues. But that is not, perhaps, on our agenda for tonight."

"Agreed," said Harriet. "Let's give ourselves time to talk with one another and with Sheldon."

"That Friend speaks my mind," said Hugo.

Elizabeth nodded, and the decision for the Meeting was made.

There was a long pause, and Friends were silent. Jane Thompson rose to her feet. "Clerk," she said.

Elizabeth looked up and recognized her.

"I have the report here from the First Day School Committee, finalizing its changes for this coming school year."

Elizabeth gratefully asked her to proceed to this, the item on the official agenda for which the Meeting for Business had been called.

Jane read the report and called on Harriet Parker to explain one point about the new division of the First Day School classes for the younger children. As Elizabeth listened to the report she remembered the many years she had worked in the First Day

School and had never taken responsibility for issues that brought the Meeting into conflict with the society outside Longfellow Park. She now envied those who still did not deal with the IRS, the police, and the law. By the time she came out of her day-dreaming on this subject, Harriet had finished speaking.

Jane Thompson asked if there were any questions for the committee. Hugo Coleman asked one polite question, and no one else seemed to have anything to say.

"We accept the committee's report with gratitude," said Elizabeth, "and express our thanks for all the work the teachers in the First Day School do on behalf of our community." She looked around the room. "Do Friends approve the change in class organization for the younger children as it is recommended to us?"

There was a murmur of approval.

"Let us close with worship," said Elizabeth, unable to keep the fatigue from her voice any longer. The room was silent. Around her she felt the strain in the community, the divisiveness at which she was the center. Sadness welled up in her.

After the Meeting broke up and most Friends departed, Elizabeth found both Neil and Bill Hoffman at her elbows.

"Don't be alarmed, Friend," said Bill as encouragingly as he could. "Policemen and Business Meetings both make mistakes. That's why we have judicial preliminary hearings and Quaker committee meetings. This Meeting has confidence in its Clerk, though a few Friends who worry about appearances will need a little time to adjust. But I'll be there on Thursday evening, and I'm sure we'll move forward on this in a reasonable way. Meanwhile, I hope you can get some rest. You look done in."

Elizabeth nodded. "Very little sleep last night," she said groggily.

"I'll drive you home," said Neil.

"I have a car here," she said, shaking her head. "But on second thought, let me accept a ride. I know I'm not in any condition to drive. Everything is hazy."

Neil put his arm around her and steered her toward the front door of the Meetinghouse. Elizabeth did not care to think of herself as an invalid but was too tired to object to his protective arm.

"I'll lock up," said Bill, stopping at the door and thus leaving the pair of older Friends to themselves.

Neil guided Elizabeth to his Buick, parked on Longfellow Park, unlocked the passenger door, and held it open for her. She gratefully sank into the well-cushioned seat and reached out to close her door.

"I've got it," he said, swinging it shut. He walked around and slid in on the driver's side, speaking to his companion as he fastened his seat belt.

"You shouldn't overdo things," he said in concerned and gentle tones. "You tire yourself too much."

She rallied against his mothering. "I do as I choose, Neil, and I do what I think is best for me and for the Meeting."

He sighed. "Please try to remember that you're more important to me as Elizabeth than as Clerk. That's all I meant to say." He started the car as Elizabeth groggily wondered if the Clerkship were more important to her than Neil could ever be. She had been called to be Clerk, had she not? As the Buick turned onto Brattle Street she lost track of her thoughts, momentarily dozing off in the quiet car so unlike her own. She awoke as he pulled up in front of her house.

"I'll help you inside."

"No, I'll be fine."

"I insist!"

"So do I!" Anger at his wish to impose his will on her flared hot. "And, thank God, I am still competent to make decisions. Good night." More gently, she added as she rose stiffly from her seat, "But thank you very much for the ride. Good night, my friend." She closed the car door and walked up to her house without looking back. "I'm too old and too tired for solicitous men," she said to herself. "At least tonight."

9

❀

Many Friends feel a responsibility to present their witness in as public a way as possible. Along with reporting their actions to their friends, business associates, congressional representatives and the media, Friends may approach the IRS directly in an attempt to be clearly understood.

Friends Committee on War Tax Concerns, 1988

Elizabeth slept deeply but awoke early the next morning, so early that it was still dark. She turned over under the damp and sweaty sheet, awakening Sparkle, who was at her feet. The distress of the previous evening's Meeting for Business welled up in her mind. With a weary sigh, she considered the chaotic and alarming events of this terrible week, still only halfway over. Realizing how distressed and confused her mind had become, she recited the Twenty-third Psalm to calm herself. Slowly and deliberately she said aloud,

> The Lord is my shepherd; I shall not want.
> He maketh me to lie down in green pastures: he
>   leadeth me beside the still waters.
> He restoreth my soul: he leadeth me in the paths of
>   righteousness for his name's sake.
> Yea, though I walk through the valley of the shadow
>   of death, I will fear no evil: for thou art with me;
>   thy rod and thy staff they comfort me.

Here the Quaker departed from the text into wordless prayer.

When she woke again it was after seven o'clock. Sparkle was gone, and the sun was flooding in the eastern window. Elizabeth rose slowly, dressed, and went stiffly downstairs. On her desk she saw a familiar envelope, and her mind briefly reviewed the letter from Rebecca, her college roommate. Serious evil in religious life, especially of the sort Rebecca had reported about her pastor, was devastating. Self-justification and rationalization were as deeply imbedded in Quakers as in Baptist preachers, she was sure. As soon as the crisis at the Meeting was past, Elizabeth promised herself, she would call her old friend and offer what comfort she could.

In Elizabeth's opinion, the most frightening thing about the fall from grace of persons who held a position of trust and authority was the realization that, but for the guidance of the Spirit, anyone might be in the same shoes as the worst sinner. No one, after all, was safe from temptation. No one, therefore, could be sure they were not lying to themselves about the important, the fundamental, aspects of life.

She walked out into the backyard to enjoy the summer morning and to replenish the bird feeder. Year-round bird-feeding had been so objectionable to her husband that only in her widowhood had she felt free to corrupt the juncos, cardinals, and finches of Cambridge with the dubious blessings of summertime food for the taking. Now and then she felt guilty about making wild animals dependent on her, but she so much enjoyed watching the birds from her kitchen window that she fed them despite her conscience.

Content that the feeder held all it could, she returned inside and put water on the stove for tea. She had just finished her breakfast when the doorbell rang. Detective Burnham was on her front step. For the first time in her life, Elizabeth hesitated to invite a person into her home.

"Don't be alarmed, Mrs. Elliot," said Burnham through the aluminum screen door. "I haven't come to take you in."

"I'm glad," said the Quaker, opening the door. "I'm a little too old for sleeping in cells."

Burnham stepped inside and stood in the front hall, awkwardly jamming clenched hands deeply into his pants pockets. "I apologize for my anger the last time I was here. I get pretty worked up sometimes by a case, and this is the type to send me a little around the bend. Even a police detective isn't so hardened as to be able to see a young wife and mother shot down in her own kitchen, without being upset."

"That I can appreciate," said Elizabeth. "I've been feeling close to desperate about the whole matter myself." She added quietly, "I'm sure we both want to see justice done."

"That's what my job is about. I'm sorry that I sometimes don't do it so well. But anyway," he went on in a rush, "the tests the lab boys have run on your clothes show you didn't hold the murder weapon when it discharged. Your hands are confusing to us, you see, but we know you didn't have time to wash and dry your clothes, and there's no powder on your blouse's sleeve. Your fingerprints on the telephone are clear and overlay all the others except for those of the IRS guy, which confirms your story about starting to call for help. All of that, plus the fact the gun was outdoors while you were discovered inside, means I won't be considering charges against you anymore. I never actually suspected you in a serious way, but I have to go with the evidence, by the book, and I thought you might know a lot more than you were telling."

"I'm glad there will be no renewed charges," said Elizabeth simply.

"I realize you were only trying to help when you spoke to the Laughton child, though I hope you can appreciate that destroyed her usefulness for me."

Elizabeth nodded, realizing it was her turn to apologize. "I was thinking mostly about Sheldon's reputation in the Meeting. I didn't consider the legal side of things, and I'm sorry about my actions."

The detective nodded. "I've come to ask who it was you were

concerned about, so concerned you felt you needed to interview a three-year-old within an hour after leaving the police station. What was your motivation for wanting to know the child's story?"

Elizabeth was silent, considering her answer.

"May I ask you again: Did you see something, anything at all, at the house which you've not told me about?"

"No," answered the Quaker honestly.

"OK." Burnham sighed. "I hope, in exchange for my explanation and apology, you'll trust me enough to tell me what Otto Zimmer's relationship to the Laughtons was."

"He was, as far as I know, a close friend of the family. He's committed to war-tax resistance, you see."

"We found a book belonging to Zimmer under the kitchen table. It was open, facedown on the floor. The deceased probably had it in her hands when she was shot, or when she saw the murderer's intent she may have flung it at him. Zimmer's name is in the front of the book. It's called *From Meetinghouse to Countinghouse*. Is that surprising?"

"Not at all. It's a good historical account of early Pennsylvania. That was an important time for Friends. Quakers held the reigns of power in colonial days, you see. It's our only experience in government. Friends made decisions not to build forts and not to fight the Indians, and those decisions didn't sit well with the other Europeans in Pennsylvania at the time. All of that we tend to remember with pride. I think the book you found details some of the more embarrassing parts of our history, though, like the fact that many Quakers in Philadelphia became quite wealthy and put their energy into commerce instead of Meeting life. The Spirit is often compromised by love of money in the Society of Friends. Both Otto and the Laughtons would be sympathetic to that message, I'm sure, and would like the book."

"I see. So it's not unusual to read even such heavy subjects in your Meeting?"

"No. We find our history endlessly fascinating, which must be some sort of sin. But good books in a Meeting get handed around a great deal. I'm reading a history of the early days of Pennsylvania at the moment. And when I was a young mother, with a little one taking up a great deal of my time, I read whenever I could grab a minute. It's not surprising Hope might have been reading while having her breakfast and waiting for me to arrive."

"Do you like Otto Zimmer?"

The question was unexpected, and Elizabeth's guard was down. She sputtered.

"You've answered my question," said Burnham. "The book and your opinion of its owner were all I was wondering about at the moment. Thanks for your time. I mean that." He turned and opened the screen door to let himself out.

Elizabeth closed the front door, first glancing at a piece of peeling paint clinging to the surface as if by faith. Returning to the kitchen, she promised herself that she would call painters in the spring. As she watched a junco pecking at seeds that had fallen from the feeder to the grass, her sense of guilt grew. Her personal antipathy for Otto, she thought, should not be transplanted into a policeman's mind. Finally, she went to the telephone and called the younger Quaker.

A groggy voice answered the phone with a semiarticulate greeting.

"Good morning. I'm sorry if I've awakened you. This is Elizabeth Elliot."

"Hello," said Otto flatly.

"I'd like to get together with you today. Is there any time we could meet?"

There was a pause. "I'm working the swing shift at the hospital now. I was thinking of coming in to the Meetinghouse about noon to give Harriet the registration money people have been sending me for the Peace and Social Concerns retreat. Then I'll have lunch in Harvard Square and get the bus that goes out Cambridge Street."

"Could I meet you at Longfellow Park? We could walk over to the square and have lunch together."

"OK," Otto said in the same monotone.

Elizabeth, content for the moment that she was trying to relate to Otto in a more productive way, cleared her mind of Meeting life and mixed up a double recipe of dough for molasses bread. The gentle smells of milk and flour began to permeate the small kitchen as she carefully exercised her arthritic hands in rhythmic kneading. It wasn't long before the dough was sitting on the counter in a large, pregnant mound, oiled on top and further protected from the air by a damp tea towel. Elizabeth hummed to herself and felt more centered and at ease than she had since Meeting for Worship on First Day.

"A sense of proportion, that's what we need around here," she said to Sparkle, who sat mutely on the floor by the refrigerator door. "The Meeting will weather this tragedy."

As she was washing measuring cups, the telephone rang. It was Harriet at the Meeting's office.

"I'm just calling to say hello," she began, "and see how you're doing. I'm sorry about the tone of last night's Meeting. I'm sure that was tough on you. I want you to know that a lot of Friends have every desire that you continue as Clerk."

"Oh, thank you!"

"Hugo Coleman and his minions always get alarmed by anything they can't control in advance. Don't take it all to heart, Elizabeth. We asked you to be Clerk for good reasons, and we've not forgotten that in the excitement of the moment."

"That's good hearing."

"I wish Patience had been able to be there last night. She would have had something to say, I'm sure. A good woman, she is, when people start to fly off the handle."

"Do you have any news of her, Harriet? I haven't been over to visit since Monday. I hope she's making progress."

"I called this morning. The nurse said she's been resting poorly. She's actually in more pain now than when she was admitted. They don't know why."

"Oh, really? I'm so sorry."

"I'll go by after I get off work."

"Good. Please give her my love. Tell her my life is a little confused at the moment, but I'll get over to Mt. Auburn as soon as I can."

"I'll do that. You've got some mail here, by the way, that you might want to pick up. Something first class from Friends United Meeting and a package from Philadelphia, too."

"Fine. I'll be over about noon. I'm going to meet Otto Zimmer at your office." Elizabeth paused, then lowered her tone slightly. "May I ask you a direct question?"

There was an affirmative noise from the phone line.

"Can you think of any reason Sheldon Laughton would harm Hope?"

There was a long pause. "It's not conceivable, of course, that Sheldon could have killed anyone. But at the time of the auction last spring, one couldn't help but notice there was something between Hope and Otto."

"The question is, something that was constructive or destructive?"

"I couldn't say. You could almost turn your first question around. Can you envision Otto harming Hope?"

"I don't know Otto well, but it's time I got to know him better. I'll see you in a little bit."

Elizabeth looked at the clock and the rising bread. She estimated the heat's effect on yeast activity. After a moment, she cleared a space on the first shelf of her refrigerator, no easy task, and put the dough in to retard its rising. Better too little rising while she was away than too much.

The walk to Longfellow Park was hot, and Elizabeth moved slowly. Her car was still at Meeting and could stay there until she needed it. The sun was high in the sky, and the humidity was approaching saturation. New England in October was a blessing to everyone, but a Massachusetts August was a trial to even the most long-suffering Yankee. She liked to walk, but the recent heat had often dissuaded her from her discipline. She had time now, and she resolved to go down to the river to stretch her legs despite the heat. Putting off exercise, after all, simply led to procrastination about more important matters.

The Charles lay slack and still as Elizabeth walked along it. She looked carefully at the river and had the impression that it was not flowing. Thick green algae covered the surface of the water near the Anderson Bridge and shimmered repulsively in the heat. Although in recent years efforts had been made to clean up the Charles, in August it looked as fetid as ever. Harvard's riverfront dormitories, always called "houses" in Ivy League parlance, stood in pretty contrast to the water. Their blue, white, and gold cupolas all but sparkled in the intense sunlight. Even Harvard's unpleasantly expansive business school building, across the river from Elizabeth, looked better to her than the natural world on this day.

A trickle of sweat from her forehead ran down between her eyes and under the bridge of her glasses. She pushed her spectacles as high on her nose as possible, but within a few steps they were slipping down again. She lost track of this indignity for a moment because she felt dizzy. She paused in the shade of a great sycamore.

I'm not cut out for the greenhouse effect, the Clerk thought as she continued on her way. *Or perhaps it's the air pollution levels the radio was warning about this morning.* She finished her walk and turned her steps toward Longfellow Park.

It felt no cooler as she stepped into Harriet's office, but a fan on the windowsill was churning the heavy air. Otto was there speaking to the secretary. Both nodded at the Clerk but continued their business.

"These are the registration forms for the Labor Day retreat. They've been coming in for two weeks now." Otto put a stack of paper on Harriet's desk. "We're going to pack Woolman Hill's facilities this year. And here are the checks for fees." He handed Harriet a separate envelope. "Please deposit them in the Peace and Social Concerns account."

Harriet took out the checks and began to count them. "They should all be for forty-two dollars, right?" she asked.

Otto nodded. "Oh, and two people have handed me cash rather than mail in checks. I've got their money here." He brought out his wallet and opened it.

Out of the corner of her eye Elizabeth saw movement before she heard the alarming crash. Harriet stood up with a shriek, and Otto's wallet spun toward Elizabeth's feet. The fan on the windowsill had fallen to the floor and was making deep grinding noises as it lay prostrate on the linoleum. Otto stepped quickly over and unplugged it. Elizabeth, to be helpful, stooped and picked up his open billfold. While still crouched down, she saw that the contents of the main pocket were partly exposed.

With shame blossoming inside her, the Clerk quickly thumbed through the billfold, Harriet's desk screening her from Otto's view. In addition to cash, the wallet contained two receipts from a photocopy store, a coupon for a haircut in Harvard Square, and a small picture of Hope Laughton.

"It doesn't quite balance there, I know," said Harriet. "The fan is wider than the sill."

"I think it's broken," Otto said, looking critically at the fan.

"Don't trouble yourself about it. I'll deal with it." The secretary sat down at her desk as Elizabeth stood up.

Elizabeth handed Otto his wallet. While he counted out the money due his committee's account, she silently berated herself for her sins. In an instant, she felt self-justification rising within her and postponed the battle with her conscience. She picked up her stack of mail and put it into her purse. She looked at the package which had come from Philadelphia and deduced that it was only informational pamphlets that could be placed on the Inquirer's Table. She put a note in the box of the Oversight Committee asking it to take care of the pamphlets. By then, Otto and Harriet had completed their business. Otto and Elizabeth departed.

The air was heavily humid as the pair walked toward Harvard Square. "I'm sorry I woke you up this morning," said Elizabeth. "In this heat, a person needs all the sleep he can get."

"It's OK. A cop came to my door just after you called, so it was a good thing I was up."

"Detective Burnham?"

"Yup. He wanted to know why a book belonging to me was in Hope's kitchen Monday morning. Almost made it sound like a crime. I guess the cops found it near her." Two nearly naked young women passed them on the blistering sidewalk. Both Quakers felt embarrassment at the exposure of flesh and carefully looked at the sidewalk as if to avoid stumbling. Otto continued, "I said I'd lent it to Hope last week. Then Burnham asked me a lot of questions about where I was on Monday morning. I was at home, asleep, during the time that seemed to interest him. But I live alone, and I can't prove where I was."

"You don't start work until the afternoon?"

"That's right." Otto's work as an orderly at Cambridge City Hospital often involved odd hours. "I'm on the swing shift now. Burnham took it all down and went away."

Elizabeth felt a trickle of sweat move on her forehead as she inclined her head. She brushed it away. "Let's go to the Stockpot, Otto. It will be cool." The pair turned at JFK Street and walked toward the basement-level restaurant. Miraculously, they got a table, and, familiar with the menu as both of them were, quickly ordered. Elizabeth fixed her gray-green eyes on her companion. "What was your relationship to Hope Laughton?"

Otto blinked rapidly, then looked down at the place mat in front of him. He picked up his paper napkin and folded it several times. "I don't mind what people know now," he said at last. His tone was leaden and lifeless. "She meant the world to me. Nothing can take her place."

"No," said Elizabeth softly. "We can't take one another's place."

"We weren't lovers," he said tonelessly, as if she had not spoken. "I wish now that we had been. But I loved her in my heart these past two years like I've never loved a woman. The sound of her voice made me glad to be alive. Glad just to be there."

"She was a married woman."

He crumpled the napkin. "That's what kept me in check. I never spoke to her about what I felt. I never touched her. But if thoughts are sinful, I was in the wrong for a long, long time."

"You may have harmed her, in a way, if she knew what you felt. And wronged Sheldon, if he guessed."

"I think they both knew. Maybe they talked about it. It wouldn't surprise me. But, you see, we were all friends, good friends. How many Quakers are there who are serious about war taxes? We were a small minority at Meeting; we had the same goals. And the same troubles, too. Living with the IRS, when it comes down on you, isn't easy."

Elizabeth murmured assent. The waitress brought their orders. Both Quakers bowed their heads over their food before eating. Elizabeth was silent as she ate her pita sandwich and cup of gazpacho. Otto spoke only when he had finished eating.

"She was the best woman I've known, and I miss her with a

longing I've never had before. But neither she nor I acted on what we felt for each other."

Elizabeth wondered if Hope had felt anything, or if Otto only assumed she had. On the good side, she thought, Otto had not had any position of authority over Hope which he might have been tempted to exploit for his own gratification. The relationship among equal Friends had many advantages over the hierarchies of church life.

"You're in no position to judge me," said Otto, "unless you've always been able to control your thoughts. And your emotions."

"I'm not judging. You are doing that, and will probably do more and more of it, I'd guess. But if you seek forgiveness, I know you will find it."

"You have that much faith in Sheldon?" he asked.

Elizabeth was startled. "I was thinking of God," she said.

Otto stood up angrily and reached for his billfold.

"You go catch your bus," said Elizabeth steadily. "I'll pay. And Otto, don't let others see that picture of Hope in your wallet. Especially not Mr. Burnham."

Otto's pasty face turned instantly crimson. He began to speak but then abruptly turned and walked away.

10

We declare our faith in those abiding truths taught and exemplified by Jesus Christ—that every individual of every race and nation is of supreme worth; that love is the highest law of life, and that evil is to be overcome, not by further evil, but by good. The relationship of nation to nation, race to race, class to class, must be based on this divine law of love if peace and progress are to be achieved. We believe in those principles, not as mere ideals for some future time, but as part of the eternal moral order and as a way of life to be lived here and now. War is a colossal violation of this way of life. If we are true to our faith we can have no part in it.

Philadelphia Yearly Meeting, 1934

Elizabeth stayed in the restaurant after Otto had left and ordered a glass of ice tea. She mused that the bond between war-tax resisters at the Meeting was much stronger than she had known. In her life, only her friendship with Patience could compare to it. She slowly drank her tea and read the Meeting's mail from her purse. When she was finished, she paid the bill and went outside, deciding to walk to Lee Street and see Sheldon at the Bakers' house.

As Elizabeth walked, she felt a vague sense of unease. She looked around her more carefully, making eye contact with people. Seeing this unusual behavior, a homeless man rose from a bench to ask her for money. Elizabeth shook her head, still with a sense of unreality.

Then it occurred to her. Harvard's summer program must be finished. In the excitement of the last few days Elizabeth had lost track of the time, and the marvelous drop in the student population had taken her by surprise. Cheered by the lack of crowds, she took a few steps back and gave the homeless man a dollar. He was startled, but smiled his acceptance.

With a quicker step, Elizabeth was leaving Harvard Square when she saw a young woman loitering on the sidewalk in front of a tobacco store. It was Kelly, disheveled and dirty and wearing a black eye, but smiling.

"So you got out, Liz!"

Elizabeth stopped and with genuine gladness replied, "Yes, the charge against me was dropped at the preliminary hearing."

"Great!" said Kelly. "I knew you didn't belong there."

Elizabeth looked around at the passersby on the sidewalk, a mixture of Ivy League yuppies and the homeless of Cambridge. "And I'm not sure you belong here, Kelly. In the heat, I mean. And you look the worse for wear. Has someone been misusing you?"

"Yeah, the man I live with," said Kelly matter-of-factly.

"Is there nowhere else you can go?"

"Hey," said Kelly crisply, "it's my home, you know? And this is my life."

"Yes, I'm sorry." Elizabeth thought rapidly. "Do you know where Longfellow Park is, just beyond the square?"

"I slept there a time or two, when I first came to Cambridge."

"Ask at the Quaker Meetinghouse if you ever want to speak to me. You don't have to live where you do now."

Kelly laughed. "Guys are all the same, at least from what I know of 'em. And my man isn't the worst." She backed up a step and turned toward the street. "But it's good to see you, Liz. I'm glad you're out."

Elizabeth said good-bye as Kelly trotted across Massachusetts Avenue. The Quaker found Lee Street, in the neighborhood between Harvard and Inman Squares. She walked up to the small house belonging to Titus and Constance Baker. The front door was open, and through the screen door she heard little Cathy's laughter. Elizabeth rang the doorbell, and Sheldon's voice called, "Come in!" She stepped into the front hall.

"Hello, Elizabeth," said Sheldon, beckoning her into the living room, where Cathy was crawling along the floor pushing a wagon in front of her. "This is Jose, whom you met at the auction."

"Yes," Elizabeth said quickly to the large man lumbering to his feet to shake her hand. "I do remember. Pleased to see you again."

"And you, Mrs. Elliot. I meant to write to you after the auction to say how impressed I was with the way you spoke to the reporters. Not an easy job, since they want extreme statements for headlines."

"That's exactly it. The press doesn't understand the religious framework behind Quaker action. Or they don't want to include that in their stories."

"No. And there aren't many of you Quakers trying to get your message out. It's a shame. I respect your tradition. There are a lot of us Catholics, but even Catholic teachings, like the ones coming out of Central America, don't get serious treatment in the press. Just a headline when a priest gets shot, then nothing."

Cathy, wearying of the wagon, picked up a teddy bear and crawled onto the sofa next to her father. She bopped him on the head with the stuffed toy to get his attention. Jose, with an agility surprising for a man his size, scooped her up, holding her high in the air. Catherine was apparently familiar both with Jose and with the heights to which he could raise her, for she laughed with delight. He carried her out to the front hall, and soon Cathy's voice was heard, still laughing, in the kitchen.

"It's not going to be easy being a single parent," said Sheldon to Elizabeth. "Last night I told Cathy that Hope is dead. She doesn't really understand, I'm afraid. She cried a lot last night, but this morning she's been her normal self. She hasn't mentioned her mama at all."

"It will take time for her to understand the absence is permanent," said Elizabeth. "Little ones don't think about the future like we do. Even the differences between 'soon' and 'now' and 'tomorrow' are hard for a three-year-old to comprehend."

"That's true. When she grows up, I hope she'll be able to remember her mama." He closed his eyes, squeezing out tears.

"She will. Especially if you speak of Hope and keep her picture where Cathy can see it." Sheldon cleared his throat, and Elizabeth continued. "I'm glad to see that your friends know how to help. And I take it Constance is devoted to Cathy. Is she here, by the way?"

"No, she's out this afternoon. An appointment somewhere. Titus is in San Salvador. So far, Constance hasn't been able to reach him to tell him the news. There's more trouble down there, and the phones are out. Jose came over to keep me company."

Jose carried Cathy into the living room, just below ceiling level. She laughed and made noises Elizabeth assumed were airplane sounds. When she was put down on the floor, she ran over to her father and tugged on his hand.

"I need to go potty," the small, pure voice announced.

Sheldon sighed, then smiled and said, "Thanks for saying so." He looked up at the adults. "We'll be back in a moment." He and Catherine disappeared up the narrow stairway of the old house.

"Hope's death is a tragedy, not just for your community, but for everyone who knows Sheldon," Jose volunteered and sat down in an overstuffed chair. He spoke calmly but with feeling.

Elizabeth murmured assent.

"I've known Sheldon a little more than a year now," continued the big man, "and I respect him deeply. His war-tax witness, while it isn't exactly what I do for Pax Christi, has been a blessing to see. He's an inspiration."

"As was Hope," said Elizabeth.

"I knew her less well, but I'm sure that's true."

"Do you know about Sheldon's AIDS prevention work?"

"Of course. I helped him get started. The group he works with is Catholic."

Elizabeth was startled. After a moment's reflection she said, "I had the impression that Catholics wouldn't participate in a program that distributed birth control."

"And I didn't know a Quaker would hand out needles to drug users!" Jose said with good humor. "It's only the pope who feels certain that condoms are as bad as gas chambers. The rest of us make up our own minds."

"But not with the blessings of your church?"

Jose smiled. "My friends and I can live without the cardinals' approval. And many priests are sympathetic to what we're doing. But even if they weren't, all we need from our clergy is the sacraments. And that they always give us. Are dissident Quakers so different? Sheldon hasn't felt his war-tax witness was appreciated by much of your Meeting."

Elizabeth was not sure how to respond, especially to the word "dissident."

Jose continued. "But he knew his witness was right, at least right for him."

"Yes," said Elizabeth slowly, "I know the Laughtons didn't receive as much support from Meeting as they should have. Sheldon and Hope made some of us uncomfortable because their actions forced us to look at our lives. Quaker lives are rather comfortable these days."

"It sounds like Quakers have many of the same problems as Catholics."

Elizabeth was silent, considering this new perspective.

"The Spirit is moving in Sheldon Laughton," said Jose softly. "It's a privilege to see him awakening. His work with us has been faithful, and I hope to see him continue to grow, wherever he goes now. I know it's foreign to you as a Quaker, but the ritual of the Mass is central to Catholic worship, and it's clearly been helpful to Sheldon. He was learning the liturgy when I got to know him, and I think his awakening dates from that time."

Elizabeth, who had never imagined Sheldon—or any other Friend—at Mass, repressed her surprise.

"It may seem a formal and stiff form of worship," Jose went on, "but Quaker silence feels that way to me. I've been to one of your Meetings at Longfellow Park."

Elizabeth smiled weakly. "I know that Quaker prayer is difficult for many visitors to understand." She summoned up her generosity. "Perhaps it's best we each do what speaks to us and let the theologians worry about what it all means. Speaking of theology, Jose, may I ask you, is Saint Augustine important to Sheldon in some special way?"

He frowned. "I know he was reading Augustine's *Confessions* last month. Yes, I remember now, he said he had written a poem about Augustine's conversion. I saw it. Good verse, as usual with Sheldon, but I thought it seemed rather Protestant. That kind of conversion, I mean."

"I gather it was a seeing-the-Light experience," said Elizabeth. "But in past years, Sheldon's poetry was published in Quaker magazines. It was always about early Friends."

"His early friends?"

"Early Quakers, I mean. Excuse me. George Fox, for example, and Quakers like that. I didn't know he now is being inspired by early Catholics."

Jose smiled easily. "Poets use whatever grips them."

"Exactly. I am simply surprised that he finds something gripping in that saint."

"Well, lots of people have, but not me. I'm not a reader."

The patter of small feet and the steady tread of larger ones announced that Cathy and her father were descending the stairs.

Jose rose and, stepping over to where Elizabeth was seated, held out his hand. "I must be going," he said. "I'm expected at the Catholic Worker house in Boston. But I'm glad to meet you again. I thought you did an excellent job that day at the house auction, and it's a pleasure to get to know you a little bit better." Cathy and her father came into the living room, hand in hand. "Good-bye, Cathy. I'll see you soon."

"Bye-bye," said the little girl solemnly.

"Thanks for coming. It was a great help," said Sheldon. "Keep in touch."

Jose lightly tousled Cathy's hair and then turned away to the front door. He let himself out as Sheldon sat down on the living room sofa. Cathy pulled at the shoelaces of his left foot. She seemed fully absorbed by her game.

Elizabeth looked steadily at Sheldon and said, "Did you know, this past year, how Otto felt about your wife?"

Unperturbed, Sheldon looked up from Cathy and, holding Elizabeth's gaze, replied, "Yes. Hope and I discussed it several times."

"He was smitten, from what I can tell. It was destructive."

"To him, destructive. But these things happen. We spent a lot of time with Otto over the past several years. He's the only serious war-tax resister at Meeting, other than us, so it was natural we were good friends. I'm spending a lot of time now with Jose, in the same kind of way."

Elizabeth knew firsthand that religious life could lead to intense friendships. She had had such a relationship with Patience Silverstone for several decades. Patience was a companion, someone in the same struggles, someone with whom Elizabeth could sojourn. A strong friendship of some sort between the Laughtons and Otto was natural, but the nature of it was still unclear to her. "I think our Meeting does foster intense friendships," she said carefully, "more so than most churches. I know that if some disaster arose in my life, I would have the help and support of a dozen good Friends. Just as I would do anything I could for a number of our members. But when a man falls in love with another man's wife, no matter how good and godly the friendship may initially have been, things must change. For all concerned."

"Oh, yes," said Sheldon. "They do. It's a strain for everyone. All three of us suffered, I'm sure. But that's not a reason to send someone like Otto away. Things change, and his feelings would have run their course. Worn themselves out, basically, without encouragement from Hope. She valued Otto as a friend, but not in other ways. The person who was hurt the worst was Otto."

"It's good of you to see that," said Elizabeth. "He lost something, and that's tormenting him."

"I'm sorry if he can't be at peace about it."

Elizabeth looked at him critically. "Are you?"

Sheldon answered easily. "I'm at peace about Otto, if that's what you mean. He doesn't distress me. But I'll never be at peace about Hope. Last night I fell asleep choking on grief. This morning, when I woke up, I actually felt angry with her. Angry that she left me alone and abandoned Cathy. That's absurd, I know, but that's the way it was."

Elizabeth said sympathetically, "I can remember being angry with Michael after he died. I think anger is part of our response to death. It's a loss, after all, and losses make us both bereft and hostile."

Sheldon stroked Cathy's head.

"I don't really mean to pry," Elizabeth continued, "but I need to understand, Sheldon. Did Hope express concern to you about Otto's feelings?"

"We talked it through, on more than one occasion. No one can control their feelings. Hope felt a bit sorry for Otto, I think. I was more annoyed, I admit. But not really distressed with him. Hope knew how to respond to it all."

Sheldon handed Cathy the teddy bear, which had fallen from the sofa.

"Did Hope know how to handle herself?" asked Elizabeth quietly, once more with a note of apology in her voice.

Sheldon looked up sharply. "Absolutely."

"You had a good marriage, Friend," said Elizabeth with respect.

"Yes," said Sheldon simply. He shook his head and sighed. "I miss her terribly."

Elizabeth sat quietly, remembering her own sense of loss after her husband's death. Then she took a deep breath and asked, "Where were you on Monday morning? After you dropped off Cathy, I mean?"

Cathy pushed a book onto the sofa and then crawled into her father's lap. "Daddy, read!" she commanded. Sheldon gently turned the book around so it was right side up, and Cathy settled into place.

"I'm talking to Mrs. Elliot, but I can read if you'll be quiet."

Catherine put a finger in her mouth and nodded her head in agreement, then flipped to the first page.

"There once lived an emperor who was so interested in new clothes that he could not think about other things," said Sheldon softly, lowering the pitch of his voice. *"One day two men came to town. They told the emperor that they were weavers, and that the cloth they wove was very unusual."*

Catherine studied the picture book. Sheldon looked up at Elizabeth and said in his normal tone of voice, "I did, of course, already give a statement to the police about my movements." He looked down and continued, " *'The cloth we weave cannot be seen by silly or stupid people,' the two men said. The emperor ordered them to set up their looms and weave him their cloth."*

"And when you visited me at the police station, you gave me an account of that morning, too," said Elizabeth. "May I assume your statements to the police and to me agree?"

"I hope a Friend would assume that." Sheldon lowered his voice. *"The next day the emperor went to see how the weavers were progressing. He looked at the looms but saw nothing. 'Goodness!' he said, 'I can't admit that I don't see the cloth.' "*

"The day will come, I'm sure," said Elizabeth, "when you will explain what you did that morning. Truthfully, I mean."

Sheldon's head jerked back, and he looked straight at his harasser. Cathy squirmed in his lap, turned the page in the book, and said, "Daddy, read!"

In a toneless voice he read softly, " *'It is just as beautiful as I could wish'*, said the emperor. *'You are doing an excellent job.' 'We will make you the finest clothes in the kingdom,' said the two men.*" Cathy turned the page of the book.

Elizabeth said matter-of-factly, "I've been to Lexington and talked to Professor Whiting's neighbor. She knows when you arrived Monday morning."

He looked up and said, "These aren't the circumstances to confront me."

"On the contrary," said Elizabeth quickly. "You want to tell where you were, I'm sure. Your reason for truthfulness is in your lap."

Cathy again called her father's attention to the book. He lowered his voice and said, *"The day came when the two men said the cloth was done. They showed the emperor the new clothes and offered to dress him in them."*

"Sooner or later it will come out, Sheldon. And when you face it, whatever it is, we can all adjust and begin again."

"The emperor took off his old clothes and allowed the two men to dress him. He did not want to admit he could not see their clothes because he did not want anyone to think he was silly or stupid." He looked up and said in a normal tone, "The trouble is, Friend, this is a new beginning many won't understand."

Elizabeth considered. "If so, delay won't help. You can count on me, and I hope the Meeting, to try to understand."

"Very few will try," Sheldon said with venom. Then he collected himself and softened his tone. *"The emperor went out on his balcony so that all his subjects could see the wonderful new clothes the two men had made for him. Everyone could see he had nothing on, but no one wanted to be thought stupid or silly, so they all said the emperor's new clothes looked marvelous."*

Elizabeth stood up. "My number is in the telephone book. For this matter, anytime is a good time to call, Friend."

"*Everyone, that is, except one little girl,*" continued Sheldon doggedly, slowly turning the page.

"*But he has nothing on!*" cried Cathy in delight at remembering the line for little girls.

"*When the emperor heard the voice of the little girl, he knew the truth.*" Sheldon looked at Elizabeth, and in a different and strained tone he said, "I'm doing my best. This is not the time to discuss Monday morning."

"At the time of your choosing, then," said Elizabeth. "But the sooner Cathy's father is free of his burden, the better." She turned and walked toward the door.

"Bye-bye, Izbit!" said a small, clear voice.

The Clerk turned quickly, ashamed of her neglect of the third person in the room. "Good-bye, Catherine," she said. "God be with you."

11

No person can decide for another what his or her witness shall be. But it has always been the practice of Friends to act upon the leadings of their consciences and to support each other in their right to do so. The conscription of tax money to build weapons of destruction is something many Friends find immoral. William Penn, in refusing to send money to England for war with Canada, said, "No man can be true to God and false to his own conscience, nor can he extort from it a tribute to carry on any war, nor ought true Christians to pay for it." Therefore we stand in loving support of any of our members who are called by conscience to oppose and refuse taxes that are to be used for military purposes.

Minutes of the Iowa Yearly Meeting (Conservative), 1983

The wind, which had been gentle in the morning, was blowing more strongly as Elizabeth emerged from the Bakers' house. The heat, or at least the sense of oppression, had lessened. Her pace became brisk as she walked toward home.

A gust of wind and a sudden darkness made Elizabeth look up at the sky. Storm clouds were rolling in from the west and had just intercepted the sun. Elizabeth wondered which of her windows she had left open. As she came up Concord Avenue she saw that a large branch of the elm in her neighbor's yard had blown down. The Quaker looked with apprehension at her slate-tiled roof. A thunderstorm in June had blown down several tiles, and Elizabeth feared more might be lost. She sighed at the thought of new expenses she might have to meet on her fixed income.

She hurried to her front door as thunder boomed in the west. She went inside and then all around her house, closing windows. Sparkle streaked by on her way to hide in the basement. Elizabeth settled down at her kitchen window to watch the storm. No rain had yet fallen. Her neighbor's elm swayed in the wind. Leaves, torn off the tree, disappeared upward into the sky. Elizabeth watched sunflower seeds blowing out of the feeder; birds themselves were not to be seen. *Well,* she thought, *the juncos and other ground feeders will find the seeds after this storm is over.*

She got several candles and matches out of the cupboard and set them on the kitchen table. Although it was still daytime, she knew from experience that a power outage could last for hours. Thinking of the roast in her fridge, she decided that cooking it would be a good idea. She did not want raw meat sitting overnight in a warm refrigerator.

Elizabeth lit a burner on her gas stove. She unwrapped the roast from Star Market's layers of plastic and Styrofoam and put the meat, fat side down, into her heavy cast-iron pot. The meat began to brown as she got out onions, celery seed, and cooking wine. She turned the roast and then added the other ingredients, plus some water, to the pot. She put the heavy cast-iron lid in place. With windows closed against the storm, the temperature dropping every minute, and a pot roast on the stove, Elizabeth felt better. She took her bread dough out of the refrigerator and set it on the counter to warm. In keeping with her wishes that morning, the bread had risen only slightly in her absence, but as it warmed to room temperature, she knew, the yeast would work rapidly.

Rain was blowing against the window. Two claps of thunder banged against the house, and she looked critically at the elm. Lightning flashed in the sky. As an old Yankee, she automatically began to count *one-one-thousand* and had only reached the last syllable when the thunder again rocked the house. Never able to remember the speed of sound, she did not know exactly how close the lightning had been, but she realized it was near.

The electric light above the kitchen table burned on calmly. She could not hear her pot roast gurgling on the stove because of the noise of the storm. The Clerk's mind turned back to the eventful week. She tried to remember the facts she had learned and organize the conjectures she had made.

Rain was now falling heavily. It was no longer blowing horizontally against the window, however. As she watched, the rain's volume increased, as did the noise on her slate roof. The thunder was more distant. She saw the leaves from her neighbor's elm falling heavily with the rain. Suddenly, the scene was a bit dimmer, and, turning, Elizabeth saw that the kitchen light was out. She felt vindicated in her decision to cook the pot roast.

As the rain fell steadily but less violently, Elizabeth cracked several windows to let in the cool, freshly washed air. She felt a spasm in her back while opening the last window and gingerly lay down on the sofa to wait for an hour or two before turning the roast and adding carrots and potatoes. She dozed off thinking again about Hope's death.

Elizabeth awoke suddenly with a new idea about the murder. Like the practical housewife that she was, however, she remembered her kitchen work and immediately rose to tend to the food. She shaped the bread dough into four loaves and set them in greased bread pans to rise. The meat was doing well. She added more water, several bay leaves, and a little cooking wine to the pot and turned the meat. An hour later she added potatoes, carrots, and a slice of onion and shortly after that put the bread in the oven to bake. By the time she had finished her supper, the sweet smell of baking molasses bread began to fill the kitchen. When the wind-up timer rang, Elizabeth peeked into the oven. She was glad, though not wholly surprised, to see that all four loaves looked perfect. She took the duck-shaped hot pads her daughter-in-law had given her the previous Christmas and removed the loaves to the bread board, one by one, turning the pans on their side as she set them down. She closed the oven door, turned off the gas, and then gently knocked each loaf from its pan.

The sight and smell of fresh bread, and the cool air after the storm, gave Elizabeth new energy. As if in keeping with her spirits, the lights came back on. She put away the candles and then, on an impulse, went to the telephone and called the Bakers' number. Constance answered on the third ring. Elizabeth iden-

tified herself, explained that she had just taken a batch of molasses bread from the oven, and asked if she might bring over some
to Constance in light of her unexpected houseguests.

"That would be lovely," said Constance. "And it's good of you
to think of me. Everything is so distressing, I can't help but think
about Hope all the time."

"I can understand that, and I'd like to give you my condolences.
Could I bring the loaf over right now? I don't mean to disturb
Sheldon," Elizabeth added hesitantly. "I talked to him this afternoon, and there's no need for him to have to deal with someone
outside the family again today."

"It's no problem. I'm sure Sheldon doesn't count you as a disturbance, Elizabeth, and anyway, he's not here. He's gone to
Foster Place to pick up more of Cathy's clothes and toys. He's
bringing all of her things over here. I want her to stay where she's
safe. I don't know how to say this," she added in a lower tone,
"but I'm beginning to wonder about Sheldon. Who else would
have a motive for doing something to Hope? It's Cathy's safety
I worry about. Husbands are the likely suspects, aren't they? And
under this cloud, I'm not sure what sort of father he will be."

"Aunt Consanse," said a voice in the background.

"Yes, honey."

Elizabeth could not hear what the little girl said, but when she
judged Constance was listening to the telephone again she said
that she and the bread would be right over.

Elizabeth walked briskly to the Meetinghouse to fetch her car.
She coaxed the 1977 Chevrolet into starting. The two loaves of
warm bread in a paper bag sat beside her on the passenger seat.
The trip to Lee Street went quickly, and Elizabeth found a place
to park not far from the Bakers' home. Constance met her at the
door, divining her presence by some means before she had pushed
the bell.

"Thank you, thank you," said Constance, holding out her

hands for the bread. "And do come in. It's so good of you to make bread."

"Kneading the dough is one thing I can do with my hands that doesn't make my arthritis worse. And today it was doubly thera-peutic. Since the police tested my hands, I haven't felt good about them. Now I feel clean again."

"The police tested your hands? What's that mean?" asked Con-stance as Elizabeth stepped inside.

"It wasn't painful, just disagreeable. They rub your hands with wax, trying to see if there's some chemical on them that comes from gunpowder. If you hold a gun and fire it, you get sprayed with invisible traces of things."

"I see," said Constance thoughtfully. "I suppose the whole moviegoing public knows that, but it's news to me." She contin-ued in a blurred rush of words, "It's all so unreal, Friend! Do you think some prowler could have killed my sister?"

"The gun that was used came from the house," said Elizabeth gently, not wishing to further grieve Constance but wanting to be fully honest. "I think that means it's likely the murder is con-nected with the household in some way, or with those Friends who were often in and around the Laughtons' home."

"It's hard to think about who else could be involved," said Con-stance, holding the bread but beckoning Elizabeth further into the house with a free finger. In a surer tone she added, "Cathy and I are in the kitchen. Please come in."

Elizabeth followed the mistress of the house into the kitchen, where Cathy sat on the floor playing with a dollhouse.

"Hi, Izbit!" said the child gaily but instantly returned to her game.

"Isn't she a darling?" Constance said as she put the loaves into plastic bags. Elizabeth was not sure the bread was cool enough to be sealed up in something that did not breathe, but Constance seemed so proficient, energetic, and young, the elder Quaker hesitated to speak.

"This is a pony," said Catherine, raising a tiny hand toward Elizabeth. In it was a red, rectangular building block.

Elizabeth smiled and asked, "Does the pony have a name?"

Catherine nodded seriously. "He's Jack."

"Everyone in the dollhouse world has a name," said Constance. "Cathy has been coming over here since she was a baby, and we've built up quite an imaginary community together."

Elizabeth smiled. "Making up companions is the best part of being young," she said over Cathy's head. "Only writers get to do that sort of thing as adults, and I envy them." Then, sitting down on the chair nearest the dollhouse, she asked if she could be introduced to its residents.

"Dis is Sarah," said little Catherine, holding up a full-sized doll. "An' dis is Sarah's mama." A small doll, easy to grasp in one small hand, was displayed. It was dressed in early American style.

"Oh," said Elizabeth, "may I see her?"

Cathy gave her the diminutive doll.

"One of the things I so appreciate about my Cathy," said Constance in approving tones, "is that she'll always share her dolls with whoever is interested."

Cathy returned her attention to Jack, the Cubist horse, as Elizabeth admired the clothes on the small doll. "Where did you get a Quaker doll in 'plain dress'?" she asked.

"I make all the clothes for Cathy's dolls."

Elizabeth nodded. She had not had daughters, only sons, and hence had not made any doll clothes since she herself was in elementary school. She remembered the activity fondly and would gladly have sewn a full wardrobe of tiny clothes if only her grandchild had been a girl.

The telephone rang. Cathy handed Jack and two other wooden blocks to Elizabeth as Constance spoke into the phone. But, with the fickle whim of young children, she retracted her gift of the toys and retreated with them to the corner of the kitchen. Not wanting to disturb the child, Elizabeth looked around and idly picked up a children's book that lay on the kitchen table. It was a volume of verse, given by Sheldon to his daughter on the occasion of her second birthday. Below the inscription, and in the same hand, was a short poem carefully printed on the bright-yellow flyleaf:

She thought she saw a Quaker Clerk
Walking toward the train.
She looked again and saw it was
The sunny coast of Spain.
Precipitation there, you see, is mainly in the plain.

She thought she saw a Quaker Clerk
Reading from a book.
She looked again and saw it was
A shaded Inglenook.
"You righteous, righteous Friend," she said, "You cannot be
forsook!"

Elizabeth was startled. Nonsensical poetry featuring a Quaker Clerk was new to her, and she did not appreciate it. For one thing, she wondered if she could have been Sheldon's inspiration. She read the poem again as Constance talked into the telephone and Cathy played with her toys. The verse seemed reminiscent of some book her boys had had as children, but she could not remember the author's name. In any event, this seemed to be Sheldon's work. On second reading, prepared for the non sequiturs, she did not find the stanzas so offensive.

"That was your uncle Titus, Cathy. He's got a ticket, and he'll be home two days from now," said Constance, hanging up the telephone. She looked at Elizabeth and said, "I finally reached Titus and told him the news. He said he'd call when he got a ticket."

"Good. I'm very glad. But now I must be going," Elizabeth said, closing and putting down the book. "I'm happy to see you both doing so well. Good-bye, Cathy."

"Bye-bye," said the small girl.

Constance showed Elizabeth to the door, and she drove back to Concord Avenue.

Enjoying a slice of one of the loaves of bread she had kept, Elizabeth considered, with some jealousy, the scene of domestic tranquility she had just witnessed. Sparkle appeared from the basement and rubbed against her ankles. The feline attention only increased her loneliness. The telephone rang, sending Sparkle scampering away, and Elizabeth answered it quickly, hoping to hear Neil's voice.

But it was Ruth Markham. She inquired how Cathy was doing. Elizabeth explained that Sheldon had been coping with Cathy quite handily during the day and that Cathy's aunt seemed to be providing the child with lots of affection.

"She's a most devoted aunt," Elizabeth concluded. "She's distressed, of course, by her sister's terrible death, but I think taking care of Cathy is keeping her on an even keel."

"I'm glad. Cathy talks a lot about Constance and Otto Zimmer sometimes, in Sunday School. I'm glad he isn't horning into this situation. I've never liked him."

"Well, there's no sign he's doing much for Cathy at present."

"The loss of her mother is going to cause a real scar for that little girl," mused Ruth.

"Yes, it will. But children are adaptable. She was clinging to her father this afternoon, but just now when I went over to the Bakers' house, she was doing just fine, with only her aunt around."

"I'm glad. I've been thinking more about the cause of all this grief, Friend. It seems to me that if the gun was just dumped be-hind the bushes, like Bill Hoffman said, the murderer wasn't try-ing to frame you or Sheldon. It's his gun, right?"

"Yes," answered Elizabeth.

"So leaving it by the body would be a better ploy for anyone but Sheldon himself. See what I mean? If I were in Sheldon's shoes and I had just killed my wife, maybe not really meaning to, I'd wake up to what I'd done and try to put suspicion elsewhere."

"Putting the gun in the bushes doesn't change things much. But I suppose it means the murderer wasn't trying to frame me, making me discover both the corpse and the gun."

"No. And the IRS would have to be in such a plot, since they discovered you with Hope so quickly after you arrived. I guess it's not likely that the government's tax collectors are that diaboli-cal. Although they sure do cause some Friends a lot of grief."

"I think they're not devils at all, just ordinary functionaries. Certainly not plotters. No, it wasn't me anyone was after." Eliz-abeth's voice trailed off for a moment. "Ruth, you just said that if you were Sheldon and you had murdered Hope, you'd do this or that. Let me ask you: If you were Sheldon, why would you kill Hope?".

Ruth was uncharacteristically silent for a moment. "I don't know," she answered slowly, "but I wonder a bit about Sheldon's feelings toward Otto. I know Otto was around that household a lot. I don't know him, really, and I don't know what was hap-pening on Foster Place. But I do know there's something about Otto that always grates. His self-importance, I guess. He's com-pletely wrapped up in Otto Zimmer, if you want my opinion, de-spite all his noble talk about pacifism and tax resistance."

"Yes, from the little I know of him, that's a problem."

"Damn it!" said Ruth abruptly. "That reminds me, I never did reach him!"

Elizabeth decided against eldering her friend for her language.

Ruth explained, "On Sunday I brought my registration form and my money to Meeting for the retreat on Labor Day."

"I saw Otto turning in those forms and checks to Harriet on Tuesday," said the Clerk.

"Drat! It was in my purse on Sunday but I forgot all about it. I didn't see the form until Monday morning when I was digging for a subway token on my way to work. Since Sunday was the deadline for registering, I tried to call Otto as soon as I got in to work, but I couldn't reach him. Then Bill Hoffman called about you being arrested and needing new clothes and it went completely out of my mind."

"I'm sure if you call Harriet she can still add you to the list. When did you call Otto, by the way?"

"Monday."

"No, I mean what time on Monday?"

"Nine o'clock, as soon as I got to work."

"Was the line busy?"

Ruth thought for a moment. "No, there was just no answer. I remember letting the telephone ring a zillion times. I was at work, and there wasn't much to do."

"I see. The reason I ask is that what you say conflicts with what Otto told the police. He told me that he told Mr. Burnham he was at home, asleep, all Monday morning."

"Maybe he's a sound sleeper. My boy sure is. He'll miss the Second Coming, I think, by sleeping through it." Ruth had been a Baptist in her childhood, so Elizabeth ignored the sacrilegious exaggeration and said good-bye. She had much to consider.

12

❦

Can we reach unity in supporting an individual act of conscience about war and violence without requiring that all individuals take the same position? Do we recognize the distinction between unity and unanimity in reaching a corporate decision?

What is the relative importance of supporting individual witness as opposed to concern for upholding the law?

There are many crosses, and we are not called to die on all of them. How do we choose our witness? Is this the one where we feel called to take a stand?

Queries for Consideration at Meeting for Business,
Friends Meeting at Cambridge, 1993

Otto Zimmer's small apartment building was in a poorer section of Cambridge south of Central Square informally known as Cambridgeport. Built shortly after the Second World War to house the influx of working-class people into Cambridge, it was a cheaply constructed three-decker on a busy thoroughfare. Cars and trucks droned along the street as Elizabeth walked slowly down the sidewalk on Thursday morning, looking for the street numbers displayed on small, grimy signs. She found number 21 and walked up to the door. She pushed the doorbell for Otto's apartment, but, as a truck roared behind her, she was unsure if she had heard a ring from within. She pushed the button again and this time was certain she heard ringing inside the apartment. She waited.

In a minute, Otto appeared at the door, dressed only in a pair of gym shorts, his hair falling into his eyes. Elizabeth, who had often seen her boys in similar disarray when they got up in the morning, was not embarrassed, but Otto blushed deeply. His usually pasty face turned gradually more crimson as he opened the bent screen door to admit Elizabeth. He stammered that he would put on something and grabbed a couple of pieces of clothing on the back of a chair, then disappeared into the bathroom.

Elizabeth was left standing in the middle of the small studio apartment listening to the traffic. It was an unkempt and crowded dwelling and smelled strongly of cigarette smoke. Like all Quakers of the old school, Elizabeth had never smoked. She disliked the dirty and unhealthful habit but recognized that, in these modern days, some Friends succumbed to nicotine and had a difficult time overcoming their weakness. Nonetheless, she had always been sensitive to the smell. Otto emerged from the bathroom in cutoff jeans and a T-shirt and invited Elizabeth to sit in the chair that had, a moment before, had his clothes draped over it.

"I expect I've awakened you, Otto, but when I got up this morning I realized we needed to talk again. Before the police question you further."

Otto sat on the edge of the unmade bed in the corner of the room and looked silently at her. He reached to his nightstand, opened a pack of cigarettes, and lit one.

"You told me of your feelings for Hope, but said you had never acted on them."

"That's right." He stopped and looked around the room as if searching for something, then shook his head. "All this past night I've been tormented with the idea that I precipitated her death."

"How do you mean?"

"Jealousy is a powerful emotion. The more I think about it, the more convinced I am that Hope and Sheldon both knew how I felt." He looked down at his feet and wiggled his toes on the threadbare carpet. Elizabeth waited.

"Look," said Otto, "we know she was killed by Sheldon's gun, right? That was the big revolver I saw the cops finding, wasn't it?"

Elizabeth nodded.

"Well, whoever murdered Hope knew where to find the gun and how to use it. Nothing else was taken, I gather, so robbery wasn't the motive. Not that the Laughtons really had much by way of possessions anyway. No one had a reason to kill Hope, no one at all, unless you consider jealousy as a motive. Sheldon may have feared he was losing her. Maybe he just couldn't stand that."

"Perhaps. But it could be that both Hope and Sheldon knew of your feelings but weren't threatened by them. Maybe you were the jealous party?"

He tapped his cigarette on an ashtray in the center of the cluttered nightstand. Then he looked directly at her. "I never harmed Hope. Never. I loved her."

"Sheldon loved her, too. No one doubts that. But love can go wrong. That's what you've been suggesting." Otto glared at Elizabeth, but she continued evenly, "There was a question on my mind when I came here, and now there are two. First, I'm not sure you were here on Monday morning as you said to the police."

She waited. Otto, for once in his life, confined his anger to silence. When he had considered carefully, he said, "I don't know why you say that. I can't prove where I was, you're right, but the fact of the matter is that I was here, asleep."

"Ruth Markham called you on Monday morning about nine o'clock from her office at Harvard. She had forgotten on Sunday to give you her money and registration form for the Labor Day retreat. There was no answer here."

"I often sleep through telephone calls. I work the swing shift, as you know," Otto answered quickly.

"But you woke up when I called you the other morning. And you woke up now to the sound of your doorbell. Despite the traffic noise."

"Maybe so. But I don't always wake. I know, because I've missed a lot of phone calls from my mother in Baltimore. She gets pretty distressed about it. The truth is, Friend, I was here, but asleep." He ground out his cigarette.

"Whose hat is that?" Elizabeth pointed toward the corner of the room where, on a lone hook, hung an odd-looking knit cap of natural colors which she recognized as Peruvian. "Have you ever been to South America?" she asked.

Otto shook his head.

"She used to meet you here? Last winter, it must have been, to need such a hat." Elizabeth looked the younger Quaker directly in the face and unashamedly asked, "Were you lovers?"

"No!" he shouted. "No! Don't say that! We did nothing wrong, ever."

"Why is her hat here?"

"I couldn't help myself," said Otto miserably. "She left it at the Meetinghouse last winter. Accidentally. Most people aren't aware of this, but Hope and Sheldon planned to move west when they lost their house." The apparent non sequitur was spoken with equal misery.

"I didn't know."

Otto nodded. "Their house was their only asset. They figured that in a small town in the Northwest they could live much more cheaply than around here. And Sheldon wanted to go back to being a geologist. That work is mostly in the West. But their moving was going to be hell for me. I've been dreading it for a year. So, you see, I saw the hat on a bench in the worship room and knew Hope must have left it. I took it home with me."

"If that's so, you weren't wise to torture yourself with her possessions. And neither of us knows how much you may have been torturing her. There's a lot of healing needed, Otto. It's no shame to be in need. On Saturday we have a Meeting for Healing."

He looked dejectedly at his bare feet, which now lay still on the grimy carpet. Elizabeth rose and said good-bye. Otto did not move, and she let herself out of the apartment, glad for some smoke-free air. She caught a bus from Cambridgeport to Harvard Square and transferred to a Watertown bus that took her up Mt. Auburn Street.

Elizabeth got off at Mt. Auburn Hospital and went up to the fourth floor to Patience Silverstone's room. The elder Quaker was awake but not animated. She was lying flat on her back, one leg enveloped in a plastic monstrosity. There was also an IV bottle hanging above her. Patience looked, for the first time in Elizabeth's long memory, frail and peaked.

"It's good to see thee," said Patience softly as Elizabeth sat down beside her bed.

"And good to be here," said Elizabeth warmly. "But I gather things are not going as well as might be hoped."

Patience smiled slightly, then coughed. She motioned with one hand toward her leg. "They've discovered what has been giving me so much pain. I have poor circulation, even in the best of times, and with this broken leg, and lying here, there's an open sore, a deep wound really, in my flesh."

Elizabeth said sadly, "I'm so sorry, Patience. What is this thing they've put on your leg?"

"It's a chamber, sealed off from the air. The metal tank there is connected to it, you see? It keeps pure oxygen all around my leg, which helps it heal, they say."

"And this?" asked Elizabeth, motioning to the IV bottle.

"It's either antibiotics or glucose. They switch back and forth between the two. I've got a touch of pneumonia now, the doctor says. I've not been able to eat much. The pain is bad." The last words were almost lost in a sob. Elizabeth reached out and took her friend's hand. "I'm sorry," Patience said with tears in her eyes. "I'm just worn out."

"Naturally. It must be difficult. Are the people on the staff still kind?"

"Oh, yes. Especially the night shift people. I don't know how they manage it."

"What can I do for you?"

"Pray with me."

Elizabeth, still gripping Patience's limp hand, immediately closed her eyes and, taking a deep, slow breath, sank into silent prayer. She asked God to be present to them both and to show her some way to be useful to her friend. She heard Patience quietly crying and coughing and prayed even more deeply for God's presence to be clear to the suffering Friend. Gradually Patience's weeping eased, and Elizabeth heard her breathing more steadily.

Elizabeth had the sensation of diving, in slow motion, into warm water. She relaxed into the depths of wordless prayer. A long time later, a knock at the door forced her to open her eyes. A large, rotund nurse was coming into the room, pushing a small cart in front of her. Elizabeth let go of the patient's hand.

"Vital signs," said the nurse matter-of-factly and began strapping a blood pressure cuff around Patience's free arm, the arm without the IV tube.

"Thee should go, Elizabeth. I'll sleep after this nurse is done." As Patience finished speaking the nurse put a thermometer into her mouth, effectively stopping conversation.

Elizabeth rose and nodded to the nurse. "I'll be back, Friend," she said, "and you will be in my prayers between now and then."

Patience nodded. The nurse began to pump the blood pressure cuff as Elizabeth left the room.

She caught the elevator to the first floor and walked down Mt. Auburn Street toward Harvard Square. Although she did not want to succumb to the sin of pessimism, Elizabeth realized that the worsening of Patience's condition was significant. She was sorry that her friend was suffering, and underneath that sorrow lay a fear that if Patience's condition deteriorated, she might die. She was not young, after all, and she now had three serious obstacles to regaining her health and strength. Elizabeth believed that death was only a temporary parting, or a shadow that veiled people from one another before everyone could be united in the Light. But, despite her faith, separation from those she loved also provoked sorrow and fear. Even with a firm religious faith, death was difficult to contemplate, since Patience was a dear friend.

"I'm being selfish," said Elizabeth aloud. "She is in God's hands, and if death does come, it will only be after a long and full life."

A teenager passing her on the sidewalk looked askance at Elizabeth as she spoke to herself. With a bit of embarrassment, the Quaker stopped her lecture.

As she neared her house on Concord Avenue, she saw Neil knocking at her front door.

"I'm here, Friend," she said from the sidewalk and smiled as he turned toward her. "And I'm glad to see you." She *was* glad, especially glad, perhaps because she wanted to tell someone that Patience's condition had worsened. Standing on the sidewalk, she explained how her friend had looked and what the doctors were now doing to her. "It's not a desperate case, perhaps," she concluded, "but at her age it is surely serious. I'm worried."

"I'm very sorry to hear that things aren't going well. I know how close the two of you have been." Neil looked at her carefully, then changed his tone. "I think you need to get away from all this for a while, just for a break. Let's go for a drive. My car's right here. Anywhere you want, just out of Cambridge."

Elizabeth decided to view Neil's solicitude as kindness, not patronizing masculinity. The idea of a drive sounded good.

Seeing her smile, he asked hopefully, "Where could we go?"

"Let's go to Walden Pond. I haven't been there for years."

"Walden it is."

The blue Buick took the pair to Route 2 and out of the city. Elizabeth leaned back in the passenger seat and tried to relax. She marveled at how quiet the car was. Compared to the rattles, squeals, and occasional roars of her '77 Chevrolet, Neil's car was as quiet as Meeting for Worship. Elizabeth, after serious study, turned on the many-buttoned radio. She tuned to WBUR, and classical music surrounded her.

The miles to Concord flew by.

"You're a good friend to me," Elizabeth murmured as Neil turned left off Route 2 onto the access road to Walden. "It's good to get away. I'm less tense already."

"I'm glad you could come." Neil laughed softly as he pulled into the parking lot. "I'm only sorry our destination isn't deeper in the country. Concord Township is hardly rural anymore."

"No. Quite different from when I was a girl. But still a change from Cambridge."

The two got out of the car and walked toward the water. As soon as the Clerk's feet left concrete and touched the earth she felt another part of her tension leave. There was a steady breeze from the east, and the warmth of the sun was easy to bear. Elizabeth took Neil's hand, and the pair walked along the edge of the pond.

"How long did Thoreau live here?" Elizabeth asked as she looked around at the small world of water and woods in which they were walking.

"A year or two, I think," answered Neil. "Without much company, which seems a shame," he added, squeezing Elizabeth's hand.

"Did he live here before or after his tax troubles?"

"After. The two things weren't connected. He wasn't evicted from his home in town, if that's what you're wondering."

"What was the story about his taxes? Do you remember?"

"Yes, I do. I loved Thoreau's writings when I was young, and I still remember a lot about his life. He objected to the poll tax Massachusetts was collecting in those days. Part of the funds raised through that tax went to return runaway slaves to the South. So he felt he couldn't pay."

"So he refused?" Elizabeth steered her companion around a child playing at the water's edge.

"Indeed. And was arrested and put in jail here in Concord. His friend Emerson paid his tax, and Thoreau was released. I think he spent only one night in jail, but he got a lot of mileage out of it as a writer. It was part of what made him famous."

"How odd," said Elizabeth. "The Laughtons suffered a great deal more than that last year, with their house auctioned and court orders for eviction. Imagine raising a child in the midst of such stress and uncertainty! But the world isn't paying their act of conscience much attention. Even Friends don't always seem to respect their stand."

"No," responded Neil. "That's true. Sheldon, I suppose, could try writing a long book about a small pool of water. Then the world might be more sympathetic."

"Having friends like Emerson is always useful if you feel called to tax resistance."

"Indeed."

"Neil, tell me seriously. What did you think of the Laughtons' witness?"

He thought before answering. "They both seemed serious and faithful people to me. If they felt called to tax resistance, and clearly they did, I could only wish them the best and support them in my prayers. I did so. And still am doing so, for Sheldon."

"But why don't people like us follow their example?"

"Fear of prison," answered Neil simply. They walked on a moment before he continued. "It's not an irrational fear."

"No," she replied. "But fear is not a positive way for a Christian to live."

"William Penn said 'Wear your sword as long as you can.' I think that's a good approach. We should cooperate with the law as long as we are able. The Laughtons just weren't able to cooperate anymore. They had been called to something more challenging."

"That's what I tell myself, too. But I think, sometimes, that we are all called to such things. The difference between me and the Laughtons is that they have the courage to hear. Or the faith."

"The Apostle Paul tells us that faith is a gift."

"Indeed," said Elizabeth. "What would have happened, do you think, if Hope had lost her faith in the witness? Could she have decided that Cathy deserved to be raised in a more normal, se-

cure atmosphere?" Neil did not respond, and Elizabeth continued more quietly. "Still, even if that had happened, I don't see
how it could have led to her death."

"We left Cambridge to give you a break from Meeting worries.
Could we talk of something else?"

Elizabeth sighed inwardly but smiled.

"I'd like to take you to New York on the Labor Day weekend,"
said Neil. "My brother lives in Manhattan, you remember, and
I'd like you two to meet. We can go to the museums and a show."

Elizabeth smiled more broadly. She was glad to know that she
merited family introductions. But then she laughed. "You
promised a topic that wouldn't be difficult, and now you bring up
visiting relatives! Neil, you brought me here for your own purposes, not to give me a break."

"A little bit of both," he admitted with a smile.

"I'll think about it, of course, but I do have to go to New England Yearly Meeting at the end of the month." Elizabeth was re-
ferring to the annual, week-long gathering of Friends in central
Massachusetts, which it would be seemly for her, as Clerk, to attend. "Let's only talk about what we'll do with the remainder of
the day. We need to eat. I propose the Howard Johnson on the
highway for an early supper. Then I have to get back to Cambridge for the Ministry and Counsel Meeting."

Neil accepted the idea of supper after Elizabeth promised to let
him pay for the meal.

13

So far did Friends carry their conviction that God revealed himself to groups that in their monthly, quarterly, and yearly meetings they always acted in accordance with "the sense of the Meeting" as gathered by a clerk; the corporate judgment thus reached was regarded as having greater validity than the often imperfect and clouded light of an individual.

F.B. Tolles, historian sympathetic to Quakerism

Elizabeth had received a telephone call from Bill Hoffman, the legal expert in Meeting, offering to walk with her to the committee meeting that evening. Neil, too, had offered to escort her, but Neil's company seemed inappropriate. He had no official reason to be present, and she did not want to be frequently escorted by him to Meeting business as long as he was only a friend. A fiancé would be different.

Bill Hoffman lived in the neighborhood, and he came on foot to Elizabeth's door. She was waiting for him and ready to depart. As they walked down Concord Avenue, he did his best to reassure her.

"All charges against you were dropped, and I'll say that to anyone in Meeting as many times as it takes them to understand."

"Thank you. I can, of course, appreciate some of the concern Wally and Hugo feel. It does look unseemly to have a Clerk charged with murder."

"The police have to suspect everyone. It's their job, completely routine. I've talked to Doug Gibson, and it's clear Burnham has no solid evidence against you. You simply had the misfortune to discover the body."

"Bill, I'm sure you've thought ahead to the next step in all this. I may not be guilty, but we know that someone is."

The pair cut across Concord Avenue and walked onto the grounds of the Episcopal Divinity School as the judge considered his answer.

"That's the next hurdle. But tonight the issue is just your Clerkship. Focus on that and don't let Hugo and his type crowd you into resigning."

"Don't say such things. We all have to listen to the Spirit and be guided by what we hear. I shouldn't have to remind a Friend that's how we do business. Silence will begin and end tonight's meeting, and that silence is meant to speak to our condition."

"Indeed. And I'm here to make sure the Spirit understands there's no mark against your name as far as the law is concerned."

Elizabeth shook her head and sighed as they crossed Longfellow Park. "Legalistic thinking differs from what's right. That's the crux of many of our troubles." Her voice drifted off as they walked up to the building next to the Meetinghouse.

Most of Ministry and Counsel's members were present when Elizabeth and Bill stepped into the parlor at seven o'clock. Chairs had been pushed into a lopsided oval in the center of the room. Bill took a seat on the far side, while the Clerk walked over to the narrow end and sat down. No one spoke to her, but Jane Thompson smiled in her direction. Mary Linkler, her eyes closed, was seated to Elizabeth's right. Wally Orvick and Hugo Coleman were opposite each other at the other end of the oval, where a lamp illuminated the gathering darkness.

Hugo, Clerk of the committee, cleared his throat and said, "Patience Silverstone is hospitalized and therefore can't be here. But everyone else is present, so let's begin with worship." He closed his eyes, not without an air of drama.

The period of silence which Hugo was in the habit of choosing was generally so short that Elizabeth despaired of true prayer. Nevertheless, she closed her eyes and tried to clear her mind of static. Just as she was beginning to progress, Hugo's voice interrupted her.

"Tonight we have a serious issue to consider. We were all present at Business Meeting, so there's no need to rehash what was said. Have there been any new developments since Tuesday, Elizabeth?"

"The police have taken no further action against me or anyone else," said Elizabeth carefully.

"For which we can be grateful," said Mary.

"Yes, of course," said Hugo, "except that it means that our community is still under a cloud. Both yesterday and today the *Boston Globe* had articles on this murder. In the back pages, to be sure, but there they were. And yesterday's article mentioned that charges had been filed, but then dismissed, against the Clerk of our Meeting."

"No," Judge Hoffman cut in, "that's not the case, Hugo. The article said that charges had been filed, but then thrown out, against one Elizabeth Elliot. The newspaper did not identify Elizabeth in any way with Friends Meeting at Cambridge. Our Meeting was not mentioned at all, in either article."

There was a pause before Hugo responded. "Thank you for the correction. But since Elizabeth is our Meeting's Clerk, anyone familiar with our community knows that its head is under suspicion of first-degree murder."

"Yes," said Bill. "Anyone who discovers a body is suspected by the police until more evidence comes in. The same thing happens in other cases. Any employee who reports embezzlement will, at first, be suspected of having something to do with the theft. But that's as far as such routine suspicion goes."

"In any event," said Wally, "we're not here tonight to consider the police investigation or police suspicions in themselves. We're here to find a sense of what's best for Friends Meeting at Cambridge."

"That's my view, too," said Mary quietly. "Our focus tonight is the Meeting. And the Meeting, in my opinion, has not been showing any signs of distress under Elizabeth Elliot's Clerking.

Perhaps a few Friends are more sensitive to appearances than I am, but when I looked around Business Meeting on Tuesday, I saw no cause for alarm. By the way, I spent quite a bit of time yesterday at the hospital with Patience. She has seen many storms come and go around Longfellow Park, and she feels confident this situation will be resolved soon."

Elizabeth was glad to hear that her friend had been filled in on the events of Tuesday evening, although it had been a topic she had not wanted to bring up with someone struggling with pain in a hospital bed. A sense of calm filled her mind as she thought of the Meeting's oldest member, and again she asked God to be present to her.

"We all hope the situation will soon be resolved," said Hugo. "But for the present, we still have the problem of appearances. How does this look to our friends and neighbors?"

Jane Thompson spoke for the first time. "Somewhere in the Gospel of John, Jesus tells us not to judge by appearances, but judge with right judgment. Can we actually have any doubts about someone we've all known for decades and trusted to be Clerk?"

"In a sense," said Elizabeth slowly, "I think you must have doubts. It's difficult to grasp, I know, but someone killed Hope Laughton. Deliberately killed her. There's good reason to think the murder was done not by a passing thug, but by someone who knew her and her household well. None of us, without an alibi or proof of some kind, can be simply eliminated from the list of suspects because of our good reputation. Remember the terrible time when Bill's uncle was found dead and suspicion naturally focused on Friends? Without proof of innocence, we'll soon be in that mess again.

"What I would hope is that our community be able to look at this problem squarely. We must be honest with one another. Some Friend may have killed another Friend. How can we, as a

Meeting, respond to that? I've been considering this situation since Tuesday, and I feel clear about resigning as Clerk."

Bill violently shook his head, but Elizabeth continued quickly.

"I don't understand the concern Hugo and Wally seem to feel about appearance, but I do think we all need to look at the community's role in what has happened at Foster Place. That's my reason for wanting to resign. There's not been as much support for the Laughtons' tax witness as one might hope. I'm beginning to understand that the Meeting has been alienating some of the best members it has. And now there's been a tragedy in that household. Instead of concern about the spiritual welfare of those involved, including the killer, we seem to be bogged down in superficial considerations. Newspaper reports, for example. Perhaps my resigning, by clearing up these lesser issues to the satisfaction of all Friends, could help us refocus on what's important. We are not supporting our war-tax resisters as we might, and if someone in our Meeting is a killer, we desperately need God's help to respond to such evil."

There was silence. Elizabeth relaxed into a solid sense of peace, sure that all she had said was, by her Light at least, of the Spirit. Minutes ticked by, and finally Hugo spoke.

"It may be that, in this unusual situation, so suddenly thrust on us all, my first concern is not the central one. The spiritual welfare of the Meeting, which is the responsibility of Ministry and Counsel, depends on the spiritual welfare of all its members. Some of us do feel hesitation about the Laughtons' witness. Their actions, after all, are illegal. I don't think that, as a Meeting, we've let that spill over into our feelings about the Laughtons as Friends. I hope not, and I'm sorry if Sheldon feels otherwise."

Mary interrupted softly but steadily. "If the Laughtons think we have been backing away from them and their witness, I'm sure they're right. They're in the best position to know. It's easy, in these situations, for the people not involved in a difficult witness to be guilty of hypocrisy. But, as I recall, many of us did support them with our presence last spring when their house was auctioned."

"It's a little difficult for me," interjected Jane Thompson. "I always feel hesitant about war-tax resisters. They show us what courage can do in serious Friends, but the witness never changes anything. I often feel our energies should be going toward something more constructive, something that will make a difference."

"We're getting off the main point here," said Wally.

Bill Hoffman nodded and said, "Orderly discussion of a problem is positively un-Quakerly. That's one of the reasons I've always tried to avoid committee work."

Several people smiled.

"I hadn't finished what I was saying," said Hugo.

"Forgive me, Friend," said Mary. "I interrupted you. Please continue."

"I wanted to say"—Hugo coughed slightly and cleared his throat—"that we need to consider what Elizabeth said more carefully. We don't need our Clerk to resign. We need her to continue."

"You speak my mind," said Jane quickly.

Speaking, alternating with periods of silence, continued around the oval for the next half hour as Friends examined the question of the Meeting's attitude toward the Laughtons and toward the problem of violence in their midst. It was decided to report to Business Meeting that no action need be taken about the Clerk, but that the Peace and Social Concerns Committee be urged to have a workshop for all members to discuss war-tax questions. Attendance at the workshop would be most strongly recommended to everyone. Additionally, a minute in support of those suffering for conscience's sake was drafted to be brought to Business Meeting.

Bill smiled, nodded at Elizabeth, and rose from his chair when

Hugo had finished summing up the sense of the committee. He looked at his watch and said, "I still have an opinion to rewrite this evening, so since I'm not a committee member, I'll slip out now."

"Of course," said Hugo. "And thank you for coming."

Bill's departure was silent but swift. Everyone else settled down for closing worship. Elizabeth closed her eyes and centered her mind. After a minute or two of silence, Mary intoned, " 'The wolf shall dwell with the lamb, and the leopard shall lie down with the kid, and the calf and the lion and the fatling together.' "

Elizabeth smiled at the verses from Isaiah. Silence returned and filled the parlor. Hugo ended the worship by clearing his throat and standing up. He said good night, and, followed closely by Wally Orvick, left the room. Mary shook her head ever so slightly and rose to leave just as Jane and Elizabeth stood up.

"This must have been a fatiguing evening for you, Elizabeth. Can I give you a ride home?" asked Jane.

"No, thank you, Friend. A little walk will do me good, and now it must have cooled off a bit. I have to use the women's room. I'll lock up when I leave." All three women walked to the front hall-way, where Elizabeth turned left and went to the small women's room tucked under the stairway. The main women's room, one flight above, was much larger and more pleasant, but after this stressful day, Elizabeth chose to avoid the stairs.

She stood before the sink, looking at her damp face in the cracked and smudged mirror. It had been a long and warm evening. She took off her eyeglasses and set them on the narrow wooden shelf above the sink. She cupped her hands, filled them with tepid water from the cold water tap, and splashed her face. Twisting her head from side to side to loosen her neck muscles, she again wet her face. This time some water got into one of her eyes. She shook her head gently and groped for a paper towel. There was none in the dispenser. She saw what she thought was a stack of them on a shelf above the wastebasket and stepped toward them, but she knocked over the metal wastebasket as she reached. She retrieved her glasses and dried her face and hands, then righted the can. A number of wadded paper towels had rolled out of it and lay at Elizabeth's feet. In the bottom of the can, Elizabeth saw a pair of heavy work gloves and a soiled handkerchief. But the paper towels were what attracted the Clerk's attention, not simply because they were scattered across the floor. She gathered them up and tossed them back in the basket, thinking it was irresponsible of Friends to throw out paper products when reusable cloth towels were available. She was surprised that none of the hard-core Greens in Meeting had taken up the issue. But perhaps they soon would, she thought, with their usual shrill certainty.

"The problem," said the Clerk aloud, "is to find the time and energy to deal with everything the Meeting should do. If it's not homelessness and recycling it's tax resistance and domestic violence."

Out of habit, Elizabeth checked the Clerk's box before she left the building. There was a small scrap of paper within it which read: *"The lady here said I could leave a note for you. I'll stop by again, OK? Kelly."*

Elizabeth shook her head in chagrin, because it was unlikely that Kelly would find her at the Meetinghouse when next she came. She wished she had a way to respond but could think of none. She left a note for Harriet requesting that Kelly be given Elizabeth's address and phone number if she stopped by again.

Elizabeth walked out into the darkness of the warm and humid night. For once, she did not cut through the deserted grounds of the Episcopals' property. At this late hour, it seemed prudent to stay near automobile traffic, so she walked on the streets to Cambridge Common and then up Concord Avenue. The walk helped ease her tensions from the Ministry and Counsel Meeting.

As soon as she unlocked the front door and let herself in, Sparkle greeted her. Elizabeth went to the kitchen to make sure the cat had ample water and food. Sparkle accompanied her mistress, and Elizabeth bent over to stroke the cat's back, wondering as she did so if she should call Neil. If she did not tell him the results of the committee meeting, she knew he would be hurt, but she was tired and strongly wanted to take a cool bath and get some sleep.

The ringing doorbell made Sparkle bolt for the basement and brought Elizabeth quickly to the front of her house. Anticipating Neil on the doorstep, it took her a moment to recognize Sheldon Laughton through the screen door. As soon as she did, she invited him in.

"You said I could call anytime, Elizabeth, and I decided to call in person. I'd like to explain what's been happening lately."

Elizabeth's fatigue slipped away quickly as she silently motioned Sheldon into her small living room and invited him to sit down. She turned on two lamps and took her place in the rocking chair her boys had given her on her sixty-fifth birthday. It was a good place from which to listen.

"I admit I've been guilty of quite a bit of deceit this past year. I'm sorry about that, truly sorry, but I got into it one step at a time. There's the business about working for the AIDS action group in Boston. I don't apologize for the work, but I suppose that keeping that kind of thing secret from Meeting wasn't wise."

"Understandable, but not wise," agreed Elizabeth gently. "Such things become known sooner or later. And although some Meeting members would have reservations about encouraging extramarital sex or condoning drug use, I think you underestimated our community. We would have responded, I hope, with understanding and respect, even if specific Friends had reservations about some points of the work."

Sheldon thought for a moment before saying, "I can see that

you believe that. And I wish I could! But remember, Friend, there hasn't been as much understanding and respect about my war-tax resistance as I had anticipated."

It was Elizabeth's turn to think. "I'm sorry the Meeting has disappointed you. That's been our failing and a much more significant one than I was able to admit in the past."

Sheldon shook his head and ran his hand through his hair. "It's been terribly disillusioning. It was harder on me than on Hope, I guess, because I expected more from the Meeting. It used to be the center of my life, after all! But the way some Friends have treated us over the past year . . ." His voice, cracked with pain, trailed off.

"I'm sorry we've been so slow, and maybe mostly off the mark," said Elizabeth. "I spoke to Ministry and Counsel this evening about the way the Meeting has failed to support your witness. I can assure you there was a good response, even from some Friends you might think most unsympathetic to your perspectives."

"Meaning Hugo Coleman?"

"The very same," Elizabeth said with a small smile. "We will, I give you my word, start working on the problem. We will be asking the Peace and Social Concerns Committee to lead the Meeting as a whole in a workshop, both on war-tax issues and on the Meeting's responsibilities to its members when they run afoul of the IRS. I'm sorry we've been slow and off the mark on this, Sheldon, and as Clerk I certainly feel responsible. I apologize. I hope you can believe that we are working on our transgressions."

Sheldon Laughton stared vacantly across the end of the sofa toward the window.

"But now the time for all deceit is over," Elizabeth continued gently. "You can't hide things indefinitely from the police. I don't know what the problem is about Monday morning, but I do know that you can't hide anything from the Spirit. And I hope you can share with the Meeting anything you can acknowledge to God."

"That's the whole problem, Elizabeth," said Sheldon with sharp hostility. "You identify God with the Meeting. That's the kind of thing I have to get away from!"

Elizabeth was startled. She rocked slowly back in her chair. "God is complete unto himself. I only meant to say that, just as He knows and loves us, the Meeting tries to know and love its members. But our efforts are imperfect, I do admit." She paused.

Sheldon looked down at his feet and again ran a hand through his hair. "You don't understand," he said.

"True, I don't. And I won't unless you explain. My not knowing where you were on Monday morning, and other mornings as well, is much more damaging than anything you could tell me. And what you say to me here need not be passed on, not to the police, not to any Friends, unless circumstances require it for someone else's welfare."

Sheldon glanced up briefly into Elizabeth's face. "I've been going to Saint Paul's for some time now." He spoke without his previous anger.

"Saint Paul's?" Elizabeth rocked forward with a frown on her face. The name seemed dimly familiar, but she couldn't place it. "Should I know where that is?"

"In Harvard Square! A ten-minute walk from here!" said Sheldon, not without exasperation.

Enlightenment swept through the Clerk's mind. "Oh, yes, the Catholic church in the square."

Sheldon nodded. Elizabeth waited in silence.

"It started several years ago, when we first became publicly known as war-tax resisters. Two men from the Boston chapter of the Catholic Worker came to visit us, just to visit and talk. It was such a relief to talk to people who view tax resistance as the normal thing, a way of life. I am weary of trying to talk to defensive and self-righteous Quakers about taxes. All Friends can spout the words of the peace testimony, and they all would be beside them-

selves if their sister married an army officer. But they don't want
to actually follow Quaker teachings about war and the money that
pays for it. They aren't willing to sacrifice even the tiniest bit of
their comfort to uphold the Gospel."

"It's true," said Elizabeth, "that self-sacrifice is not popular
among Friends. Other denominations have the same trouble, I
would guess. Very few people actually live up to the teachings of
the New Testament. Or even seriously try."

"But Quakers claim to be superior, special and set apart from
the common horde of Christendom. That's what I can't stomach
about Friends, and that's something you don't find at the Catholic
Worker. Taxes are not the real problem, you and I both know
that. Look at how many people in Meeting are businessmen and
lawyers, making big money and not caring where it comes from!
That's not consistent with the peace testimony! Think of John
Woolman and all he said about the connections between money
and war."

The Clerk knew little about the Catholic Worker, but she felt
on firm ground where Woolman was concerned. He had been an
eighteenth-century Quaker, famous for his deeply spiritual life
and his campaign in colonial America against the slave trade. He
had set aside his private life and traveled to the Caribbean and
England to preach to Friends who made money conveying slaves
from Africa to the New World. He was credited with beginning
the American movement to abolish slavery and with ridding the
Society of Friends of any involvement with the institution of slavery. John Woolman's name was revered by all Quakers in the
United States, and Elizabeth often read Woolman's journals.

"I remember his writing on money and war," she said calmly
and certainly. "He thought that wealth and violence were directly
linked, that the holding of 'great estates,' as he put it in his day,
led us into conflict with the poor and powerless. Conflict that
was, or could be, violent. Therefore he lived very simply. In
poverty, one might say."

"Exactly. And how many Friends live in keeping with that idea?"

"Very few," replied Elizabeth firmly. "A handful in each generation, perhaps. We're all of us human, Sheldon."

"Yes, that's not the trouble. It's the hypocrisy that got to me!" Elizabeth noticed the switch to the past tense as he continued intensely, "Don't you see, the more Hope and I did as war-tax resisters, the more isolated we were from the main part of Meeting. We were seen as dangerous. Not really because of taxes themselves, but because you and I and the Meeting know full well that a lot of Quakers live nicely, with money in mutual funds, invested in godforsaken enterprises that enrich us at the expense of the less educated, the less fortunate, the folks around here who don't manage to be white or Ivy League." He shook his head vigorously. "Businessmen and lawyers, good Meeting members all!"

"True. But may I point out, as an acknowledged hypocrite myself, that you and your wife accepted the inheritance from your parents of a very handsome piece of property. Many people would have given their right arm for what you owned, outright, on Foster Place."

"Yes, yes." Sheldon was silent for a minute, and Elizabeth listened most contentedly to the silence, trying to hear its voice. As if influenced by her, Sheldon spoke more softly. "We had our money worries at times, and we were glad to have a house. It was not, of course, our doing that the house happened to be so large and on such a valuable piece of land."

"That's true," conceded Elizabeth.

"And we neither of us had any hesitation about putting it at risk because of our tax witness. I'm not saying it was easy. I know it was the hardest thing I ever did. But Hope and I didn't have doubts."

"And I admire you for living rightly, as Woolman and others have shown us. The tax problem is a complex one, since we Friends aren't anarchists who can ignore the law whenever we choose, but you did what you felt led to do. I think you are a true Friend, Sheldon."

"But the Meeting didn't think so!"

"Your witness made others uncomfortable. They had to look at their own lives more critically, simply because you and Hope were choosing to live in keeping with your conscience." Elizabeth smiled. "You were a great blessing to Meeting, but you were a challenge to us, too."

"In the Society of Friends," said Sheldon bitterly, ignoring her smile, "those who follow Woolman and other early Friends are not treated as blessings. I was repeatedly eldered by nearly everyone over fifty around Longfellow Park. Was I doing the right thing? How could I be sure? Didn't I understand the importance of obeying the law whenever possible? What about Catherine's life? Didn't I know that small children need security? The people who were helpful to me and Hope were almost always students and young Friends. People like Otto. And you, too, Elizabeth. You never were a problem."

"I'm glad," said the Clerk, grateful not to be lumped with Hugo Coleman and Wally Orvick. Or even, perhaps, Patience Silverstone.

"But wealthy Friends and a lot of the older members," Sheldon continued, "refuse to think in economic and political terms or take a stand on any public issue. They know what side their bread is buttered on. Hope and I felt their rejection. The important people in Meeting, the weighty Friends, never had us over for supper after our war-tax situation became public! They didn't even speak with us seriously. If they spoke to us on Sunday mornings, it was only to give advice. The people who prayed with us, and for us, were always those on the fringe of the Meeting."

"I'm sorry if our community let you down. I've said that." Elizabeth's tone, still gentle, became more focused as she added, "But you haven't explained where you were on Monday."

"The Catholic Worker people were a joy to us, you see. They came to our house and were present to us."

Elizabeth recognized the significance of the phrase about being present, and she decided this might be the beginning of Sheldon's answer to her question. She said, "Anyone truly present to you would be wonderfully helpful. I'm glad you felt support coming from somewhere. The Catholic Worker organization follows voluntary poverty, is that right?"

"Like Woolman," answered Sheldon.

"And if the people themselves were helpful, that would add tremendously to the way you would perceive them," Elizabeth mused aloud.

"They came, again and again, to our house. They were with us when the Meeting was not. They prayed with us and ate with us and rejoiced with us. Hope didn't feel as strongly about them as I did. She was more afraid, you know, of all the things we Quakers say about Catholics. But I started to go to Haley House, the Catholic Worker house in Boston, just for the sake of the company of people like Jose. It's a different world. A Catholic soup kitchen in Boston, with all kinds of people present, versus the lily-white and wealthy Friends Meeting at Cambridge. I couldn't help but compare the two."

Elizabeth waited for more.

"I started to go to services with the people there." He hesitated, then stammered, "To M-Mass." Once the word had escaped, a word diametrically opposed to so many words describing Quaker worship, Sheldon went on in a torrent. "It took me a while to understand what the liturgy was about. It's so different. But it spoke to me, more and more. And what we talked about at the Catholic Worker was the Gospel and the New Testament. At Friends Meeting, all you hear about is Quakers, Quakers, Quakers. And it's all hypocrisy, if you ask me. Or nearly all. But there, in Boston, I found people who valued the Bible and the teachings of Jesus.

We studied the Bible together. Then I started to really appreci‑
ate the Church calendar. I went through Lent and Holy Week
for the first time in my life, two years ago. Holy Thursday and
Good Friday and then the Vigil and Easter morning Mass. I tell
you, Elizabeth, it was of the Spirit. Do you know the only obser‑
vance of Holy Week that we have here at Meeting?"

"We have none at all."

"That's not true. We do. We have an Easter egg hunt for the
children on the Meetinghouse lawn on Sunday. Think about it!
Friends like to say all days are holy, so Quakers don't need things
like Palm Sunday and Good Friday. But what are we teaching the
children? The only thing that Friends, as a community, do about
Easter is that egg hunt!"

Elizabeth considered carefully before responding. "I've often
thought the eggs were unfortunate, too. Pagan, really. But the
young children love them, and it gives the adults in the First Day
program something they like to do. Easter is observed here,
Friend, in true ways, don't forget that. That's what each Meet‑
ing for Worship is about. But you're right, many of the children
may not understand."

"Many of the adults don't understand that! How many weighty
Friends around here read George Fox and early Quakers?"

"Quite a few."

"How many read the Gospel?"

Elizabeth considered when she had last carefully read Scripture.
"Not as many," she admitted.

"I liked what I found with the Catholics. Those experiences
in Holy Week convinced me," Sheldon concluded, using the
Quaker word for the process of conversion.

"So you're a Catholic now?"

"I'll be baptized at Easter." Sheldon moved on the sofa and
stretched his big frame. "This school year I'm enrolled in the
preparation class. It's called the Rite of Christian Initiation for

Adults. And I'm happy like I've never been before. Hope wasn't enthusiastic about what was happening, but she respected it. It was right for me, and it was of the Spirit. She liked many of the Catholic Worker people. People like Jose are a blessing whether you are a Quaker or a Catholic."

Elizabeth nodded her understanding.

"Hope did the best she could not to hinder me, to support what I needed to do. I started meeting with Father Tom Enagonio last month. He's an excellent man. He's taught me the catechism and the responsive prayers. So on Monday morning, you see, I was at Saint Paul's, meeting with Father Tom. We have a regular schedule, early in the morning before I go to work. Because I was raised as a Quaker, there's just a tremendous lot about church life that I don't know. Father Tom is a good teacher.

"I only wish Hope were alive to see me this happy and this sure. I planned to write to the Meeting's Membership Committee this week so they could drop my name from the Meeting's list. Because of Hope's death, I didn't write the letter, and I didn't want Hope's relatives and all our friends to learn of my conversion in the midst of this murder investigation. You know how bigoted Friends can be about Catholics. Hope's sister and brother-in-law will never understand what I've done. So I told the police I went straight from Cathy's day care to my job in Lexington. I did go to the job, but I went to Saint Paul's first. It's a wonderful thing, Elizabeth, preparing to be part of the body of Christ."

There was no stopping Sheldon now that he was in confessional mode. "Birthright Friends like me really never make a choice about their identity. I was born into Quakerism, and I simply never looked carefully at it. Now I've finally made a choice for myself. I've chosen the church of the poor, the church that goes back to the earliest days of Christianity, the church that speaks to me, both as a pacifist and as a human being. I'm glad I'm home."

There was a small pause, and Elizabeth wondered if Sheldon's enthusiasm would dampen in time. Not all Catholics, she was sure, were members of Pax Christi.

"I've often thought that we birthright Friends miss an important experience," she said. "Those who convert to Quakerism, it seems to me, have quite a different journey from those of us who grow up in it and become members by default. I've envied convinced Friends. I've never thought about a lifelong Quaker converting away from Quakerism, however. I'll have to get used to the idea. But I do wish you well. You're a man of integrity. It would have been easy enough to close your eyes to the failings of the Meeting. That's what most of us try to do."

"Thank you."

"What you've done will not be understood by most Friends, you're right. I daresay that if you had always been a good Catholic and you converted to Quakerism, you might not have wanted to mention that to your old friends, either."

"That's true," said Sheldon slowly.

"But whether Quakers can understand your journey or not, you need to tell them about it. And tell the police. The deception makes it look like you are implicated in a terrible crime."

"I know that now. Early in the week, I was so confused by everything that I just didn't know where to begin. I kept things simple, and that was easy to do with just one lie."

"I urge you, as a friend, to tell the truth."

"I'm not a Friend now. You shouldn't say that."

"I don't urge you as a Quaker, Sheldon, but as your friend."

He smiled. "I see. Thank you. I hope we will always be friends. I wish Hope and I had known you better. Although we may have disagreed with you about taxes, we always respected the work you did around Meeting."

"Thank you. That's generous." There was an awkward silence, finally broken by Elizabeth. "Again, I wish I could give you more than condolences about your loss. Your life has been forever changed."

"Yes, I'll always miss her. And so much of my life was part of hers. She was the reason I started writing poetry years ago. We were courting, you see, and I decided to try to put down what I felt. That's led to many other poems. And of course it was Hope who gave me Cathy."

"You still have the child."

"That's a comfort. She has always looked like her mother to me. And she'll be OK." He stood up and stretched his large frame to its full height. "So," he said, a note of conclusion in his voice, "to get back to what brought me here: I've brought a letter of res-ignation." He dug in his back pocket and produced a creased piece of yellow legal paper, which he handed to Elizabeth.

"I'll give this to the Membership Committee," said the Clerk. "As you know, when we welcome a new person to our Meeting, we appoint two or three Friends to speak with them. I think we'll want to do the same in the case of a resignation. Especially the resignation of such a serious and trustworthy Christian. I hope you'll meet with whomever the Membership Committee ap-points."

"I'm not sure what such a meeting could accomplish."

"It would help us understand each other. And it would be a for-mal way for the Meeting to wish you well in your new spiritual community."

There was a pause. "OK."

Elizabeth nodded. "God be with you," she said.

Sheldon turned and walked slowly to the front door. After he left, Elizabeth rocked in her chair for a long time. Sheldon's con-version, of course, did not make her happy. She was sorry her Meeting was losing a serious member. She had seen a number of young people attracted to the silent worship of Quakerism or to pacifism convert from various denominations and become

Friends. Like Sheldon, she had been raised a Quaker. She had never considered belonging to any denomination other than her own. More clearly than ever, Elizabeth realized that birthright Friends were missing an important step toward responsibility for their spiritual lives, the crucial turning point of making a choice.

"But Catholicism?" she said aloud, her dismay disturbing Sparkle, who had come in and curled up at her feet. "A real Friend like Sheldon?" She sighed, her earlier fatigue again taking hold. She slowly stood up, careful not to tread on Sparkle's paws.

Sheldon's story about Monday morning was unusual enough to be true. Because she liked and respected him, she had a hard time thinking he could be lying about anything that might have occurred on Monday morning. But the police would have to carefully check the times of his alibi. Harvard Square, after all, was just a ten-minute walk from Foster Place.

"Do I believe him because I like him?" said Elizabeth to the cat. "But someone killed Hope! I can't lose track of that simply because I can't bear to see the murderer for who he is. Is it too much to imagine that one of the Catholics in Sheldon's life could have committed the crime? But for what motive? If that is the case, I might feel better, God forgive me, but I must still try to understand what various Friends around that household were doing. As Clerk, I have to do all I can to clear things up as far as the Quakers involved are concerned." She rubbed her temples. "What needless pain we bear," she muttered in conclusion.

14

Letters to Congress in support of the Peace Tax Fund Bill are always appropriate; such a fund would allow citizens to contribute the military portion of their taxes to a special fund earmarked for peaceful expenditures. The fund is an analogue to conscientious objector service in times of war (and the bill is introduced before most sessions of Congress).

Leaflet on War Taxes
Friends Meeting at Cambridge, 1989

The morning dawned dark and wet. After the long and tiring evening before, Elizabeth stayed in bed longer than usual. But the clock radio promised Boston rain until midday, with appropriately cooler temperatures, and that was enough to get Elizabeth stirring before eight o'clock. After feeding Sparkle indoors and the birds outdoors, she made tea and toast, promising herself a more nutritious lunch. After the teapot was drained, she called Neil.

"I wondered, of course, how things had come out at Longfellow Park last night." There was a long pause before he added, "I was hoping you'd call me."

"I thought of it, but it was just too late. I had Meeting business other than Ministry and Counsel after I went home." She went on quickly, not caring to discuss what Sheldon had told her until the man himself had informed the Meeting of his action. "But the good news is that I think everyone on Ministry and Counsel did some listening to the Spirit. Even Hugo Coleman. Maybe even me. Ministry and Counsel wants to work toward a broader and better understanding of war-tax questions for our whole community. Hugo himself is going to ask Peace and Social Concerns to set up a Saturday workshop, or something along those lines, where we all could discuss the issues. Included is the idea that, whatever our own personal decisions about war taxes may be, we need to be supportive of those who are called to witness to the government about military spending."

"William Penn would be behind us there."

"Indeed. And if Penn and Hugo and I can agree on anything, I'm certain it must be of God."

Neil laughed softly. "I'm delighted, of course. Truly delighted. I'm glad Ministry and Counsel did the right thing. To celebrate the outcome of the meeting, let's go to lunch. Someplace nice. What about the Charles Hotel?"

The Charles Hotel, in Harvard Square, was new and expensive. Elizabeth had never been there but was sure that conspicuous consumption was its main theme. She began to say something about a simpler lunch being much more to her preference, but then she remembered that she had not called Neil the evening before, even when she knew he would have wanted it. She accepted his proposal to ease her conscience.

"Good. I'll come by at noon, then."

Elizabeth and her friend hung up, and she settled down to look at the mail that had been accumulating during this busy week. She was at her desk writing to her sister-in-law, Pearl Curtis, when the doorbell rang. It was Detective Burnham standing on her front step in the drizzle.

"I was on my way over to Harvard Square," he said, "and stopped by for just a moment. I hope I'm not disturbing you."

"Not at all." Elizabeth motioned him inside. They sat down in the living room, Elizabeth returning to her chair of the previous evening.

"This morning, bright and early, Sheldon Laughton was at my office. He told me quite a strange tale. He said he told it to you last night. I'm on my way to Saint Paul's to talk to the priest there and see if he can confirm what Laughton says. I suppose he will, or Sheldon would not be putting forward this story."

Elizabeth slowly rocked her chair. "I know the people involved in this case, Mr. Burnham. It is, now that I think of it, a rather obvious place for Sheldon to have been. It's not surprising to me that, initially, he was reluctant to speak about it. He still values the Meeting and its opinion of him, you see, so confessing that he was leaving was difficult. And he was shocked and confused earlier this week. The sudden death of a spouse, let alone violent death, must be tremendously disorienting."

"Do you believe what he says about his conversion? That's what I came here to ask. It all seems rather unbalanced to me, at his age, to change churches like that. Could it be a sham?"

"Not at all!" Elizabeth laughed, without malice. "Conversions happen when they happen! The Lord works in mysterious ways. My only problem with what I learned last night is that, in my own narrow and bigoted way, I long ago accepted the idea of people converting to Quakerism but never considered an active Friend converting to something else! So much for my understanding of the Spirit!

"I do believe what Sheldon told me last night. Absolutely. I realize he may still not be above suspicion, since he might have had time to return to his house. You will have to consider that, I'm sure, Detective. But his religious life is not unbalanced, nor is it a fake. Quite the contrary." She paused for a moment, at a loss for words to describe a Quaker's realignment of faith. In the end she simply said, "The Spirit is always at work within us. Failing to acknowledge where he was Monday morning will bother Sheldon for a long time. And I know his misstatement to you concerning his whereabouts may be technically criminal. But I still greatly respect him and Hope for following conscience rather than convenience in their tax resistance. Sheldon is now simply following his conscience into a different part of Christendom, one where he feels at home. I wish him well and will be glad to rejoice with him for what he has found as a Catholic, as well as grieve with him for the loss of his wife."

Burnham sighed. "It's not easy to understand you people." His voice changed as he started a new subject. "You were most helpful to my office last year, of course, and I remember that clearly. You observe people and have an uncanny ability to discover the truth. I still feel you've not told me everything you know, or think you might know, about this case. I want to ask you another question. Perhaps you didn't see more than you've told me about when you went to the Laughtons' house, but can you tell me anything you knew then, or have learned since, that would help me with this case?" He paused, and Elizabeth was silent. "I do hope you'll tell me everything that's in your mind. I realize that may be painful, because it seems likely someone in your Meeting is Hope Laughton's killer, but you have an obligation, as a citizen, to give me all the information you can. I'm sure you appreciate that."

Elizabeth considered him silently for a full minute, quietly rocking, thinking about several different obligations she felt weighing on her. The detective, doing his best to adapt to Quaker ways, waited for her to speak.

Finally she spoke. "If I wanted to, I could say that someone at the house auction last spring or one of Sheldon's Catholic friends knew where the gun was kept in the house and came back to get it, perhaps to kill Hope or only killing her because he was discovered. But that's unlikely, it seems to me. It would be convenient for Quakers, but I doubt that it's true. Maybe that's a peculiar kind of cynicism on my part."

Detective Burnham, who had never thought of Elizabeth as a cynic, was sufficiently surprised that he didn't know how to respond.

"It's much more likely that the problem rests with us," continued the Quaker, "and as Clerk, I need to understand what happened and why. That's crucial for the health of the Meeting." She looked earnestly at the detective. "I'm only beginning to understand the situation around Hope and Sheldon, a situation I should have, as Clerk, had the courage to look at more closely. But I can't tell you things I only partially know. It wouldn't be right." There was finality in her voice. "I do believe, however, that Sheldon is now telling the truth about his whereabouts. I hope you will check his story and clear him. He and his little daughter have enough to deal with now, without police suspicion."

"And you won't say more than that?"

"No." Elizabeth stopped rocking.

Frowning, Burnham stood up. He shook his head and said, "I think you're making a mistake. I won't press you on it right now because I made a mistake when I charged you. But you have a legal and a moral responsibility to cooperate with my office. Think about that. Good-bye."

He stepped out the front door into a steady rain.

Elizabeth was just clearing her desk and stamping the last bill when the telephone rang in the kitchen. She answered.

"Good morning, Elizabeth," said Sheldon's voice. "I'm afraid I have some bad news. I'm calling from Otto's apartment. But let me explain first. I went to Detective Burnham's office this morning, just like you wanted."

"I'm sure that was for the best."

"Yes, it was. And with that out of the way, I realized I'd been neglecting the one Friend who really did his best to stand by us during all our conflicts with the IRS. Because of Otto's feelings for Hope, I didn't waste much time thinking about him lately. It was easier to put him aside, I'm afraid, but that surely wasn't right. But after talking to Burnham I went to Otto's apartment to try to start building bridges. He's important to me, and, after all, Cathy is used to seeing him almost every day. It was still early enough in the morning, you see, that I knew he'd be home."

"Yes, he says his days start late," said Elizabeth.

"There was no answer when I rang his bell. I thought that was strange, because I've always known him to sleep late. There was a lot of mail jammed in his box, as if he'd not been picking it up. That seemed strange, too, since he's been in town this week. I was worried enough I looked through his window. It was open, of course, because of the warmth. The rain hasn't cooled things down terribly much. The landlord is too cheap, I guess, to have proper screens, and there are no storm windows. Otto has one of those little half-screens you prop in the window."

Elizabeth nodded, remembering the small screens her family had used during the Depression and on which, she knew, some people still depended.

"I could see him lying on the bed, Elizabeth. Fully clothed, but not answering when I shouted to him. So I crawled in through the window. It wasn't easy for someone my size, but there was no choice."

Elizabeth waited with as much patience as she could manage.

"He'll be OK. He was alive and halfway conscious. He'd slashed his wrists, during the night, I'd guess. There's blood all over the bed here. I called the ambulance and they came quickly. The paramedics said they've seen much worse, and they think he'll be fine. They've taken him to Cambridge City Hospital. He works as an orderly there, of course, so I think the staff will be as good to him as we could hope."

"I see," said Elizabeth. "I am grateful the ambulance men think he'll live. I'll go and see him."

"Do. You're a good visitor, I'm sure. If it's despair about losing Hope that drove him to this, I might not be the right person to show up at his bedside. At least not right away."

"I agree. I'll go see how he is and what caused this crisis."

"Thanks. He's a good man, Elizabeth. Abrasive, I know, and not easy to get along with, but he has good values. It wasn't his fault that he fell for Hope. And we were all of us good friends. If

I felt isolated in the Meeting because of war-tax resistance, Otto must feel the same. It would have been incredibly difficult for him to cut us out of his life, just because he was feeling some things he shouldn't have."

"I'm glad you can see the good in him. It speaks volumes about your character, Sheldon. I'll call the Bakers after I've seen Otto, and if you're not there, I'll leave a message saying how he's doing."

Sheldon thanked her, and they hung up. Elizabeth immediately called the public hospital and was told that Otto Zimmer was in good condition and could be seen during visiting hours beginning in the afternoon.

Neil's blue Buick pulled up at the curb outside Elizabeth's house promptly at noon. Waiting at her open front door, she saw the big car and went outside, opening her umbrella. Contrary to the radio forecast in the morning, the rain showed no sign of letting up.

Neil drove the few blocks to Harvard Square, where he parked in the garage of the Charles Hotel. Elizabeth reflected that the cost of parking alone would be more than the price of lunch for them both at a more modest establishment. But, reminding herself that she had neglected Neil most of the week, she did her best to put the thought out of her mind.

Umbrellas were unnecessary with indoor parking, so, dry and fresh, the pair entered the hotel's dining room. Neil spoke to the maître d', and they were quickly seated in a private corner and presented with menus. Neil recommended the orange-glazed chicken. Elizabeth accepted the idea, and the waiter departed.

"You've been here before, I gather," said Elizabeth.

"Oh, yes. My son and I often lunch here." Neil, a wealthy man in his own right, had a son who worked for Cambridge's largest bank. The younger Stevenson was vice president of corporate ac-counts, and Elizabeth knew his father was proud of his son's business accomplishments. She supposed that meals at exclusive hotels were part of a banker's lifestyle.

"I know you don't always appreciate my taste in things," said Neil quietly, as if reading Elizabeth's mind, "but thank you for coming here today. I wanted it to be a special meal, and since I'm no cook, a special lunch means this kind of establishment."

Elizabeth smiled her understanding and waited.

"I want to take you to New York on Labor Day weekend so you can meet by brother." Neil seemed to lose his place.

"Yes, you made that clear at Walden." Elizabeth laughed gently.

Neil reached into his pocket and drew something out. As he did so he said, "I'd like my brother to meet my fiancée when we go down there." He opened a small jewelry case.

Elizabeth saw the diamond flash before he had finished his sentence. She turned away for an instant, then forced herself to look at her friend. "I'm s-s-sorry," she stammered. "I wasn't expecting this."

"Not at all?" asked Neil, the pain evident in his voice.

Elizabeth rallied. She reached across the table and took his free hand. "Of course, it was something I've wondered about. And, you may be sure, you're the only fellow I think of when I consider my future. But so much has been going on with me as Clerk, you've caught me off guard."

Neil set the ring, still in its case, on the table and said, "I know things haven't been normal this past week. But I wanted to make myself clear before this trip I'm inviting you to take with me. Even in the confusion of recent events at the Meeting, I've seen what I want. I want you to marry me, Elizabeth. And I'm prepared to wait until you've had time to think." He squeezed her hand, then released it.

"You're kind. And I'm not being very gracious, considering all that you're offering. But such a decision merits clear thinking."

She sighed and said involuntarily, "There could be so many problems."

"Name one!" said Neil with the air of a man who could overcome any obstacle.

"Our children," she said quickly. "Especially, perhaps, your children. You're wealthy, and all I have is my social security and the house. Your children will be afraid they may lose their inheritance."

"That's merely a problem for my lawyers to handle. Or my children's lawyers," said Neil, shaking his head and smiling. "It doesn't affect things between us."

"It will if your children are unhappy at the thought of your marrying again. I know how much you care about them."

The arrival of the glazed chicken interrupted the discussion and gave Elizabeth another moment to think. When the waiter left she said, "Neil, I can answer the question you put to me at Walden. Yes, I'll be happy to go to New York and meet your brother. This other question, though, needs to wait until I can turn things over in my mind."

"Of course," said Neil, reaching over his plate and picking up the ring case. He closed it and returned it to his pocket, then said, "It's available anytime you want. But I won't bring up the subject until we're back from New York."

"Tell me about your brother," said Elizabeth, seizing a topic they could address more easily.

Neil launched into a description of his sibling. A question or two from Elizabeth led him into reminiscences of their childhood. The food, which proved delicious, was consumed slowly, enjoyed with plenty of conversation. As they finished the meal, the sun came out and shone through the hotel's windows. The rain had ended.

After lunch, Elizabeth asked to be dropped off at the Meetinghouse, explaining she wanted to check what mail had arrived in the Clerk's box. Neil's large, quiet car took them as quickly as traffic permitted to Longfellow Park. Before she left the Buick she gave Neil a long and heartfelt kiss. Then she stepped out into the sun and the increasing mugginess of the day.

As she walked onto the Meeting's property, carrying her now useless umbrella, Elizabeth was surprised to see that the door to the Meetinghouse was open. In the basement of the building, the Friends Service Committee ran a used-clothing room, but it was not the day for volunteers to be at work sorting and mending the clothes, and it was unusual for anyone to be inside the Meeting-house apart from times appointed for worship or group work projects. The Clerk decided to investigate. She entered the build-ing, leaving the sun behind.

Constance Baker was sitting in the stuffy Meetinghouse. She had opened no windows, only the front door to the building, and the atmosphere was more than thick. But she looked oblivious to discomfort. She rocked slowly back and forth on a bench at the far side of the worship room, murmuring just below an audi-ble level.

Elizabeth, her forehead furrowed in concern, walked quickly over to her and sat down. "What's happened?"

Constance looked up like someone drowning. She tried to speak, but her efforts led only to meaningless sounds.

"Come now!" said the Clerk in tones that were, for her, sharp. "Pull yourself together. No speaking in tongues! Tell me what's wrong!"

"I'm sorry, I'm sorry, I'm sorry! I'm so sorry about everything!" blurted Constance. "Cathy has fallen. She's unconscious at Mt. Auburn. The doctors have put a shunt in the base of her skull to drain fluid that's collecting on her brain." Sobs interrupted her for a moment. "I'm so sorry." After a minute, the distressed woman paused in her weeping long enough to mop her face and blow her nose.

Elizabeth waited patiently.

"It's my fault. She's so precious, I don't know how I could have done it! Sheldon went out this morning. To the police, for some reason he wouldn't tell me. Titus isn't home yet. He flies in this evening, so it was just little Cathy and me. I put a stepladder on the landing of the stairs to change a light bulb in the stairway. It's the only way to reach the thing. Cathy was watching me, of course. The telephone rang before I climbed up the ladder, so I went into the kitchen."

Elizabeth nodded, fully comprehending what a three-year-old would do under such circumstances. She made no sound, however, letting the distraught woman tell the story in her own way.

"I thought Cathy came with me. She usually does when the phone rings. In fact, if I'm not quick, she answers it before I get there. It was a call from Sheldon saying that Otto has attempted suicide but will be OK. I listened, of course, and I didn't think about where she was." Constance looked Elizabeth in the eye and continued. "I swear it was only a minute she was away from me!"

Elizabeth frowned at the idea of an oath in the Meetinghouse but remained quiet.

"I heard a terrible crash and ran out to the front hall. Cathy was lying on the floor, and the ladder was on top of her. She wouldn't speak to me! I pulled the ladder off and realized she was unconscious. I ran back to the kitchen to dial nine-one-one, but I'd left the phone dangling, you see, so it took a minute to get a dial tone. Then the nine-one-one operator was so slow! It took forever for the ambulance to come. I sat with Cathy, not knowing what to do. I didn't even pray for her, I was so terrified."

"The ambulance took you both to Mt. Auburn?"

Constance nodded. "I told them to go there. It's the best hospital in town. The emergency room doctor sent her in for a CAT scan. He told me she has a severe concussion and there was already fluid building up inside her skull. He said they should put in a tube to drain it, and I said go ahead and signed the papers. I said she was my daughter, covered by my Blue Cross. It's not true, of course, but it wasn't the time to explain that Titus and I will pay. I know that Hope and Sheldon have never had health insurance. Can you imagine! Either one of them could have got a real job that gave them insurance! But now the operation is done. There's nothing more to do, just wait and see."

"Sheldon must be told. He's probably gone home to your house and is wondering where you and Cathy are."

"I suppose so," said Constance, looking down at the dull and dirty cork tile floor of the Meetinghouse. She added a nonsequitur: "The doctor said he has to fill out a form about any injury a child receives. The child welfare people may have to investigate this for abuse!" Again, Constance broke down in tears.

"I'm so sorry," said Elizabeth, "but we'll face that when it comes. Come out of this Meetinghouse, Friend. With the sun coming in through these closed windows, the air in here is stifling." Elizabeth led the weeping woman out of the building and to the bench beside it. The bench was still slightly damp from the morning's rain, but Elizabeth sat down, and Constance compliantly did the same.

"I'm so sorry," murmured Cathy's aunt.

"You're deeply attached to Catherine," observed Elizabeth.

"She's like my own."

"I can see that. As Clerk, Constance, I've got to understand what happened at your sister's house on Monday morning. It's still a puzzle to me and an open sore for the whole Meeting."

"It's not a puzzle to Otto," said Constance, shaking her head and drying her tears. "He confessed to me that he had had strong feelings for Hope for a long time. Now he's tried to kill himself. It speaks for itself."

"Indeed it may. I'm going to go see him directly. In my experience, people in hospital beds, if they speak, tell the truth. Perhaps he can explain what really happened between him and Hope."

"If you're saying my sister had an affair, I think you're wrong. Otto imagined a lot in her, I think, because he wanted to. But I don't believe Hope did anything wrong."

"Not even as a mother?"

"Well, she and Sheldon had no call to disrupt Cathy's life like that, I agree, putting everything at risk because of taxes! The IRS always collects, one way or another, and it's wrong to neglect your child's interests. That house could have come to Cathy if it weren't for what my sister and brother-in-law have been doing over the years."

"Maybe they wanted to give their daughter something other than a house. A vision of what's right, perhaps."

"I thought you agreed with me! What they were doing was criminal. They were lucky they weren't arrested during the past two years. People do get arrested for not paying their taxes, you know."

"Yes, I do. And I'm sure they knew that, too. I always prayed it wouldn't come to that, and it didn't. Where were you, by the way, on Monday morning?" She looked closely at Constance, unashamedly taking her by surprise.

Constance looked at the Clerk with hostility. "At home," she said, "doing Monday's laundry like I always do."

"And Otto was asleep in his bed," Elizabeth mused aloud.

"I don't know about that, one way or another," said Constance, rising to her feet.

"Please walk home with me," Elizabeth said quickly but gently. "It's not far, and my car is there. I can give you a ride to Lee Street. Sheldon deserves to know where his child is and what's happened."

Constance agreed to the plan. The minds of both women

turned as one to Cathy Laughton's situation. The pair walked across Longfellow Park and up Concord Avenue. The younger Quaker was near tears, and Elizabeth gave her what comfort she could. As they got into Elizabeth's car, she told Constance the story of a concussion her son Mark had had in fourth grade when he had fallen from the top of the jungle gym at school. He'd been unconscious for three hours, and Elizabeth had been nearly driven to distraction as she waited at the hospital. But he did awake and was fine. A week later he and his younger brother were running and laughing in the Elliots' backyard. Constance listened with as much attention as she could to the story, but her mind was clearly at Mt. Auburn.

"I'll tell Sheldon what's happened. Then he and I both can go to the hospital and wait."

"That sounds good to me," replied Elizabeth. "And I'm glad, of course, that your instincts led you to the Meetinghouse in a time of crisis. I'm sure the Lord will hear our prayers for Cathy. We must do all we can to accept His will. I'm certainly glad I stopped by Longfellow Park." Only now did the Clerk realize she had not collected her Meeting mail. She put it on her mental list of things to do another day as she pulled her car up in front of the Bakers' house. "You'll have to straighten out the hospital about Cathy's lack of insurance, Constance. That can't be postponed any longer. I'm sure that if you'll sign for financial responsibility, they'll let her stay, at least until she's stabilized enough to be moved to the public hospital."

"I'll sign anything. Titus and I will remortgage the house, if need be."

"The public hospital isn't a bad place. There's better medicine available there than anything we had when I was a child. But it's your decision. Please give Sheldon my greetings. God be with you both while you wait."

Constance thanked Elizabeth for the ride and got out of the old Chevrolet.

Elizabeth drove to Cambridge Street and, after parking at the lot of the Cambridge City Hospital, inquired about Otto Zimmer at the main desk. She was directed to the third floor. Before going to the elevator, she stopped at the hospital's small gift shop. She bought a vase with one rose and, on an impulse, a copy of the *Boston Globe*. A nurse on the third floor told her that Otto was doing very well. The psychiatrist on call had already seen him and cleared him for release when he was physically ready, requiring only that he agree to be an outpatient at the hospital's mental health clinic.

Otto Zimmer was sitting up in bed at the end of a long room that held four beds, all of which were occupied. One of the other men was snoring loudly, while another was speaking softly to himself. Elizabeth could not help but be glad her friend Patience was enjoying a little more privacy at Mt. Auburn.

"I never thought I'd be here like this," said Otto without preamble when Elizabeth arrived at the foot of his bed, "and I don't want to speak to you." His arms were folded in his lap, bandages wrapped thickly around his wrists.

"I understand," said Elizabeth. She needed a moment to think of how to respond to the situation, and she patiently waited for her thoughts to become clearer. "Let me just give you these, if I may." She put the bud vase on the stand beside Otto's bed and held out the paper. He shook his head. "I'll leave you in peace, Otto, if that's what you want. I just came to express the Meeting's concern for your welfare and say we shall all be rejoicing that you've survived this day. If there is something I can do for you, I hope you'll contact me." She tucked the unwanted *Globe* under her arm.

"There's nothing anyone can do, but as I told the doctor, I won't try this again." He looked out the window and added in a rush, "I've lost everything I've ever valued."

"Is it really that bleak?"

"Yes! The one person I loved is gone. And now I think that I harmed her and her marriage. Sheldon must have been jealous and killed her in a moment of rage. I can't see any other motive for her death. And I was the cause of his anger."

"Possibly. But could Hope have been killed by the man who loved her but could never have her?" said Elizabeth tentatively. Otto did not reply, and she ventured, "Could it have been the man who knew she was soon to leave for the West, where he wouldn't see her again?"

"No." There was disgust in his voice.

"I want to believe you. But I know for a fact that you haven't told me everything about that day. Is there anything about Monday morning you want to explain now?"

"No. I didn't kill her. That's the truth. Now please leave."

"Of course," said Elizabeth quietly, moving a step away from the bed. "I know there's something about Monday you need to tell someone, but I'll leave you in peace. Do call me if there is anything I can do for you when you're released."

Elizabeth drove home and went into her house. She brewed a small pot of Earl Gray and sat down at the kitchen table. The tea sharpened her mind, and she perused the pages of the *Boston Globe* she had carried home. On a back page of the paper, squeezed between two advertisements, she saw a headline: *Woman Dead in Cambridge*. She read the short paragraph with close attention, her heart sinking at each sentence.

> A young woman, apparently homeless, was found dead in an alley in Central Square last night, badly beaten and stabbed. Although she carried no identification, the police believe her to be Kelly O'Connel. She had been arrested earlier this week for drug possession but was released. She was also suspected of working as a prostitute. The authorities have no leads in the case but suspect the death was drug-related.

Elizabeth's stomach contracted with nausea. She had seen Kelly in Harvard Square two days ago, and Kelly's note to her had been written yesterday. She looked around the kitchen for the small comfort that Sparkle could provide, but the cat was nowhere to be seen.

15

Other Friends actively resist the [federal] telephone tax which Congress instituted in the 1960s to help pay for the war the United States government was waging in Vietnam.

Leaflet on War Taxes
Friends Meeting at Cambridge, 1989

It was a hot and humid Saturday morning. Elizabeth felt oppressed when she awoke. Her mind reviewed the recent events in the Meeting, and she stayed in bed much longer than usual, hoping to delay the day. At nine A.M. the clock radio, tuned to National Public Radio, greeted her with boisterous banjo picking. As if to remind her of more normal days, the theme of her favorite program, *Car Talk*, was coming over the air.

As the owner of a '77 Chevrolet, Elizabeth had frequent automotive complaints but no mechanical expertise. On Saturday mornings since her husband's death it had been her habit to listen to a pair of car mechanics, two Italian-American brothers, who had a call-in radio program broadcast out of Cambridge. Dispensing advice about repairs, the pair used the nicknames Click and Clack, and their conversation, filled with biting humor, attacked the sacred cows of the automotive industry. The show was more fun than Elizabeth could fully admit. She thought that Click and Clack were clever, albeit un-Quakerly, young men, irreverent in all senses. Nevertheless she listened to the program, and she was glad to take her aged car to the garage in Cambridge near M.I.T. which one of the brothers ran. She preferred The Good News Garage to any other shop.

"You know why the British haven't built a computer yet?"

asked one of the brothers. The other grunted no. "Because they haven't found a way to make it leak oil!"

Both men laughed loudly. Elizabeth smiled, remembering all the oil-guzzling dinosaurs she and her late husband had driven. She knew it would make sense to trade in her '77 Chevrolet for something more reliable, as her sons urged. But because the car was familiar and her husband had purchased it, she was reluctant to consign it to the scrap heap. Besides, it ran almost all the time, and her Yankee spirit balked at the thought of walking away from a car that still worked. Her boys talked of antilock brakes and air bags and urged her to get something new. Neil concurred, saying he would gladly help her look. But so far, Elizabeth had resisted all the excellent automotive advice from the men in her life.

Her mind drifted back to the Meeting's problems, and she missed the remainder of the radio program. The closing theme music broke in on her reverie, and she got out of bed. Despite the warmth, she wrapped a robe about her to cover her thin, somewhat threadbare nightgown and went downstairs. She called Cambridge City Hospital. Otto Zimmer's condition had been upgraded to excellent the previous day, a nurse informed her, and he was being discharged this morning. Genuinely glad, and heartened that she could be pleased by anything connected with Otto, Elizabeth dialed Mt. Auburn Hospital. Catherine Laughton was listed in guarded condition, still unconscious. Patience Silverstone was in critical condition, her pneumonia worsening. Elizabeth felt the need of prayer and, glancing at the clock, was encouraged to see it would soon be time for the Meeting for Healing. Such Meetings were held on an occasional basis. This one, scheduled long ago by Ministry and Counsel, could not have come at a more appropriate time.

Elizabeth put out seeds for the birds and fed Sparkle. She had a quick breakfast of tea and toast, then put on a pale blue linen dress. As she left her house and walked down Concord Avenue, the warmth of the day hit her.

Entering the Meetinghouse, Elizabeth discovered that the heat was even worse inside the barnlike building. All the windows were open, along with both doors, but there was no wind to provide any cross draft. The sun forced itself through the windows, and, since it was also scorching the black roof above, the temperature inside the building could have been described as hellish, even in Elizabeth's vocabulary. The presence of a hundred Quaker bodies in the worship room only added to the heat. Quaker breath and sweat gave tangible weight to the humidity. It was a day for tropical fish to attend Meeting, but not human beings, thought Elizabeth. But then she put such complaints aside. Quakers, after all, must gather. If anyone collapsed in the torrid atmosphere, he could be carried to the relative cool of the basement.

Elizabeth walked across the room and sat next to the side door, which was standing wide open. She did not have Care of the Meeting and was glad to have no responsibilities other than prayer. She breathed deeply and tried to discipline her mind to the worshipful task at hand. There were many good and courageous Friends here, some present to pray for others, some for themselves, but most simply to be part of the process of healing in any small way they could. The needs of the Meeting community were always great. Cancer and depression, accidents and old age, all attacked the group. This week the Meeting had suffered an unusual, and unusually great, injury. The violent death of one of its members and the suspicions and fears associated with the murder were deep wounds. Elizabeth was glad to see such good attendance and was sure many Friends had come simply to pray for the Meeting.

The silence around the Clerk at first seemed empty, and she had a difficult time getting herself to concentrate. To focus her mind, she silently recited the Twenty-third Psalm several times. This helped, and she was able, after the last recitation, to concentrate directly and simply on the needs of two human beings struggling for bodily health. This, at least, was a start toward prayer, although Elizabeth would not have considered this level of thought to be true worship. Her mind became more focused as she listened to the silence around her. Young Catherine and aged Patience, the one an object of natural concern and pity because of the past week, the other an old and valued friend, were each vividly present. Elizabeth alternated between images of Catherine and Patience, holding them in the Light that could sustain them. Catherine and Patience. The Clerk moved between the two, glad to be in Meeting despite the heat, despite the crowding, despite the circumstances of murder and accusation. Catherine and Patience. Elizabeth was at home, at home with both Catherine and Patience. The two images alternated before her and embraced her mind.

Slowly, by a mysterious, gradual process which the Clerk had long ago learned to recognize but was wise enough never to examine, the silence around her deepened. Catherine and Patience were fully present in worship. The depth of the quiet room opened slowly into an abyss beneath the Clerk, an abyss she never feared. It was a canyon of peace, which slowly rose to envelop the whole Meetinghouse. She became aware of the sound of her breath in her narrow chest, each inhalation drawing her deeper into prayer. Catherine and Patience continued to be the sole objects of her thoughts. The peace which passeth understanding filled her and stayed with her, pulsing as steadily as her breath. A middle-aged Quaker rose to speak in the silence. Elizabeth did not hear his testimony, nor note how much time was passing, remaining as she did in a state she often sought but seldom reached. Then, instantaneously, Kelly was present in her mind. She heard the young woman's voice in the jail cell, and saw her again on the sidewalk in Harvard Square. Elizabeth reached out and drew

Kelly to her in peace. It was all she could do for the young and misused woman, but it was enough.

Time was no longer relevant. The Clerk was aware that the Meeting for Healing was ending only when her neighbors on the bench began shaking hands, the traditional close of worship. Her mind began to take in her surroundings, but the deep vibrations of true prayer remained within her. She shook hands with everyone in her part of the worship room and spoke to several Friends. Jane Thompson smiled and firmly shook her hand. Jane's hands were, as Elizabeth well knew, as arthritic as her own, but neither woman seemed aware of their joints at the moment. Jane asked about Patience, and Elizabeth gently but significantly explained that she planned to walk to Mt. Auburn hospital and see how the Meeting's oldest member had fared during the night.

"And what about Cathy?" asked Jane.

"I'll check on her first."

Ruth Markham nodded at Elizabeth from across the aisle, but the two did not speak. When Elizabeth reached the main door to the Meetinghouse, Neil Stevenson appeared out of the crowd and asked if she were heading to Mt. Auburn right away. Elizabeth was glad he understood.

"Let me give you a ride. It's far too hot a day to be walking in the sun," he said, taking her elbow lightly in his hand.

She had forgotten the heat. Indeed, enveloped as she was in prayer, she could notice the temperature only distantly, even when it was called to her attention. But Neil was being considerate and kind, and she accepted the ride as an expression of his love rather than as something she needed or desired. She brought the peace of the Meetinghouse with her into Neil's car, which, with the air-conditioning on maximum, took her quickly to the hospital. Neil pulled up the circular driveway to the front doors.

"I'll let you off here, then park in the lot out back. Is that all right? I'll wait for you in the lobby on the first floor."

Elizabeth nodded, squeezed his hand, and got out of the car.

Still filled with prayer, she moved through the sunlight and heat to the hospital door and stepped into the world of doctors, surgery, and suffering.

"I will fear no evil . . ." she murmured to herself on her way to the pediatric ward. She got off the elevator and stopped at the nurses' station, brightly decorated with clown cutouts.

"May I help you?" asked the woman behind the counter.

"Yes, I called earlier this morning, and I'd like to know how Catherine Laughton is doing now."

"Are you a relative?"

Elizabeth nodded assent. She did not want to discover what the hospital's rules might be about people who had the audacity to be concerned about a child to whom they were not related. She would deal with her conscience later, but at present she felt compelled by circumstance to use this small deception.

"Her grandmother, I suppose," said the nurse brightly, and moved closer to the counter. "Well, I'm glad to say that she's entirely out of danger. The shunt the doctors put in yesterday to relieve the fluid pressure has worked well. The fluid is draining just as it should."

Pure joy filled the interstices of prayer within Elizabeth. "Is there danger of the problem returning?"

"No," said the nurse, smiling. "The concussion was serious, but as long as she doesn't fall on her head again soon, she'll be fine. She was awake early this morning and was quite clearheaded. It's really much more rapid improvement than we might have expected. We're sure things are going well."

Elizabeth took in the wonderful news, always able to grasp grace with both hands when it was offered. The peace of the Meetinghouse filled her voice as she asked, "May I see her?"

"Of course. She was sleeping a moment ago, but you can look in on her. She's in the first room on the left."

Elizabeth turned to go, maneuvering around a child who was

being wheeled toward the elevator. In a full-sized wheelchair, the boy seemed terribly small and frail. But when the Quaker smiled at him, he instantly smiled back.

Elizabeth gently opened the door to the room the nurse had indicated. The first bed was empty. In the second bed, the sleeping form of Catherine Laughton was visible. The little girl hardly reached to the halfway point of the bed. Elizabeth walked quietly up and looked down at the child. Cathy's fine golden hair was partly covered by bandages. Her face, however, was clear, and glowed with the color of the young. She was fast asleep and looked as if she were getting a deep rest. The Clerk sat down on a chair near the window and offered her silent thanksgiving. God willing, the child would recover and remember her time in the hospital only as fragments from a bad dream.

Elizabeth emerged from Cathy's room still filled with the spirit of the Meetinghouse. She walked to the elevator. As the doors closed behind her she left the world of clowns and brightly colored cartoons and reentered the more somber adult world of a modern hospital. Emerging on Patience's floor, Elizabeth stopped at the formidable, modern nurses' station. The large gray-haired nurse recognized her at once from her previous visits and motioned her to sit down at the end of her desk. She came around the counter and stood near Elizabeth.

"I have bad news, I'm afraid," said the nurse quietly.

The Quaker nodded, still at peace.

"Your friend was very weak this morning."

"Yes, I know. I was told her condition had deteriorated during the night."

"We think things are near the end."

"Let me see her, please."

"Of course. You know the room."

Elizabeth got up and walked slowly down the hall. Because of her experiences at the Meetinghouse, she was unafraid. She quietly opened the door and walked over to the bed, glad her friend had a private room and was able to face this day by herself, as she would have chosen.

Oxygen lines ran from a large cylinder by the head of Patience's bed to her nose, and her eyes were closed. Even before she reached Patience, Elizabeth heard her friend's labored breathing, but the old Quaker's face was still at rest. For a moment, Elizabeth was reminded of the rhythms of her own breath during the Meeting for Healing. She sat down on a chair near the head of the bed and took her old friend's hand. The images of Cathy and Patience that had flooded her mind in the Meetinghouse returned to her as she closed her eyes. Her prayers now ebbed and flowed with the slow and difficult rhythm of Patience's breath, and Elizabeth quickly returned to the depths she had reached in the Meetinghouse. She offered her thoughts to the heavens and waited, knowing like Isaiah that those who wait upon the Lord are renewed in strength. She then looked at her friend and, with the most gentle of pressures, squeezed her hand.

Patience Silverstone opened her eyes, focused on Elizabeth Elliot, and smiled. Her labored breathing continued.

"I called this morning. The doctors said it had been a bad night. Now I've come, straight from the Meeting for Healing."

Patience nodded ever so slightly.

"You might want to know that little Cathy Laughton is here because she had a bad fall yesterday. But she's out of danger and will be fine. You were both with me at the Meetinghouse. I've just seen her and given thanks."

Again the nod was immeasurably small but perceptible to Elizabeth.

Deeper breaths exercised the chest of the elder Quaker. She opened her mouth and said, in a voice just above a whisper, "I'm glad the little one will be fine. I am going now, Friend, and I am happy. Thee must accept it."

Tears slid down Elizabeth's cheeks, and she faltered. After a moment, a painful lump in her throat slid down, out of the way, and she was able to speak, although her voice was both deep and hoarse. "Must I lose my best friend?" she asked.

Patience smiled. "I won't be far away, and you'll have the Meeting here with you."

"But who can I speak to when you're gone?"

"Neil?" asked Patience, conserving her strength by using a single word.

"I thought you could be here to help me decide about Neil!"

Patience coughed weakly.

"I'm sorry, Friend, that I'm so selfish," said Elizabeth quickly. "I meant to say that the years of our friendship have been wonderful and rich. A blessing."

"For me, too. But I won't be far away."

Elizabeth considered this statement of faith, offered for the second time. Almost overwhelmed by emotion, she slowly answered, "I know that's true. And we'll be fully together soon, in the peace that God sent me this morning."

Elizabeth watched as Patience closed her eyes. The racking breaths continued. Each inhalation was a victory; each exhalation brought the older Friend closer to her life's goal. Minutes passed, and the breathing stopped. It was quiet in the room.

Elizabeth considered calling the nurse but decided against it; there simply was nothing to be gained by medical intervention. She looked at her friend for a long while, tears flowing down her cheeks more and more freely. She moved to a chair nearer the window and thanked God that she had been present with Patience through her final moments. This death was a sorrow, and a deep one for Elizabeth, but it was not a tragedy, nothing like the loss of Hope Laughton. And it was the first time in the Clerk's life she had been able to watch death approach with a true sense of acceptance as well as grief.

She stood and quietly left the room. At the front desk she spoke to the gray-haired nurse, who immediately called for a doctor and rushed down the hallway. The Quaker, however, knew that Patience was past their care. She got in the elevator without hesitation and without looking back. The doors closed softly, and she sighed.

16

Christopher Holden and a companion arrived [in Boston] in 1656 from England. In Salem one Sunday morning he was bold enough to speak a few words after the minister had done. He did not get very far before someone seized him by the hair [and violently stopped his mouth]. [He and his companion] continued their preaching. They were conveyed to Boston, where the exasperated Governor inflicted on them a brutal punishment which went beyond all existing laws . . . First the two Quakers were given thirty stripes apiece, during which one of the spectators fainted. Then they were confined to a bare cell for three days and nights without food or drink. After that they were imprisoned for nine weeks of the New England winter without fire. By special order, the prisoners were whipped twice each week.

Daniel J. Boorstin

Elizabeth's elevator stopped to pick up people on the pediatric floor, and Otto Zimmer entered. He had much more color in his face than on the previous day, but his wrists were still bandaged.

"Are you all right?" asked Elizabeth reflexively.

"Yes, yes, much stronger. I got out of Cambridge City this morning. Released on my own recognizance, as it were. I've just been here to ask after Cathy; I looked in on her a moment ago. Sheldon called me last night in the hospital. To say hello, I guess, and report the news about the kid. He was upset for her, of course, and upset because he has no way to pay her bills. But the good thing is, the doctors say Cathy will be all right."

"Yes, our prayers have been answered."

"I thought Sheldon would be here," said Otto as the elevator descended. "I guess I wanted to see him." He went on in some embarrassment. "Just to say hello. Was he at Meeting this morning?"

"No," said Elizabeth slowly, thinking over the crowd at the Meetinghouse, "I don't think so. I assumed he was here. Now perhaps he's at the Bakers'. That's where he and Cathy are staying until they leave town." The elevator door opened. Otto was too absorbed in his own problems to wonder why Elizabeth had been visiting another floor of the hospital, and she chose not to bring up the subject.

Neil was standing in the lobby, as good as his word, and he caught sight of Elizabeth as soon as she emerged from the elevator. She waved him back and took Otto by the arm, gently but firmly pulling him to the wall, out of the foot traffic.

"I'm glad to see you up and about, Otto. But if you're well enough to be visiting the sick, you're well enough to tell me the truth. What happened at Foster Place on Monday morning?"

Otto's naturally pasty face lost the last of its color. "Why do you keep harassing me?" he sputtered.

"Because I know that you were there."

Otto leaned up against the wall. His will seemed to melt as his body relaxed against the plaster. "I suppose you must have seen me. I wondered about that. I knew you were expected early in the morning, but I didn't see you."

Elizabeth did her best to hide her surprise at Otto's assumption. She had not seen him, only remembered the faint smell she had encountered in the Laughtons' front hall and matched that with the pervasive odor in Otto's smoky apartment. The cigarette butts she had seen by the telephone pole on Foster Place might not have been smoked on Monday morning, of course, but she could easily imagine Otto hanging around the Laughtons' house, waiting for Sheldon to depart, smoking to kill time. Sneaking around like that was in keeping, she had thought, with his secretly cherishing one of Hope's Peruvian hats. But why Hope, who ran a proper Quaker household, had allowed him to smoke in her front hall, Elizabeth had not been able to puzzle out.

Otto rushed on. "I'm glad you didn't tell the police you saw me. That took some guts, especially when they arrested you!"

Elizabeth was filled with consternation at Otto's misunderstanding and put a hand out to the wall to steady herself. Her silence with the police had never been a lie. The notion that Otto had been at the Laughtons' that morning made intuitive sense to her, and fit with the faint smell in the front hall and the butts on the street. But she could not have testified to the precise identity of a faint odor in a court of law, and therefore she had not mentioned it to Detective Burnham. She did not, however, consider herself to be a liar, and Otto's misplaced praise stung.

"I admit, I was there," he continued, both unabashed by his admission and oblivious to her distress. "I waited until Sheldon and Cathy drove away. Then I dashed up to the house. I had been awake most of the night, and I was a wreck. Hope let me light a smoke in the front hall, and that helped my nerves. I said I didn't want her to leave Cambridge. I thought she should stay here. The West is so far away! I begged her, really begged her, to stay for my sake."

"And her response?" asked Elizabeth.

"She said I must leave right away. What I was asking wasn't right."

Elizabeth felt relief for the dead woman.

"I was angry. It had been a night of agony for me, and she dismissed it in just a moment. I left, all right: I ran out of there. If she wanted me to go away, I figured I would."

"That was the best thing you could have done," agreed Elizabeth.

Otto, slumped against the hospital wall, looked pathetic to the older Quaker.

"Do you know what time you left?" she asked.

"No. It would have been just a few minutes after Sheldon drove away. Our conversation didn't take long. My cigarette was only half-burnt when I got to Willard Street, I remember that. I suppose you saw me on Willard from Brattle?"

Elizabeth was silent.

"Anyway," continued Otto, lost in his own thoughts, "I owe you a lot for not mentioning it to the police. When I left Hope she was alive and well, but I don't know how I could prove it. I appreciate your lying for me."

Disgust overcame Elizabeth. *I didn't lie.* She waved Otto away with a dismissive hand, then turned away without explanation and went to her friend. He had, as she had wished, remained in the middle of the lobby while she talked to the young, foolish Quaker. She put her head against Neil's chest, and he put his arms around her. Otto, still leaning against the wall by the elevator, realized there was more happening than he understood and, for once in his life, had the sense to retreat with grace. He turned and went out the front doors of the building.

Elizabeth became both numb and dumb. She quickly and easily put the distasteful young man out of her mind. Patience was much more important. And Patience was gone. Neil spoke to her gently, asking about her friend, but she did not reply. After a minute she backed out of his embrace and, taking his hand, led him in the direction of the door. He interpreted her silence correctly.

After getting into the Buick, she spoke. "The odd thing is, I don't feel much grief. I know that I'll miss her, but the sadness hasn't hit me yet." With mechanical detachment, Elizabeth noted that Patience's death had closed a long and important chapter in her own life. It was possible, she supposed, that Neil represented the next chapter.

Neil steered his car toward Harvard Square.

"Let me off at the Meetinghouse," said Elizabeth. "I want to be alone in the worship room."

"It's very hot, and all the windows there will be closed. Let me take you home."

"No," said Elizabeth with determination.

Neil recognized her tone and turned down Brattle Street to Longfellow Park.

But the heat *was* a problem. Elizabeth sat in the empty room, on the same bench she had earlier in the day, but she could not find any sense of peace. Her mind was scattered and prayer was impossible. The windows were closed, and she did not have the energy to wrestle with their stiffness, even greater than her own. She had propped open the door, but even so the building was an oven. For the first time since leaving Patience, Elizabeth felt a rush of deep grief. In the stifling heat of the Meetinghouse, everything in life looked futile.

She gave up and locked the building, then slowly walked up Concord Avenue in the heat. Conflicting emotions washed through her. Patience Silverstone, her oldest friend, would never come to the Meetinghouse again. She would never call Elizabeth or invite her over for tea and a confidence. Their relationship, if it were to continue, had to be transformed into something new. At the end, Elizabeth hoped to be united, in some sense, with everyone she had loved, but for now she felt the pain of separation keenly. Her mind turned to her husband Michael and the many years of marriage they had shared before death had claimed him. As she crossed Garden Street, grief and loss threatened to overwhelm her, and it was only by an act of will that she continued homeward. By the time she reached her front door she was calmer, and she let herself into her quiet house. Mechanically, she sat down at the kitchen table and poured herself a cup of tepid tea from the pot, left over from breakfast. She was halfway through the cup when the telephone rang. Elizabeth hoped desperately it was Neil calling, but the voice that responded to her strained "hello" was not his.

"Mrs. Elliot, this is Jose Condoro. I don't understand what's been happening, but I thought you should know about it."

Elizabeth braced herself for more bad news.

"Sheldon Laughton has been arrested. Taken away by a man named Burnham. Sheldon and I went to Mt. Auburn this morning, to see Cathy. Things seemed to be going well with her, but when we got back to the Bakers' house, a police detective was there. I guess Constance had called him. She found something in Sheldon's things, but she won't explain to me what's going on. The detective arrested Sheldon as soon as we turned up. The cop wouldn't explain anything to me. I'll try to get a public defender for Sheldon. Constance says he's being charged with Hope's murder."

17

Public prayer, thanksgiving and praise ought ever to spring from a living sense of the wants and condition of the congregation. In this solemn service, may all be impressed with the importance of their words being few and full.

London Yearly Meeting (1868)

Elizabeth said good-bye to Jose and quickly dialed the Bakers' number. Titus answered. Elizabeth said she was glad he was back in town and asked to speak to Constance.

"I'm sorry, she's gone to Mt. Auburn to visit Cathy. I don't understand everything that's been going on while I've been away. But I expect Constance home in a few hours. Shall I have her call you?"

Elizabeth realized she did not want a protracted conversation with Titus, and she was not sure what she would have said to Constance had she been home.

"Please say that I called," she responded, "and thank you. Good-bye." She quickly hung up. As she sat in her hot, humid kitchen, looking at the telephone, she felt the dizziness of Monday returning and, to combat it, immediately dialed Detective Burnham's office. He answered on the second ring. She gathered her scattered thoughts together at the sound of his businesslike voice.

"This is Elizabeth Elliot. I'm calling because I just learned you've arrested Sheldon Laughton for murder. Is that correct?"

"Yes," said the detective, "and I'm glad you called. There's something odd about this whole business, and I'd be happy to fill you in. You understand the people involved a lot better than I

do. Constance Baker called us this morning. Sheldon Laughton
has been staying with her, but I gather something has happened
to his child, and he was at Mt. Auburn this morning."

"Yes," said Elizabeth. "Thanks be to God, the child will be
fine."

"Good. Were the circumstances of her injury curious to you in
any way?"

"No," said Elizabeth firmly. "It seemed an understandable accident for a little one left alone for a moment with a stepladder.
And Constance was deeply sorrowful about what happened, holding herself responsible."

"OK, I'll accept that, at least for now. Mrs. Baker called me and
asked me to come to her house this morning. She said she had
found something in Sheldon's things that I should know about.
A bloodstained handkerchief and a pair of gloves. I got my search
warrant for Sheldon renewed right away and went over. There,
in a box of his clothes, were the things Mrs. Baker had told me
about. She said she had been looking in his room for dirty laundry to add to the wash. Sheldon showed up and I arrested him.
He's in custody now, refusing to say anything until a public defender gets here. I've had the lab boys busy on what Constance
found. The handkerchief has human blood on it, blood of the
same group as Hope Laughton's."

Elizabeth nodded to herself. Everything was becoming clear.

The detective continued. "The gloves have perhaps a trace of
blood, no more, but there's powder on both of them. A forty-five-
caliber revolver discharges a lot of hot gases and burning powder, both down the barrel and backward through the cylinder
chamber. It looks like whoever wore those gloves fired a gun, all
right."

"I am sorry, of course, that those items were found in the belongings of a former member, a man I consider a Quaker in the
best meaning of the term. And everything, from the start, has

pointed toward this being a murder within our community. But of course it would make no sense for Sheldon, if he were the murderer, to keep those things."

"That's true in a way," answered Burnham, "and I would be interested in your thoughts about that man. Clearly what we have here is crucial physical evidence. I have to go by the book, and that means I had to bring Sheldon in."

"If you say so, I'm sure that's true. But that indicates the limitations of the methods the police have to use."

"Perhaps. But there are good reasons for our rules. Killers do stupid and irrational things. Perpetrators who keep incriminating evidence are not as rare as you might guess. But Laughton seemed bewildered by the things when I showed them to him at the Bakers' house. It seemed they had no meaning for him. I don't know, maybe he's a good actor."

"Or maybe he was actually bewildered," responded Elizabeth. "Mr. Burnham, tell me, if a person like me, who doesn't know anything about guns, went upstairs at the Laughtons' and found that revolver, could he load and fire it even if he'd never handled a gun before?"

"Sure. Everyone has seen the things on TV. And guns like that are incredibly simple. They're easier to operate than a microwave and lots easier than a VCR."

"I see. One last question: Are these powder-charged gloves you found what you would call work gloves? Tan colored?"

"Yes," said the detective, clearly startled.

"I see it all now, Mr. Burnham. I'm sorry I've been so stupid. It was just so hard to believe."

"Spill it, Mrs. Elliot! What do you understand now?"

"I can't tell," she said, thinking furiously. "I'd look like a suspect to you and your rule book if I did. But by this evening we can have all this straightened out." For the first time in her life, Elizabeth Elliot hung up the telephone without saying good-bye or waiting for the other person to close the conversation. She looked intently at the telephone, wondering what she should do. After a moment, she called Ruth Markham and reached her at home.

"This is Elizabeth. I need your help right away, about the Laughtons."

"What's up?"

"I now know what happened on Monday morning. I need you to help tie things up."

"I'm your man," said Ruth cheerfully, "although, these days, I guess I've got to learn a new phrase. I'll come over."

"Good. In your car, please. We have to move quickly."

"Roger, I'm on my way," said Ruth.

Elizabeth cautiously and quietly pushed open the door to Cathy Laughton's hospital room. Constance was seated by the bed. The door behind Elizabeth stayed slightly ajar as she crossed the room. Constance put her finger to her lips and nodded toward the child.

"She's been awake much of this afternoon," she said quietly, "but now she's sleeping again. I signed for all her bills. They won't discharge her until she's fit to leave."

"Good. I'm glad that's on a more honest footing. Are the doctors still pleased with her progress?" asked Elizabeth softly.

"Yes. They say she's out of all danger."

Elizabeth stepped back and sat down on a chair near the door, beside the unoccupied bed. She motioned for Constance to come nearer.

Constance rose and quietly carried her chair near the door and sat down. In a more normal tone of voice she said, "It's good of you to be so concerned about little Cathy. I know there have been other things on your mind this week."

"Indeed. And that's what I've come about," said Elizabeth.

"Oh?" Constance was startled.

"Sheldon's arrest—"

"Oh, yes!" interrupted Constance. "So you've heard. It's such a pity. Almost impossible to understand."

"It was difficult to understand at first," agreed Elizabeth. "But I spoke to Detective Burnham about what you said you had found in Sheldon's things."

Constance caught the caution in Elizabeth's statement and replied, "Mr. Burnham came to my house himself and saw where they were."

"Of course. But you know, you wouldn't have been looking through Sheldon's belongings if you didn't want to find something there."

"I was looking for dirty clothes, that's all, to start doing the laundry."

"Monday is wash day. You said so yourself when I asked you where you were this past Monday morning."

Constance snorted. "I was getting an early start on it. It's quite a chore with extra people in the house."

"Yes, that's true, I'm sure. But, you know, I had seen the gloves, and the hanky, too, earlier in the week."

Constance grew pale.

"In the trash in the women's room at Longfellow Park," Elizabeth continued. "Early on Monday morning, just after seven o'clock, the building would have been locked, of course, but like most of us old-timers around Meeting, you have a key. And you knew that Harriet doesn't come in until nine. You needed somewhere to catch your breath, didn't you?"

"I don't know what you're talking about," Constance spat.

"I wish you didn't. You can say what you like, but I'll testify that I saw tan-colored work gloves and a soiled handkerchief in the trash of the women's room at the Meetinghouse. How they got from there into your house is the only relevant question. Sheldon could have gone into the women's room and taken them, to incriminate himself in some fit of guilt. But it will seem much more likely to the police, and to Friends, that you collected them from where you had left them, after you learned from me that the gloves would have traces of gunpowder on them. You didn't know that when you left them there, any more than I understood the police's test of my hands at first. You planted the gloves in Sheldon's things as soon as you knew about the traces of powder on them. Calling the police and having your brother-in-law arrested, you hoped, would remove the last obstacle to your being given custody of Cathy."

"I don't know what you're talking about. Gloves in bathrooms. Why would I have done that?"

"You were afraid and acted impulsively. I don't think you did this out of careful premeditation. You probably weren't clear what you were doing when you went to your sister's house that morning. Did you plead with her about the house? About paying taxes and raising Cathy more normally? But after what happened there, you ran out of the house, dumping the gun behind the rose-bushes as soon as you realized it was still in your hand. It would have been better to leave it in the house, I think, if you wanted to implicate Sheldon. But you panicked. The roar of the gun, I suppose, or the sight of Hope's body had been terrifying. So you ran. You ran to the same place you did when Cathy was injured, and a good refuge it is, too. You ran to our Meetinghouse. Maybe you wanted to wash your hands. I know I would have. And you needed to catch your breath and think. I can understand everything, in a way, except why you did the killing. She was their child! Would you really eliminate them both for a chance to raise Cathy?"

"What you say isn't true, but what if it were?" said Constance hotly. "What of it? Do you think Cathy was going to have a normal life with my sister and brother-in-law? They wouldn't do any of the regular things, like hold a real job. Sheldon never had Blue

Cross for his child! Titus has always done that for me. Does going to prison because of taxes, leaving a little child to care for herself, seem like God's will to you?"

"The chances of them both being sent to prison were remote, I think. And if it had come to that, I'm sure Cathy would not have had to care for herself. The Meeting would have done so, in one way or another."

"I would have done so, of course."

"And gladly so."

"Yes!"

"Are you able to have children, Constance?"

The question made the listener freeze. Her face, turned halfway toward her interrogator, was outlined in the sunlight from the window. "I don't see what business that is of yours," she said at last.

"Someone in Meeting told me she had heard you and Titus had tried to have children."

"What of it?" said Constance again, beginning to rise. "It's no business of yours."

"I remember last year Hope came and talked to me. It was the only personal discussion the two of us ever had. She was wondering about having another child, but really, I could see, she was in the process of deciding against it. She wasn't young, and Sheldon is fifty now, isn't he?"

Constance moved to the edge of her chair. She said nothing.

"She mentioned to me last winter that she had decided against more children and was going in to have a tubal ligation."

"That didn't concern me."

"No, not at all. But maybe it hurt."

"Everything hurts when you can't have children! And your husband always, always, always doing Friends work in godforsaken places, leaving you alone." Constance was pale with intensity. "I so much wanted a child! You had kids, Ruth and Harriet and Jane

Thompson and everyone else around Meeting! High school girls have them left and right! It hurts terribly when your sister has the luxury of getting herself sterilized and keeping a beautiful baby."

"And she was going to take that baby away from you, wasn't she? Take her out West?"

Constance pulled back her head and stood up. She looked contemptuously at Elizabeth. "That was for them to decide."

"Was it?" asked Elizabeth. "Were you comfortable about that? Or did she seem almost like your own child, and yours by rights because you were sterile and loved her so much? You knew about Otto and Hope. You knew about that situation for a long time, and you watched it grow, even if it was pathetic and one-sided. You shot your sister, Constance, rather than lose the child you thought of as yours. I think you probably pleaded with her to stay in Cambridge. But she had already heard that plea earlier in the morning and rejected it. Did you plead with her to pay her taxes? Even if she had to ignore God's leadings?"

"God doesn't lead us to crime!" whispered Constance fiercely.

"Certainly not to killing," said Elizabeth simply. She paused for a moment and looked at the overwrought woman before her. "You used Sheldon's gun. It was what was available, and you knew where it was kept. After the murder, when you started to think it all through, you knew Sheldon would be a top suspect for the police, and you hoped he'd be arrested. When he wasn't, you adapted, and invited him into your house. You, of course, could take care of Cathy, in your sister's stead. And think about how to implicate Sheldon.

"Sheldon will never let you see Cathy again when I speak to him about all this. I don't know what the police and the prosecutor will be able to prove. I don't understand the legal system. But I know what happened, and Sheldon and the Meeting will listen to me. You won't have custody of Cathy. After today, I doubt you'll ever even see her again."

Constance looked at Elizabeth as if she were ready to kill her. "Titus and I went to all the best doctors in New England, years ago. But I just wasn't able to conceive. Cathy was all I had. My sister had no right to take her from me, not after all I'd done for her. I'm the older one. I always took responsibility for things in our family. When our parents died, it was me, not Hope, who took charge of everything. She never even thanked me. That baby of hers should have been mine. I love her so much!" Silent sobs shook her frame.

"But you hoped Sheldon, an innocent man, would be convicted of murder, leaving you with their child?"

"My child! She was more mine than theirs! They didn't provide for her. Neither or them ever took serious jobs. They didn't have health insurance for her! Do you call that good parenting? And they continued with this stupid tax thing to the point where they lost that beautiful house. Worth hundreds and hundreds of thousands of dollars. That could have been Cathy's when she grew up, but no, it was sacrificed to their self-righteousness. . . . And you know, I could have killed you, too, Elizabeth. I guess I should have."

"What happened before I arrived?" asked Elizabeth calmly.

"Hope and I argued about taxes and about their going away," Constance blurted. "It wasn't the first time, but I could see that it was really at an end between us. They were going to give up that house and move thousands and thousands of miles away. I went upstairs to the bathroom to cry. A pair of Sheldon's pants was on the hook on the back of the bathroom door, and they fell down when I closed the door. I picked them up, and two condoms slid out of the pocket. So, you see, I knew he was having an affair with someone. Hope couldn't have more children; he was seeing someone else."

Elizabeth did not stop Constance to point out her error.

"They were both terrible parents," continued the younger Quaker, "and they were taking my Cathy away! I could see I didn't have any choice. There were no other options, Elizabeth. That's just the way it was. I knew where that gun was kept—I helped Hope clean the closet one day. I put on some old work gloves that were in the same closet. I knew I shouldn't leave fingerprints, you see. It was easy enough to get it down from the shelf, but I wasn't sure I had it loaded right. I don't know anything about guns. But I came down and pointed it at Hope as best I could. When it went off it pushed my whole arm backward. I barely hung on to the thing. The noise was so loud in that little kitchen my ears were ringing. I sat down on the floor to collect my senses. I didn't look at Hope. I didn't care about her anymore; I had done what I had to do. But it took a while for my head to clear. Then someone rang the front doorbell and knocked and knocked. I was paralyzed and just sat there. After a minute I saw you in the backyard. I scooted behind a counter when you started coming toward the window. Then a moment later I heard you knocking at the back. I turned and ran for the front. I got out the door before I realized I still had the gun in my hand, and I threw it away. I don't know where it went."

"Into the rosebushes," said Elizabeth.

"I just ran down Foster Place and then over to the Meeting-house. That was stupid of me."

Elizabeth shook her head. "Not stupid. It was the instinct to run toward something that was certain, something that was good."

"I would have taken good care of her!" cried Constance, for the first time raising her voice to a point where it might disturb the sleeping child. "It made more sense for her to be mine. Titus and I would have provided for her, much better than a pair of war-tax resisters ever could!"

"Hope and Sheldon loved that child more than anything but

God. You had no right to even think of yourself in their place!"

"I'm not sorry about what I did."

"Take one last look at your niece," said Elizabeth Elliot, rising from her chair. "You can do nothing but harm to Cathy from here on, and I'm sure you won't be allowed to see her. It was you I should have prayed for at the Meeting for Healing, Constance. Your needs are far greater than any I was aware of this morning."

The door opened fully, and Ruth Markham entered.

18

And his father Zechariah was filled with the Holy Spirit, and prophesied, saying . . . "And you, child, will be called the prophet of the Most High; for you will go before the Lord to prepare his ways, to give knowledge of salvation to his people in the forgiveness of their sins, through the tender mercy of our God, when the day shall dawn upon us from on high to give light to those who sit in darkness and in the shadow of death, to guide our feet in the way of peace."

The Gospel of Luke, Chapter 1

I heard everything that's been said. I'll testify to the police, to the child welfare people, and to the Meeting," said Ruth hotly as she entered the room.

"Despite what you said, I think you will be sorry, Constance," Elizabeth said quietly, "when you fully understand what you've done. But that may not be for some time now."

"Goddamn you both!" cried Constance, her words carrying their full, literal meaning. "You can't keep Cathy from me!"

"We can and we will," said Ruth fiercely. "You're not fit to even be in the same room with her!"

The child, still asleep, stirred in her bed in response to the noise.

"Come out into the hall, both of you," said Elizabeth firmly. She walked out the door, followed by Ruth and then Constance. To Elizabeth's surprise, Constance seemed to falter as she came into the hall. She slumped against the wall of the corridor. Ruth looked at her skeptically, but Elizabeth saw that the transformation was genuine.

"I didn't do anything to harm Cathy," said the child's aunt.

"Yes, you did," Elizabeth said, quietly but intensely. "You tried to take her mother's place. And because of that, you murdered her in cold blood." Constance looked at her accuser in a daze as

Elizabeth continued. "You'll never see her again, and that's a good thing. You've brought true darkness into Cathy Laughton's life."

"As I stood there in the kitchen, there was no other choice, nothing else I could do. That's the way it was," said Constance, tears now flowing down her cheeks.

"That wasn't true. I know it felt that way, but that wasn't reality, Constance. You couldn't see what was real."

"I didn't want to hurt Cathy!" Constance sobbed. She staggered and almost fell forward, but Ruth, a strong and quick woman, caught her.

Constance sobbed deeply and clung to Ruth.

"We've got to get to the cops while she's talking," said Ruth quickly to her friend. "Come on!"

With Ruth guiding the stricken woman, the trio walked to the elevator and were carried down to the first floor. Ruth left the sobbing Constance in Elizabeth's care as she went out into the heat and brought her car to the front door. On the short trip to Central Square, Constance cried, but no one spoke.

Ruth parked immediately in front of the main doors of the police station, on a yellow curb. She helped Elizabeth extract Constance from the automobile, and then, abandoning the car to its fate, the two women guided Constance up the stairs.

Stewart Burnham happened to be standing in the hall when the trio arrived. He waved all three women into his office and looked questioningly at Elizabeth.

"What's all this?"

"This is the truth," said Elizabeth as Ruth sat Constance down on a chair beside the detective's desk. "And the truth will make us free, when we can bear to look at it."

"Constance!" said Ruth sharply. "Tell us what happened."

"I never meant to harm Cathy," said Constance, looking at Elizabeth as if for confirmation. The detective intervened and gave all three Quakers the Miranda warning. Then he led Constance, question by question, through the events of the morning of the murder. With pauses for sobs, Constance related what had happened in her sister's house, her avoidance of Elizabeth, and her flight to the Meetinghouse. The detective took notes of everything.

Finally, Detective Burnham had Constance led away. He called down the hall and gave his handwritten notes to a secretary to type.

"I should have seen it long ago," said Elizabeth. "I'm sorry I was so slow. It's a good thing she didn't try to harm Sheldon, only to frame him for the murder."

"It's a good thing she didn't kill you," said Burnham. "If she had started to worry about what you might have seen through the kitchen window, she could have put a bullet through you."

"Most of us might kill to save our lives," mused Elizabeth. "But not Constance. Her deepest desire wasn't self-preservation, just a purely selfish love focused on little Catherine Laughton."

"I still find it hard to grasp that the child was a motive for murder," said the detective.

"Maternal love is strong, Mr. Burnham," Elizabeth said quietly. "The strongest love in the world, actually. I've often thought it's a shame you men never get to give it to anyone. You really don't know what it is, how it grips a person."

"That's right," interjected Ruth. "Men never understand."

"You see," continued Elizabeth, "Constance had begun to think of herself as crucial to Cathy's life. She wasn't, of course. Cathy had a mother and a father. Not the most usual mother and father in the world, but good parents, as far as I could see. Constance and her husband have been unable to have children. Cathy became a surrogate child for her aunt. I'm sure that she didn't want to kill her sister. She had nothing against Hope, but she could not stand to see Cathy taken away from her."

"If you two care to wait at the end of the hall, I'll have Shel-

don Laughton released," said Burnham, rising from the chair behind his desk. "It will take a little while for the formalities to be
observed, but you're welcome to stay until he comes down from
the cells."

The same small lounge in which Ruth had spent the best part
of Monday morning now held both Quakers as they waited.

"I'm so weary," said Elizabeth. "Constance was motivated by
love, but it was perverted into sickness long ago."

"Yes," said Ruth with surprising gravity.

"Can all love turn into evil?" Elizabeth looked steadily at her
friend. "Was Otto's love that different? Yes, surely it was. It may
not have been proper, but he didn't do anything based on the
longing he felt. He did no deliberate harm to Sheldon, not even
with words."

"There's a world of difference between the two cases," agreed
Ruth. "Morally speaking, Otto should have left the Laughtons
long ago. But he was useful to them, helping them at the time of
the auction, helping to beat the Meeting over the head with
war-tax issues so long and so hard that even Hugo Coleman and
the like have had to think a little about it. Otto did the Laughtons
much good and was a friend to them both. And little Cathy.
What Constance did is something else entirely." Ruth spoke
slowly, with uncharacteristic thoughtfulness. "But, still, love is
more dangerous than we like to admit around Meeting. We are
always saying 'Love one another.' We ought, perhaps, to say
something about respecting one another."

"Yes," said Elizabeth. There was silence in the little room, broken only by the ringing of a distant telephone somewhere down
the hall.

"Well," Ruth mused, "our Meeting is going to have to decide
what to do about Constance. She can't keep her membership, can
she?"

"That's up to the Spirit," said the Clerk automatically. "If the

Meeting thinks she's repentant, I think we'll feel clear about keeping her as a member. But let's not get ahead of ourselves."

"You're right," said Ruth more briskly. "Imagine what Titus is going to go through!" The usual hard edge returned to her voice. "And all for a kid! If she had asked, she could have had mine and welcome to him!"

Elizabeth knew her friend was not serious. Still, the remark pained her, and she said, in the most gentle tones she could manage, "If Patience were here, she would elder you about such a poor joke."

Ruth was startled. "That reminds me, how is she doing?"

Elizabeth shook her head and related the news of the Meeting's oldest member.

"I'm very sorry, Elizabeth. I know you two have been good friends for many years. This has been a terrible week for you, hasn't it?"

"It has indeed," answered the Clerk, a tear escaping from the corner of one eye. "A week without end, each day adding pain to the last. My only comfort is that Patience is no longer suffering, and that Sheldon and his daughter will have the chance to start a new life. God help them find what they need in the West."

19

Nurturing the processes of peace takes . . . the skills of arbitration, mediation, and conflict resolution in the context of the practice of community, of neighboring. We must develop these skills . . . [and the skill of] prophetic listening.

Elise Boulding, twentieth-century Norwegian-American Friend

The heat had abated. Cooler and drier air had blown down from Canada during the night. On Sunday morning all of New England had a reprieve, deserved or not, from the sodden heat of summer. Elizabeth awoke as soon as the sun rose and groggily, but gladly, noted the change in weather. Sparkle was on the bed, and the Quaker was careful not to disturb the sleeping cat. She thought about the past week with regret and sorrow. The tragedy at the Laughtons' would always be with the Meeting, and Kelly's death was a private grief for the Clerk. Patience's peaceful passing-on was a deep loss. In the midst of all of that, how could Neil have asked her to marry again?

When she awoke later it was time to get up. Sparkle was gone, and the clock radio was playing. Although she knew it was Sunday, the week had been so long and confusing that she could not remember if she had Care of Meeting this morning. She decided to go to Longfellow Park a few minutes early and check the written list of the rotating duty of overseeing the worship gathering.

Walking down Concord Avenue in the cool, dry air was most refreshing. In her Sunday best, enjoying the mild temperature and low humidity, Elizabeth could think about the past week with more perspective. She needed time to consider what Neil had asked. It was a decision that merited careful thought from them both. The Meeting would help, the Clerk knew, by appointing a committee of seasoned Friends to meet with them and search for what was best. She had often been on such Clearness Committees in the past. She and Michael had benefited from their Clearness Committee more than forty years earlier when they had married. Patience Silverstone, Elizabeth remembered with a start, had been on that committee.

There would be so much to talk to Patience about if she were here! There was the problem of Cathy's hospital bills. Constance had promised to pay them all, but clearly that would not happen now, nor would it be appropriate. Sheldon had no assets. The Clerk thought the Meeting community, out of respect for Sheldon and in memory of Hope, would find the resources to settle all of Mt. Auburn's bills. It had to be admitted that Neil Stevenson and the other wealthy Quakers in Cambridge were most useful to the community at times like this.

Most central to Elizabeth's wandering thoughts was the problem of Constance Baker. Her actions were as great an evil in Meeting as the Clerk could imagine.

As Elizabeth cut across Episcopalian property, she looked at her watch and quickened her step. She scolded herself for not being sure who had Care of Meeting. She walked briskly down the sidewalk of Longfellow Park and onto Quaker property. Standing in the driveway next to the Meetinghouse stood a middle-aged man who looked familiar. He smiled tentatively at Elizabeth, and she stopped.

"Good morning," said the man pleasantly. "I was wondering if visitors were permitted on Sundays."

"Of course, visitors are most welcome," she said. "Please forgive me. Perhaps I should know you, but I can't place your face."

"That's OK. I'm Evan Beringar. We never properly met, but I was one of the men who came to Foster Place on Monday morn-

ing. I work for the IRS, I'm afraid, and I would certainly understand if I weren't welcome around here."

Elizabeth remembered the kind man who had spoken with her
on the sofa before the police had arrived at the Laughtons'.
"You're very welcome," she said warmly. "We're the ones who
should be unsure of ourselves. This Meeting is in no position to
judge anyone's job. Please come with me, Mr. Beringar. I have to
see if I have the responsibility of shepherding the worship this
morning."

The IRS agent followed Elizabeth inside the Meeting's office.
A written list showed that this First Day's worship was the responsibility of Hugo Coleman.

"Good," said the Clerk. "I don't have to worry about anything.
Please come, and I'll show you where we meet."

As the pair crossed the alleyway to the Meetinghouse itself,
Evan volunteered, "I got to know the Laughtons over the past two
years. I never agreed with them, but I respected their courage.
And their gentleness, too, in the face of some pretty harsh re-
sponses on our part." He continued in a rush, "I was raised in the
Church. I haven't been to Sunday services for a decade; there was
a lot of rigmarole and ritual I just didn't appreciate. But seeing
the Laughtons go through these past two years, I guess I saw again
what faith could mean. So I wanted to visit here."

Elizabeth smiled. "I remember, at a meeting here one Saturday, Hope said you had been kind to them. Warning them when
eviction was imminent, so they could prepare Cathy for what was
going to happen."

"Yes, I thought they should know. I liked the little girl."

"Children are jewels," said Elizabeth, motioning the visitor
into the front door of the Meetinghouse ahead of her. Jane
Thompson stood just inside the door, the designated Greeter for
the day. She shook hands with Evan and quietly introduced herself. Elizabeth lightly touched Evan's arm and drew him further

into the building. With the windows open and the doors ajar, the oppressive heat of the previous week had left the large room.

"You're welcome to sit anywhere you wish," said the Quaker, just above a whisper. "I'd be glad if you wanted to sit with me. The idea of our worship is to listen to the silence. We think that God's voice can sometimes be heard in that way. Someone may be called by the Spirit to speak. If the worship is deep enough, what they say may be important to many of us."

Evan looked around nervously at the big room, still largely empty. "Is that all?" he asked in a whisper, gesturing to the empty benches with plain backs and seats. "No prayerbooks or hymnals?" It was a question that had been asked many times before of Friends and will always be heard when visitors come to Meeting.

Elizabeth shook her head slightly. "We just listen," she said. "That's all we can manage. It's not such a strange goal as it may seem at first." She walked across the room to a seat near the door, and Evan followed her. A moment later, Elizabeth began to pray for Constance and for her Meeting.